T0067136

Spirits
Among Us

A Psychic's Research & Insight
Into the Realm of Ghosts

Christy Clark

authorHOUSE®

AuthorHouse™
1663 Liberty Drive
Bloomington, IN 47403
www.authorhouse.com
Phone: 1 (800) 839-8640

Published by AuthorHouse 03/17/2015

ISBN: 978-1-4969-7366-5 (sc)
ISBN: 978-1-4969-7368-9 (e)

Print information available on the last page.

CONTENTS

Foreword.. ix

Prologue... xi

Chapter 1
  "What is a ghost and do they really exist?"...................... 1

Chapter 2
  "The Beginning"..19

Chapter 3
  "The Awakening" 43

Chapter 4
  "Spiritual Attachments" 57

Chapter 5
  "Learning to Overcome Roadblocks"............................ 77

Chapter 6
  "Emotional Spirits" 93

Chapter 7
  "Spirit Dreams and Visitations" 115

Chapter 8
  "Can Our Minds Really Create a Ghost?"................... 139

Chapter 9

"Children and the Paranormal" 167

Chapter 10

Spiritual Warfare "The Attack" 189

Conclusion..253

DEDICATED TO:

My daughter, Sarah-Ann: For precious time never lost or forgotten between us. You are my heart and I will always love you!

My son, Graysen: Thank you for blessing me with you when I was older. God knew I needed healing. You are my heart and I will always love you!

Kathy Wickham: For all the help you provided along the way. I am forever grateful!

The OKPRI Team: For always being professional, striving to meet our goals and helping to make our team the very best!

FOREWORD

Ghosts. Do they really exist? Does the soul actually continue after the physical body dies? Should we be afraid of what awaits us on the other side? Is it morally wrong to believe in ghosts and the afterlife? Can we actually prove that ghosts exist? These are just some of the questions many researchers have pondered throughout their time of investigating the paranormal field.

Perhaps you are interested in ghosts and therefore the reason you are reading this book. Perhaps you just stumbled upon it and were struck by curiosity. Either way, my goal for writing this book is to share with you one paranormal team's experiences while investigating places reported to be haunted and the strange activity they encountered along the way. This isn't just another book about ghost stories. It is about actual ghosts and the personal stories they communicated to me psychically while investigating the paranormal.

One of the questions I have been asked repeatedly throughout the years is: *"How did you get started in the paranormal field and what sparked your interest?"*

We all have experiences that inspire our own individual interests, but what exactly is it that maintains my personal interest to pursue the paranormal field of study even further? I have thought about this many times and can only say that it is a passion for many investigators. For some of us, it is a calling. This field requires a lot of dedication and patience and there is a lot more involved than just taking pictures and recording some audio.

Let me begin by saying when I first had the urge to write this book, I wasn't sure where I would start, so I asked myself, "Why not from the beginning?" This beginning starts with my spiritual path which led me to be the founder and director of a paranormal investigations group called, O.K.P.R.I. (Oklahoma Paranormal Research and Investigations). This book takes you on a spiritual journey as my team and I encounter different spirits: some lost, some troubled and some with their own stories to tell.

Throughout the years I have seen paranormal enthusiasts come and go, but it's only those who have the true passion and calling for the field that remain. The calling is such a powerful way to describe what we do and it's also a great way to start my story!

PROLOGUE

The night is late and Amanda is tired from her long day. She tried to relax as she flipped through the channels on her television set hoping to find something decent to watch. Her mind really didn't want to focus on the screen in front of her. She didn't find anything to watch, so she decided to turn it off and call it a night. It was nearly 1 am.

She quickly began turning off the lights one by one in a specific order so she wouldn't see *them*. She dreaded the thought of walking down her long hallway each night, as its darkness seemed to hold something sinister in its shadows. Each time she stepped into the black abyss, she felt like a helpless victim awaiting a silent predator who would grab her as she began her decent into the darkness. She knew this was part of the reason she wasn't able to relax or rest lately, but it hadn't always been this way for her. Not until she moved into this old house.

There was something wrong with her new home but she wasn't sure what it was that lingered there. She had never really believed in ghosts, so she tried blocking thoughts of their existence out of her mind. No matter how hard she tried, she could never logically explain the experiences she was having or the images her own eyes had been witnessing.

She thought back to the first time she had seen the old house. Advertised through a classified ad in the newspaper was this quaint but lovely old turn-of-the-century home. She quickly found herself intrigued by its Victorian charm and inexpensive sale price. She was convinced it would be a good investment, especially when the realtor bragged about how wonderful the house was. At that time she had agreed with him since the home seemed to be so inviting and a place she had always dreamed of owning. Of course, it needed a few repairs and she found herself spending quite a bit of her savings on restorations. Now, she wasn't so sure she had made the right choice to buy the old house.

She had lived in the home for only a week when she started noticing strange events taking place. She thought back to all of the things that had happened to her lately. Her lights flickered or turned off and on by themselves. She heard disembodied voices, saw shadows, and sensed someone watching her and felt an occasional touch on her face or shoulder. Her cabinet doors made a habit of opening by themselves and she occasionally smelled the stench of something rotting. She also recalled an experience when an extreme coldness brushed past her.

She found herself terrified to be in her own home and she knew something was toying with her level of sanity. She had never experienced anything like this until she moved into this house. She felt helpless and alone. She didn't know what she could do or whom she could turn to for help. She couldn't afford to leave her house, as she had spent all of her savings on the old home. She thought about selling it, but she didn't think she would be able to earn back what she had invested into the home. She didn't know what to do. She was stuck in a nightmare that seemed to be draining the life right out of her.

She had switched off all of the lights except for the last lamp in the living room. That was a light she would never turn off because it was her only source of security as she walked down her ominous hallway. In the past, she had tried to leave on the lights, especially in the hallway. However, as soon as she would enter the hallway, all of the lights would flicker and turn off. She had even used a flashlight but it too would fade and become useless.

Her palms were sweaty and she felt her heart begin to race. Her room was the last door on the right and she told herself, if she ran quickly enough she could possibly make it without encountering one of *them* again. They seemed to find her best in the dark, so the darkness had become her greatest enemy. She stared at the saving light source given off by the living room lamp and prayed for it to stay on. The light began to flicker and dim and she knew the games they would play with her again tonight.

Most nights it was more of the same. She pleaded for *them* to leave her alone, but they only seemed to gain strength in toying with her. She passed the lamp and, like in the past, they had shut the light off causing darkness to suddenly envelop her. She took a step backwards and the lamp came back on by itself. She could hear *them* laughing at her because they knew her fear. It was almost as if they could smell it. She felt goose bumps crawl up the back of her neck as she braced herself for a long night ahead. She felt unseen eyes pierce right through her as her fragile hand reached for the small Bible in her pocket. She took a step forward again and found herself in darkness once more.

She closed her eyes and ran straight for her bedroom and quickly turned on her light. She had tried leaving her bedroom light on each night, but when she would return to the hall it was always turned off again. They did this with every light she tried to keep on. It was part of their game to scare her and make her feel helpless.

Her door suddenly slammed shut behind her as she ran for the safety of her bed. She put her back up against her headboard and pulled the covers up around her body. She reached for the flashlight on her bedside table waiting for the next phase of the game to begin. This is where the game would change each time. They kept her in suspense, as she never knew what the next move in their game would be.

Her hands were shaking and her heart was pounding. She couldn't stand living like this anymore and knew she had to find a way to leave this house for good. She had tried to call a priest to come and bless her house, but the priest only delivered bad news saying they couldn't help her.

She logically tried to understand what was happening to her. If ghosts haunted her house, could they really harm her? Did ghosts really torment people like this? Her mind was racing with thoughts and she felt like she was going crazy. She sat there for a few moments in silence, trying to shake the uneasy feeling she had. She tried to calm herself down by closing her eyes. Maybe she just needed to get some rest. She had been working way too hard lately and knew she needed to slow down a bit. Was her stress level the cause of this nightmare she was experiencing? Maybe her mind was just making it all up as an alternate reality. The room was deathly silent as she placed her Bible back on her nightstand and switched off her bedside lamp. Staring out into the darkness of the room, she hoped nothing would find her as she prayed whatever was causing her torment would just leave her alone. She forced herself to close her eyes and before she knew it, she fell asleep.

Amanda awoke a couple of hours later to someone tapping on her bedroom door. She sat straight up in bed and in silence, watched as her bedroom door slowly opened on its own and a strange man walked over the door's threshold and up to the foot of her bed. She knew it was one of *them*. She found herself shaking again and was scared to death. She couldn't fathom what would happen next.

She watched as the man just stood there and stared at her. Silence was her enemy. She tried to switch on her bedside lamp, but it came on with an explosion as the bulb shattered and returned her room to darkness. Frightened, she opened her mouth to scream, but nothing came out. She grabbed her pillow and covered her face. She was too afraid to look at the dark shadowy figure again and too scared to see what he might do next.

After a few moments, she mustered up her courage and peaked out from her pillow and as she did, she saw the shadow's mass standing right beside her and there were several other dark shadowy figures standing behind him. The original dark shadowy man suddenly reached out its hand as if to grab her and she hid in fear under her covers again. She began praying, but she could still hear its hellish laughter. Her bed began to shake as if an earthquake had suddenly occurred. She let out a shrill scream and demanded for the entity to leave her alone. She started to pray again. Suddenly, a quiet stillness fell over her bedroom and the shadow man and his crew were gone. Tears streamed down her cheeks and she begged for God to help her.

She realized she could no longer deny the existence of the dark ones who were tormenting her. She knew she needed some help to figure out what was going on and to prove she wasn't insane. She intended to find some help right away. The buildup of the ongoing paranormal events along with that evening's frightening experiences had finally convinced her that ghosts were real and they existed. Her search has now begun to find someone, anyone, who could help end her haunting torment.

CHAPTER 1

"What is a ghost and do they really exist?"

Some people have had encounters like Amanda but some have not. There are different intensity levels of hauntings as well. Some individuals who experience paranormal activity may only experience mild phases of strange phenomenon while others may experience frightening encounters. Whatever the degree of paranormal activity, to many who experience it, it is real and it can affect people of all walks of life differently. Usually those individuals who seek help with paranormal activity are those people who have reached their toleration limit and are not only frustrated but they are also tired of being scared in their own home. Most simply do not understand why they are being haunted and look to outside help for answers in order to put an end to the chaos they have been experiencing. Paranormal activity can range in effects but the fact remains that it is a real and widely recognized phenomenon experienced by many people all over the world.

Perhaps you believe in ghosts or perhaps you don't. Most people struggle with the thought that life ends after they die. A lot of people want to believe that after our physical death our existence does not stop, but continues on in another form. Without this believe or hope, many people would live their entire life in fear of death and dying with no continuance.

We, as human beings, are programmed to believe that there is always hope or another way of living once our physical body dies.

Some historical figures have searched for ways to prolong life. Tales of a "fountain of youth" have been told across the world for thousands of years and have even appeared in writings by Herodotus in the 5th century BC along with Alexander Romance in the 3rd century CE. In the early crusade era of the 11th and 12th centuries, John Prester told similar stories about youthful waters. Even the indigenous people of the Caribbean in the early 15th century spoke of restorative waters with mythical powers in a land called Bimini. However, it wasn't until the 16th century when Spanish explorer, Juan Ponce de Leon, was accredited with his infamous search for the Fountain of Youth in 1513 in an undiscovered area now known as Florida.

Unfortunately, a fountain of youth was never found and people in general are destined to eventually die. Humans also have a tendency to start thinking about death and the afterlife, as they get older. A comical comparison to a human's life span is said to be a lot like a roll of toilet paper because the older one gets, the quicker the roll of toilet paper reaches it end.

Many people tend to believe the soul is a never-ending life force or energy. If this is true and if the soul does truly exist, where exactly does it go once it leaves the physical body? Does a disembodied soul really turn into a ghost? If so, where do ghosts go and how are they able to exist? Do they really exist in another dimension or plane that collides with our dimension and reality? Does a soul automatically go to Heaven or Hell? Is there really factual proof that a soul can live outside its physical body and exist on this Earthly plane? If ghosts are truly real, why are they here and what do they want?

Many people are curious about these types of questions, but finding the answers has been a long-time common goal among many paranormal researchers. They hope to find clues to help answer questions about the afterlife through paranormal investigations and research. We may never know the answers to our questions until we are released from our physical bodies and transformed into spiritual ones. We also may never be able to fully understand the spirit world in our lifetime, but there will always be people asking if there is truly a life after death. The search for answers will continue as it has for centuries.

The spirit world appears to be a mysterious and mystical place that some fear exploring. They consider the unknown paranormal realm to be taboo. It is said that most people fear what they do not understand. Although, some believe the spirit world is an area we are not supposed to venture into. They believe it is a natural part of life for our continued existence. Something I often like to tell people is that the paranormal is the normal, just not yet fully understood.

There are many other people who are interested in the paranormal and with the fast-paced production of paranormal T.V. shows and other paranormal interests, it's no wonder more and more people are falling into the paranormal craze and seeking answers for themselves. Fifty years ago or more, a person would have been put into a strait jacket and placed into a mental institution for admitting witnessing paranormal activity. People just didn't talk about the paranormal long ago, but now more and more people are becoming open to the idea that the paranormal realm is real and there is more to life after death than most originally thought.

I always advise caution to paranormal enthusiasts who are determined to investigate the paranormal. The paranormal field can be one that is full of dangers. Paranormal investigators do not always find peaceful and calm spirits. Where a good side exists, there will often be a bad side. I will go into more detail about this a little later.

Modern Christianity teaches there is a Heaven and a Hell and those who do not uphold good morals and accept God/Jesus as their savior, have a fiery hell that awaits them when they die. Others believe that the present life we are living on Earth is hell, while others believe we are all destined for a resting place of peace and happiness no matter what type of life we lived. Then again, other people simply believe that when our physical body dies, life simply stops and along with our existence. Many different religions lead individuals to believe different or similar theories about the "other side" and what really happens to us when we leave our physical bodies. While there is not a lot of proof that the other side exists, we are given clues and bits of information from time to time which can help each of us decide what "theory" or "belief" system we choose to accept.

Many people throughout the world have reported seeing apparitions, more commonly known as "ghosts," hear disembodied voices or claim to see things move on their own, etc. Is all of this proof that ghosts exist? To those of us who have experienced any strange phenomenon, chances are it's strengthened our belief system to agree that ghosts really do exist. To the hard-core skeptics or to modern day scientists however, there will never be enough proof to say that ghosts exist. Modern technology has also made paranormal claims harder to prove because of easy editing programs, applications and many other technological tools that can forge paranormal photos, video and even audio recordings.

Medical scientists have conducted studies on the physical body and the possible existence of a soul. During these studies; they have discovered interesting facts that have lead up to a theory on death and the soul's existence. Their studies have involved different people who were near the time of their death. These scientists have weighed their subjects right before they died and again just seconds after death. While this may sound a bit morbid, it has enabled scientist to find a slight difference in weight right after the body dies. Could this possibly be from the absence of the soul away from the physical body? This was their theory presented as a result of their studies.

Although most paranormal researchers do not necessarily have a degree that defines us as a scientist or paranormal expert, we are all still interested nonetheless in the studies of the soul and the existence of life after death. Throughout the years, many paranormal researchers have taken a step forward to test theories about the existence of ghosts and have developed intriguing methods of study, coming up with some interesting evidence which we believe helps back our theory that ghosts are indeed real. Seasoned paranormal investigators also know that investigating the paranormal is not how Hollywood portrays it to be in movies or T.V. shows. It's not continuous experiences of paranormal activity or far-fetched happenings that keep everyone on edge but investigations are rather slow and sometimes boring. There are times when nothing at all takes place during an investigation.

Most paranormal researchers and investigators know modern science will never accept our evidence as proof that ghosts exist. In fact, the closest form of recognizing any evidence that ghosts possibly exist is through electronic voice phenomenon (EVP) or "voices of the dead". Although this method is still highly debated due to current recording methods and the lack of evidence to substantiate that ghosts are able to produce sound since no vocal cords are present. It is through this phenomenon of recorded voices that scientists have acknowledge a possibility that a supernatural realm exists, but the recordings presented are not enough "evidence" to say for sure. Those of us who research the paranormal and record voices from people who were not physically present can honestly say we believe there is another existence for us after we die; a place where our soul goes after it leaves the physical body; an existence known simply as a "ghost."

I have been asked the question, "If ghosts have no vocal cords, how then do they produce sound?" Ghosts have been known to communicate through EVP (electronic voice phenomenon.) For years many paranormal researchers believed that ghosts somehow imprinted their voices directly onto tape. This theory was debunked when technology developed digital recorders. Many also argued that EVPs were just radio waves that bounced through the atmosphere. While this theory could have been true, it did not explain why some EVPs were direct answers to questions asked or that they were relevant to the conversations held at the time of the recordings.

Researchers began looking closer at sound waves in the air and theorized that ghosts could manipulate these different sound waves to produce voices heard at frequencies outside of our normal hearing range. Through time and more research, most experienced paranormal researchers agree with this theory. The human voice generally ranges between 300 Hz and 10,000 Hz. EVPs have even been measured above and below this range, even up to 14,000 Hz. An example of the various frequency levels would be a dog and a dog whistle. While human ears cannot hear the dog whistle, a dog can hear it very clearly. These different frequency levels are what allow our audio equipment to record EVPs. Although most EVPs are not audible to the human ear, the recording equipment picks up an EVP through the various frequency levels and is converted upon playback within a frequency range that is audible to the human ear.

History suggests that it could have been Thomas Edison with his discovery and creation of the "Tin Foil Phonograph," which he built in 1877. It is said that while trying to record his voice to test out his phonograph, he actually recorded the voice of an unknown entity. The American Society for Psychical Research however, recorded the first documented EVP on April 23, 1933 through "Decca Records," which was recorded communication with the dead through so-called "dead recording equipment." This experiment was successful but when the researchers were asked to go public with their findings, none of them would come forward due to fear of being ridiculed.

There are 3 main classifications of EVPs: Class "A," Class "B" and Class "C". Class "A" EVPs are easily heard, understood and are usually loud and clear. Class "B" EVPs can be heard and understood but not with as much clarity or volume. Class "C" EVPs have voices present but are usually harder to hear and understand. This information will come in handy as you continue to read further into this book.

So what really is a ghost? Some define it as the soul of a human, a disembodied spirit, apparition or shadow. From our studies, and contrary to some peoples' beliefs, ghosts were once human and in physical form living their lives like all of us, until their passing into death. When the physical body dies, the soul continues on and if these people don't cross over, they remain Earthbound and become what we commonly refer to as ghosts. There are other theories as to what a ghost is, but this is the most common explanation.

However, ghosts are generally just like regular people, each having different personalities, etc. The only difference is they have no physical body. They usually keep the same personality traits in their thoughts, needs, wants, etc. The reasons they stay Earthbound can vary with each individual ghost. In our experiences researching and investigating the paranormal, we have learned that ghosts do not always choose to cause harm and scare people as Hollywood depicts in the movies. Hollywood has produced this stereotype of ghosts for so many years that it has etched a preconceived notion deep into our subconscious minds causing many people to make assumptions about the paranormal without having all of the facts.

Many people are not aware that ghosts have been around for a long time and are even mentioned in history. According to historical research, the word "ghost" originated before 900BC. The origin of the word "spirit" in a paranormal sense was first recorded in 1666. Who were some of the first people to document the existence of ghosts or spirits? There were several. Some that I discuss in this chapter are: William Shakespeare in his play, Julius Caesar, authors of The Bible, Anthendorus, and the Fox Sisters. These stories are interesting because they document early stories and potential true encounters with ghosts.

Shakespeare (c. 1599) in his play Julius Caesar – 44BC

William Shakespeare often wrote about true-life events and based his characters off of real people. Brutus did not like Julius Caesar and devised a plan with his co-conspirators to murder the Roman dictator. One night, they gathered together and stabbed Caesar to death. Shortly after the murder and one night before a battle, Brutus said a huge apparition claiming to be the ghost of Julius Caesar had visited him. Brutus took the vision as an omen of doom after he lost the battle and ended up killing himself a short time later.

The Bible:

Documentation referencing ghosts was found in the old scrolls that were later translated into the modern day Bible. Some of these references are found in the New and Old Testaments in the books of Mark, Luke and Samuel. There are more scriptures on ghosts or spirits found in the Bible, however these are just a few as an example.

Mark 6:48, "But when they saw him (Jesus) walking on the water, they thought he was a ghost and cried out."

Luke 24: 36-39, "While they were still talking about this, Jesus himself stood among them and said to them, "Peace be with you. They were startled and frightened thinking they saw a ghost. He said to them, "Why are you troubled and why do doubts rise in your minds? Look at my hands and my feet. It is I myself. Touch me and see; a ghost does not have flesh and bones as you and I have."

1 Samuel 28: 1-25 tells the story of Saul and the witch of Endor. These scriptures tell of King Saul who had to lead the Israelites into battle against the Philistines. Fearing the worst for his upcoming battle, he sought out the witch of Endor and asked her to bring forth the ghost of Samuel so he could give him advice for the battle. The witch conjured up Samuel's spirit who told Saul that since he had turned his face against God, he would lose the battle and the Israelites would be taking captive by the Philistines.

Anthendorus – Athens, Greece – 63-113 AD:

This story took place in Athens, Greece: Anthendorus was a scholar and writer and moved to Athens, Greece and began looking for a place to take up residence. He found a home in which he had been told was haunted by a man who rattled chains but he refused to acknowledge the stories because he did not believe in the existence of ghosts. Late one evening he had sat down with a light and writing materials. He began to hear the rattling of chains close by him but he kept writing and refused to acknowledge what he was hearing. The sounds began getting louder and closer and finally when he could no longer ignore the sounds, he looked around and saw the apparition of a man in chains, the same one that had been reported by others. The apparition beckoned to him with his finger but Anthendorus waved him off as if to say he was busy working. The apparition however would not be ignored and went over and shook his chains over the head of Athendorus and beckoned him once more. Taking his lantern, Anthendorus followed the apparition to the courtyard and watched as the man disappeared. Baffled by this, Anthendorus then placed grass and leaves over the spot where the apparition disappeared so he would recognize the spot when he returned. The next day he had the spot dug up and in the ground and entwined in chains laid the skeletal remains of a man. He was taken and given a proper burial and from that point the haunting of this house ceased.

The Fox Sisters – Hydesville, New York – 1848

It is said that the Fox Sisters were responsible for starting the spiritualistic movement and they have been documented in history as creators of the "rapping" technique for communicating with spirits. In December of 1847 John Fox, along with his wife and 2 daughters, Kate and Margaret, moved into a house that had a reputation of being haunted. There were several instances told of raps, taps and other noises occurring so often that the prior tenant, Michael Weakman, moved out of the house because of these inexplicable disturbances.

Around the Middle of March 1848, the family also began to be disturbed by the strange sounds and activities. The sounds were often so loud that the beds themselves would shake. They looked for logical explanations for the activity but could find none. One night, Kate asked the unseen entity if it would mimic the number of claps that she made and surprisingly the spirit complied and clapped back. Later the girl's asked the entity if it would rap back a certain number of times to answer questions. Again the spirit granted their request. Amazed at this new type of communication, the girls told their parents who then told neighbors. Before too long, many friends and family members would come to the Fox's home to try communicating with this spirit through "rapping."

During one of the "rapping" sessions, the ghost told them that he was 31 years old and that he had lived in the Fox's home five years prior to them moving in. He stated through rapping that he had a wife and five children, all whom were still alive except for his wife. He stated that he had been murdered in the front East bedroom on a Tuesday at 12 o'clock by a man who had slit his throat with a butcher knife in order to rob him of the $500 he had. He then proceeded to state his body had been taken down to the cellar of the home where it laid for 1 day before being buried in the floor of the cellar.

Wondering if this ghost's story was true, the Fox family along with some neighboring friends began digging in the cellar of the home on Saturday, April 1st, 1848. They hit water that forced their digging to cease until the summer months. Further digging at about 5 feet, they discovered a plank below the charcoal and lime that revealed hair and bones. It wasn't until 56 years later, however, that the Fox sisters' story was confirmed and proof was found that there had indeed been a body buried in the cellar of the Fox home. (A secondary version of this story remains the same with the exception that the Fox family never found hair and bones of a human in their basement and that their story could never be fully verified.)

Word supposedly got out about the discovery that the Fox sisters had made and a small group of spiritualists gathered at Corinthian Hall in Rochester, New York on November 14, 1849. Excitement was building over the new discovery and several committees were formed to try and prove the Fox sisters' phenomenon was fraudulent. The public was not buying the sister's story either and had no sympathy for the Fox sisters. Anger even flared and at one point where the Fox sisters were nearly lynched. Still, there were others that were excited about the discovery and many began to see a great spiritualistic movement beginning.

Since this time, sightings or experiences with ghosts and spirits have increased throughout many generations. Why is this? Could it be due to the Internet or the increased amount of paranormal TV shows? Could it be due to a more open-minded modern society who accepts the fact that ghosts and spirits might be real? What about if there is some sort of undiscovered spiritual movement that most are not aware of? The possibilities are endless but one fact remains for sure, more and more people are experiencing paranormal activity.

Whenever the topic of ghosts is mentioned, the subject of angels and demons are also included. While I definitely believe that all three exist, I fully believe there is a difference between ghosts, angels and demons. My belief is that you can't have one without the other. If you believe in good, you have to believe in the bad. If you believe in angels, then you have to believe in demons. Like the Chinese philosophy of yin and yang, in order to have balance, it takes opposing or complimentary forces to make the balance complete.

I've had some people ask me if there is a difference between ghosts and demons and my answer has always been yes. Even if one looks back on Biblical scriptures they will find that angles, ghosts, unfamiliar spirits and demons, are always referenced as separate and different entities and not one in the same. I am a firm believer that deceptive demons or spirits do exist and they can portray themselves as something they are not, such as the spirit of an innocent child. However, this does not mean that every ghost out there is a "demon."

Too many people are too quick to automatically label ghosts as demons, especially those of many various religious faiths. This could be because this is what they have been taught or because they do not have the in-depth knowledge to make a decision about the unknown. As the old saying goes, people fear what they do not understand. I am reminded of a Biblical scripture found in 2 Corinthians 11:14 – "And no marvel; for Satan himself is transformed into an angel of light." In my years of investigating the paranormal, I have learned that spirits can be deceitful as well as honest. Those who are troubled and who cause a lot of chaos are usually the ones who resent the living. Why do they resent the living? Because they themselves want to be alive in the physical form and resent those they come into contact with who are alive. I will share in depth stories of spirits later on in this book.

Francis Lawrence directed the movie, "Constantine," in 2005 where it speaks about how once one accepts pure evil's existence then evil becomes aware of your knowledge. The movie also leads one to potentially believe that those who have knowledge of the other side might have a higher chance of having an encounter with the darker realm at some point. This is one of the reasons why our paranormal investigations group has spent years encouraging new paranormal enthusiasts to conduct a lot of research regarding what they might be dealing with before experimenting with the paranormal. There is a lot more involved than what many people might think and I will cover this more in depth in a later chapter.

There are different types of "spirit entities" out there. While, again, there has been no solid proof that ghosts, angels and demons exist, there have been written documentation that states otherwise. Our group has encountered strange entities, which we remain unsure of their origin to this day. They don't seem to fit into your typical "ghost" description, nor do they fit it with the angel or demon category. Some of these entities are known as "Shadow People" while others are what we have referenced to as a "Non-Human Entity."

So what exactly are the different spirit types? While there may be more out there that many of us are unaware of, we do know of at least five different spirit types. One type I have mentioned already is "ghosts," which are believed to be the soul of man once it leaves the physical body.

Next are "Demons," who are usually considered to be a malevolent spirit, and in Christian terms, are generally understood to be a fallen angel, formerly of God. A demon is frequently depicted as a force that may be conjured and insecurely controlled.

"Angels" are more commonly known as messengers from God but other roles in religious traditions include them acting as a warrior or guard; the concept of a "guardian angel" is popular in modern Western culture.

"Shadow people" are commonly seen by many and usually appear in three different ways. Type 1 is usually seen as a small dark misty cloud and is normally below two feet in height. Type 2 is usually as a huge thick cloudy or dark mass ranging from two to eight feet in height. Types 3 is where they appear in human form and are usually seen wearing a hat of sorts and sometimes a duster or long cloak. Their appearance is around seven to eight feet in height and sometimes they are reported to either have no distinguished eyes or their eyes appear red or orange in color. Speculation for the true identity of these beings ranges from demons to aliens to inter-dimensional beings to time travelers and/or astral bodies. Their true identity may never be found in this lifetime; however there are many eyewitness accounts that prove there is something to the shadow people phenomenon. Many people associate shadow people with being bad or demonic but this theory is not always true. Shadow people are seen in a dark form but this also could be because of light refraction or the energy source being used by them to appear.

"Non-Human Entities" are fascinating and an area of research that many paranormal researchers are still studying. They seem to be able to take on any shape or character they choose for their appearance and they are usually very chaotic in nature. They have been known to be mischievous and can be harmful if they choose. There has been some speculation that they are the offspring of the Nephilim, which are thought to be the fallen angels cast out of heaven.

Nephilim is a Hebrew word for "Giants" which literally means the "Fallen-Down Ones." Scholars think that perhaps this description is for the angels that were cast out of Heaven. The main documented source for the Nephilim is found in the Bible as Biblical scriptures state in Genesis 6:1-2 "When men began to increase in number on the earth and daughters were born to them (2) the sons of God saw that the daughters of men were beautiful, and they married any of them they chose." (4) The Nephilim were on the earth in those days and also afterward the sons of God went to the daughters of men and had children by them, the same became mighty men, which were of old, men of renown.

What makes the Nephilim the "Son's of God?" In Job 1:6 "The Son's of God came to present themselves before the Lord in Heaven." Job 2:1 "Among the Son's of God is Satan...." Which indicates that the "Son's of God" are angels and then once cast out of Heaven, they were considered "Fallen Angels" or.... "The Nephilim." This is also backed up in Jude 6-7: "And the angels which kept not their first estate, but left their own habitation, he hath reserved in everlasting chains under darkness unto the judgment of the great day. Even as Sodom & Gomorrah and the cities about them in like manner, giving themselves over to fornication, and going after strange flesh...."

Biblical scholars believe it was Satan's plan to use the Nephilim to infiltrate the human race in order to mess up the DNA bloodline of Jesus. The Nephilim were said to have been chaotic and ones who caused trouble. Their "sins" and negative influences upon mankind caused great wickedness, which displeased God. This was during the time of Noah when God caused the flood. Genesis 6:5-6 "And God saw that the wickedness of man was great in the earth and that every imagination of the thoughts of his heart was evil continually. And it repented the Lord that he had made man."

The Flood - Due to the wickedness that prevailed on Earth, God sent the flood to wipe out all of mankind with the exception of Noah and his family since they were righteous. Scripture however mentions later there were still Nephilim in the land even after the flood and scholars speculate that there were many Nephilim and their offspring that survived. Modern science believes that the flood only covered a specific landmass where supposedly man was known to live. Studies have been done on the areas where the flood was said to have covered the earth and differences in stone and dirt have showed their theory to be correct. Could this be why some Nephilim remained?

Do the Spirits of the Nephilim Still Remain on Earth? Some researchers believe that they do, especially since there is scripture that states that the Nephilim cannot lift their eyes to Heaven and they are to be chained in darkness. There is however also scripture that states that there were some Nephilim allowed to roam free until judgment day. Isaiah 26:14 "They are dead, they shall not live, they are Rephaim, they shall not rise." The Rephaim is understood to be the Nephilim and scholars have interpreted "rise" to be the "Resurrection of Christ." Could these doomed "Nephilim spirits be the ones that people encounter that seem dark and ominous and full of chaos? Some paranormal researchers believe that these "unknown" spirits are indeed ones that are encountered during certain investigations. These spirits are sometimes known for causing chaos in homes/businesses and who also take on forms of strange creatures or beings.

The Giants: Offspring of the Nephilim

It is believed that Giants are the offspring of the Nephilim. Since the basic DNA structure was changed due to the inner breeding of the Nephilim and humans, research suggests that Giants were the result. Giants have been around for ages and have been documented in many photographs. Some of these "Giants" were as tall as 7 feet up to 20 feet. Some proof that Giants have altered DNA is shown through different body parts including bone and organ structure. Some were known to have 2 sets of teeth and/or 6 fingers and 6 toes. There is even on-going research being conducted today into the mystery of the Giants. Skeletal proof is being sought in order to prove they once existed.

Paranormal Investigators may not have all the answers about the spirit realm, but through our research and investigations that document our experiences with these different types of spirit entities, we can present our understanding of the other side.

We have been asked many times if we feel like every place we investigate is haunted and our answer is no. Our first method is to find a logical explanation for any reported activity or any activity that we might witness first hand. While many occurrences can be explained, there are some instances that we do not have an explanation for.

There are many different ways that research teams explore and study the paranormal field and while strict protocols should be kept, there is no right or wrong way to investigate if contamination protocols are followed. Our team developed a method of combining a scientific but yet spiritual approach to paranormal investigating and our main goal is to observe, record, and document data using the scientific method, but to also hear, see and feel things around us from a spiritual aspect. Getting psychic impressions to correlate with recorded evidence is very hard and rare, but sometimes the findings can correlate with the scientific data. While we use people with gifts and abilities, we do not always base our findings or investigative reports off of psychic impressions.

By using both methods of investigating we not only can record evidence that ghosts exist, but we can also learn about the ghosts themselves. In this book you will read about our investigative experiences and the ghost stories that accompany our investigations, told by the ghosts themselves through the eyes of the psychic investigator. While this field might seem strange to some, to others it is quite normal. I came up with a phrase for our group and it is one that I mentioned above: Paranormal: The normal not yet understood. There are so many things that are not yet understood in the paranormal realm but there are many things that we could learn if we just took the time to discover what's really out there.

Do ghosts really exist? We believe they do and perhaps through this book you will gain a bit more insight into the spiritual world by reading further about our investigative experiences. Then perhaps you can decide for yourself what you believe.

CHAPTER 2

"The Beginning"

I remember as a child growing up how I would sometimes see and hear different things that I never could quite understand. The older I got the more weird encounters I seemed to have. I was raised to be very religious, so my parents never entertained the idea of ghosts and the subject was just something that you did not talk about at home or around the church family. Still, there were questions that I had and that I wanted answers to, so I decided to be daring and I approached my pastor about the subject of ghosts.

I didn't want to cause any trouble for my church family and I did not want to become an outcast, so I approached him very carefully and let him know that I just wanted to get his opinion on the subject matter. I remember being about 12 years old when I spoke with him and feeling quite nervous, but I knew if I wanted the truth, I had to seek it out.

My pastor was quick to tell me that we shouldn't dwell on things like ghosts because the "devil" liked to play tricks on our minds. He also said that all ghosts were just demons in disguise, sent by Satan to deceive us. I never did quite fully understand where he got the information for his answer, because I knew throughout the Bible there were scriptures that mentioned ghosts and spirits and even our Pentecostal faith taught us to believe in the "Holy Ghost" or "Holy Spirit," so what was the difference? I accepted his answer but still found myself fascinated by the spirit world. Later, as I got a bit older, I found myself sneaking in a good scary ghost book or movie to keep my interest alive.

While I might have had a good imagination all throughout my life, I knew there were many things that had happened to me that I could never as assume was just imagined from my vast young mind. I think one of my first strange experiences happened when I was around 9 years old. My grandparents had moved in with us since they were getting older and my grandfather was very ill. My grandparents were wonderful people. They married when they were quite young. My grandmother was aged only 15 years and my grandfather only 19 years. They were together for a total of 48 years before my grandfather went to be with God.

However, several years before my grandfather's death, he and my grandmother had always slept in different rooms so they would not disturb each other. My grandmother was always a light sleeper and my grandfather was quite the opposite. Since our house had only three bedrooms, my grandmother elected to stay in the same room with my sister and I leaving our grandfather with our only guest bedroom. For the past 15 years, my grandfather had found himself in and out of hospitals with heart trouble and he had always said that if God was going to take him, he wanted to die either behind the pulpit preaching or in his sleep. Well in July of 1989, he was granted his wish because as we all sat around the breakfast table one morning, my grandmother came into the kitchen announcing that my grandfather had passed away during the night. We learned that his heart had finally given up and that he had passed away peacefully in his sleep.

I remember the funeral quite well and how hard it was on all of us, even for me at such a young age. I was trying to be strong for my family but it was hard watching everyone with their sad faces as tears streamed down their cheeks. I remember feeling like it wasn't fair that God had taken my grandfather away from all of us. I remembered my mother taught my sister and I if we really wanted something badly enough and if we prayed in earnest, that God would grant us the desires of our heart. I remember closing my eyes while sitting there on the benches of that old church at my grandfather's funeral and praying for God to bring my grandpa back to all of us. I remember staring really hard at my grandfather's body expecting his chest to rise and fall with breath and for his body to animate with life again. I prayed and watched throughout the whole funeral service but unfortunately my grandfather continued to lie there motionless.

When we all attended the graveside services, I didn't want them to bury my grandpa because I just knew that God had heard my prayers and that he was going to give me the desires of my little heart. When I saw them start to lay my grandfather in the ground, I cried heavy tears and found myself feeling very angry with God. Why had He let me down? I remember feeling so sad and I knew I had to say goodbye to my grandpa forever now that they were finally laying him to rest in the ground.

I remember going home and staring into the room where my grandfather had passed away. I couldn't help but wonder what it had been like for him to die. I shuttered at the thought and knew I would never look at that room ever the same way again. No matter how hard I tried to ignore my strange feelings about that room, I could never shake the uneasy feeling and from that point forward that room always sent chills up and down my spine. I never quite understood why until later when I learned that it was the essence of death that I still felt and was afraid of as my grandpa's spirit was no longer there, but his soul's essence was.

To define essence, it can be described as energy left over from someone or something. Later, I would learn that a person could leave an imprint of their energy in a place, even in different quantities. That's what my grandfather had done. I could never ever again look at my grandfather's room as the guest bedroom that my sister and I had played in once in a while, because now it resembled death to me and I wanted nothing more to do with it.

My mother began using it for storage and I remember several occasions where she had asked me to put something in that room. I would beg her not to make me, because I was so scared of the room, yet she insisted I overcome my fear and do as she had told me. I remember approaching the door and opening it only enough to get my small arm inside where I could toss the object into the room and then quickly close the door again.

The layout of our house had the room that my sister and I shared at the end of the hallway. In order to get to our bedroom, we had to pass by our grandfather's old room. I remember how I would always run by the room in order to reach my bedroom. I felt if I didn't run, something might open the door, reach out and grab me. It's strange now to think about how the death of a loved one could have such a big impact on such a small child. Death is never easy and can really be confusing to a small child who doesn't fully understand it.

That same year my folks bought some land out in the country, so we moved from our home in the city to our new 5-acre piece of land in the country. In the beginning, we stayed in a mobile home until my father finished building our new house. Something funny about my father, and those who know him can attest to this, is that he loves his antique cars. He had started quite a collection of them out on our 5 acres. I didn't mind seeing the old cars, at least not during the day, but I had grown to hate them in the late-night hours when it was dark outside, because I would sometimes see shadows passing in between them. Then at other times I would see figures actually in the cars. When I brought this to my parent's attention, they could never see what I was seeing. Of course, when I told my mother, she told me that there was nothing out there in the old cars and that my mind was just playing tricks on me again. Were these experiences just the over-active imagination of a young 9-year old or was I really seeing these strange figures?

When I was about 13, we were finally ready to move into our new house and settled in quickly. This is when I really started experiencing even more strange things. Our new house was quite large and required two heating and cooling units in order to properly accommodate the 3,000 square foot home. My parents had my sisters and I sleep in one bedroom, so they would only have to use one heating unit at night when the temperatures dropped low. They found this helped save money on utility bills. My baby sister would sleep in my parent's room on some of those nights. My middle sister and I found it nice to fall asleep in our family den right in front of the fireplace. We would pull two couches up together to make an extended bed and then we would fall asleep listening to the crackling embers of the fire. It became a nightly routine until one night when my sister and I experienced something that we both will never forget.

I had gotten up to use the bathroom in the middle of the night. Half asleep, I stumbled down our hallway and made my way to the restroom. I had just finished my business when I heard my sister calling my name. Suddenly, she stood at the bathroom door frantically stating there was a tall shadow-man in our den. I thought that perhaps my sister had just had a bad dream or that she had just imagined this figure out of the darkness that had encompassed our living room. It was logical since the glowing embers of the fire had diminished to nothing but a small orange glow. We both went back into the den and as we stood there at the entryway by the French doors, our eyes both focused on a tall figure about 7-feet in height wearing a long fedora type hat and a long duster coat. It had no facial features, just indentations for the eyes, nose and mouth and no distinguishing limbs for hands or feet. My sister and I just stood there in shock until we started seeing this figure float down towards us from the Cathedral ceiling of the den.

Whatever this was, we wanted nothing to do with it, ran to our parents' room and woke them up to tell them about this "shadow man" we had just seen in the den. My father immediately woke up, grabbed his gun from out of his closet and went into the den. When he found no one, he flipped on all the lights in the house and looked in every room and closet, but again there was no one to be found. He went outside and looked all around our property for our silent, scary intruder but, once again, found no one.

Our dad might not have been convinced there was a seven-foot shadow person in our living room, but of course my sister and I were fully convinced that we had seen him and that he was real. We knew what we had seen and refused to go back and sleep in the den. We convinced our parents to let us sleep in their room for the remainder of the night. My sister and I couldn't fall back to sleep due to the incident that had happened with our mysterious visitor. Was this just a figment of our imagination or did we really see this shadow person? We both talked about how our mother had always told us that demons existed and since this thing was tall, black and scary, we wondered if it was one of the demons our mother had taught us about. Whatever this thing was, my sister and I were both convinced that it was real and we knew that we had both seen him. It took us a long time before we would ever sleep in our den again because we were afraid that we might encounter this shadow man again.

A few months later, I had another strange encounter that I couldn't explain. I had fallen asleep one night and had been sleeping for about 4 hours when I started dreaming about myself running from this black shadow. I found myself running down a long hallway, but the faster I would try to run, the slower I was able to go. While this may sound like a movie scene right out of Hollywood, it was a very real experience to me. It is a memory that will stick with me forever.

I remember looking behind me and seeing this figure getting closer to me. I turned back around to run again and I hit a door at the end of the hallway and fell down. I woke up from this dream and immediately sat straight up in my bed. I was sweating badly and as I sat there, I could feel my heart pounding as I tried to shake off the dream. I happened to glance over to my right and there, beside my bed, was the same figure I had been running from in my dream. This really scared me so I threw my head under my covers and started praying it would go away. I couldn't make myself look out from under the covers to see if it was gone, so I laid awake until daybreak when I felt safe to come out.

I realized from that point forward that my experiences became more frequent and I wondered why all of these different spirits were tormenting me in their own subtle ways. I would see strange figures and things more often. I began to think my mother was right about these "ghosts" when she told me they were "just the devil playing tricks on my mind." I then decided I wanted nothing more to do with ghosts and the afterlife, especially if it was wrong to focus on them. I thought I could end up being like them one day, lost in a place I did not want to be or even worse, in the fiery hell my preacher had so often spoken about in all those years of church services I had attended!

Years had past and I was now an adult. It had been a long time since I had really thought about the paranormal or the strange encounters I had chosen to forget as a child. However, there were times in between where I found myself fascinated with a show I had watched on television or a book I came across on the subject of ghosts, but I remained firm in my decision to put it all behind me and ignore it.

I have often heard those who have spiritual gifts or abilities can never really forget them or shut them off completely; they stay with them forever. I had learned that these individuals could only suppress them for a while before they were confronted with spirits again. It is at that point the individual has to decide what they want to do with their so-called abilities. If the individual chose to get back in touch with their spiritual gifts, it is often times called an "awakening." This is where my real story begins.

At the age of 19, I ended up moving away from home to start my own "independent life." I ended up believing that I was in love, as most young people do, and I got married at twenty years old and gave birth to my daughter at twenty-one. As life would have it, I was divorced after three years and was on my own with my daughter who was only 2 ½ years old. I dated for a while, fell in love a couple of times. I eventually met a man named John who helped me get started with researching the paranormal field. We became great friends and had many long talks about our interests in the paranormal. He invited me to go out and try a ghost hunt with him at a local rural cemetery not to far from where we both lived. The thought of a cemetery scared me a bit and I didn't think I was ready to start actually "looking for ghosts." I remembered the time when I was younger and how they seemed to be "looked for me" and wouldn't leave me alone, so I wasn't sure if I wanted to experience those fears all over again.

A couple of months had passed and after a few more conversations about the paranormal, John invited me once again to go out with him on a "ghost hunt." I still wanted to tell him "no" however, I had to admit that my curiosity was peaked because of some things other out-of-state paranormal groups had been revealing in the way of "ghostly evidence." The state of Oklahoma, where I lived, had no paranormal research teams at that time that we were aware of. At least there were none listed on the Internet either that we could find. The field of paranormal investigation was new to Oklahoma but through research, John and I learned there were other paranormal teams outside our state who were actively investigating. I then wondered if we too could possibly find some sort of proof that ghosts existed if we conducted some investigative research ourselves. Besides, I wasn't quite convinced of everything I had seen, read or heard on the Internet. I wanted solid proof for myself. I already knew from my past experiences that ghosts did exist, but I wondered if we could record and collect the type of evidence that others were doing as well. I figured if John and I were able to record it ourselves, then I could believe the recorded claims more since I personally would have some of my own evidence to compare.

John and I made it a habit to listen to Art Bell on the radio and we gained a lot of insight into other people's encounters with ghostly phenomenon. John also showed me different websites full of insightful information about the paranormal and I became more and more intrigued with it all. I found myself finally agreeing to go out on that cemetery hunt with him, even if it was a decision made against my better judgment.

I remember this first "hunt" quite well as he and I were driving to a rural area where we would soon step foot in an old cemetery. John told me he had visited there once before and some of the headstones dated back to the 1800's, so there was a good chance we would be able to get some evidence recorded. At the time, it was thought that the older the headstones the greater chances of a cemetery being haunted.

I remember the drive there and how scared I was. I watched the road in front of us carefully, so sure that we would have a ghost step out in front of our truck telling "Beware, turn *back while you still have the chance!"* Yes, I had obviously watched too much *"Scooby Doo"* as a child, but that didn't change the real-fear I was experiencing at that moment. I became even more frightened while we were driving as I looked in front of us and noticed how the old trees seemed to warn us to turn back. Their low branches hung over the road forming a tunnel and I just knew that it was a bad omen. I felt nauseous to my stomach and felt like every muscle in my body had tightened to the point of no return. I kept looking back in my side rearview mirror at the dusty road we had just traveled and I found that every ounce of me wanted to turn back. It took everything I had not to ask my friend to turn around and take me home.

I found myself telling John I didn't think this was a very good idea and maybe I still wasn't ready for this. He was supportive and tried to encourage me to be strong and put my fears behind me. He told me the only way I could overcome my fear would be to face it head on. I wanted to tell him, "That's easy for you say; especially when you don't see ghosts!" but I didn't. However, deep inside I knew this was the night I would be facing my ultimate fears. I just wasn't sure I was ready to take that step forward. I wasn't sure what I would find at this old cemetery or what I might end up seeing. Once we finally arrived, I knew there was no way I could chicken-out and go back home.

I remember pulling up to the old cemetery and parking just outside the gate. There wasn't a "No Trespassing" sign and the gate wasn't locked, so we decided to go inside knowing it would be legal for us to do so. I was very hesitant at first and told myself I would keep my flashlight on at all times so I couldn't see *them* that well should they decide to show themselves to me. Even as a child, I could see them better in the dark than I could in the light and still to this day, I have never been able to figure out exactly why. We grabbed what simple arrangement of equipment we had with us and walked up to the old iron gate. It creaked when we opened it as if protesting its disturbance and I remember jumping a bit as I heard it groan. I was anxious and my senses were on full alert, because I felt more like the hunted instead of the hunter.

We began to walk around and the more we explored, the more I noticed this cemetery seemed to be one of Oklahoma's lost and forgotten since it looked like it hadn't been tended to in quite some time. The grass in some areas was up to our knees and some of the headstones had been knocked over and broken. There were many that had been tarnished by age and weather. Some were so bad we could barely make out the dates. Cobwebs were strung from some of the trees hanging low enough to connect to the headstones. I found its current condition sad and I wondered what it had once looked like in its beginning years. I kept watching where I stepped and, of course, in the back of my mind I kept expecting a hand to reach out of a grave, grab my ankle and pull me down into the grave with it. Again, more influence from Hollywood that was plaguing my mind, but in a situation like I was in, I imagined anything was possible. I began thinking about all the ghost and zombie movies that I had watched throughout the years and I found myself hanging on to the arm of my friend. He was a fearless police officer and a big paranormal enthusiast. Therefore, he politely chuckled at my state of mind and body.

After a short time in the cemetery, I started to feel a bit more relieved and relaxed, because I hadn't seen any ghosts and I hadn't had anything from beyond the grave grab my ankles. I found myself actually enjoying being out there as the cemetery seemed to be quite peaceful, even on a dark night with hardly a star visible in the sky. John had been taking photographs and I was left in charge of our new box cassette tape recorder with the Omni-directional microphone. It was obvious I had never done investigating before and I wasn't quite sure if what I was doing was correct. However, I held on to the hope that I would be able to record some EVPs (electronic voice phenomenon or "voices of the dead.") I began thinking maybe, just maybe, I would get the hang of this and be okay. I also thought perhaps what I had experienced as a child was just a figment of my imagination and maybe there was nothing to be afraid of after all.

We had spent a couple of hours out in that old cemetery before deciding to call it a night. I recall feeling very relieved when he said it was time to go and how I was glad when we finally walked back through the old iron gate to our truck. I hoped we were lucky enough to have gotten something recorded and I was actually looking forward to going over the evidence that we had gotten from that night. As we drove away from the cemetery, I began recalling the events from that evening and I was actually glad that I had faced my fears that night. Little did I know this was only the beginning and I would still have many more fears to overcome.

We reviewed our evidence the next day and were disappointed when we didn't get anything, but that didn't stop us from choosing to go out again. It seemed that John had developed a new drive and passion for this new field we had discovered and he was determined to continue investigating. He wanted me there with him to help, however I still found myself leaning towards the side of caution.

Our second investigation was scheduled, but this time at a different location as we had our sights set on another small rural cemetery in a different part of the county in which we lived. I again encountered the same fears I had felt that first night, but convinced myself I didn't have anything to worry about. I had done this once before and I could do it again.

The night began just as it was getting dark. We got into our truck and drove about 20 miles to this little old cemetery. This one seemed well maintained and much smaller in size. It too had no visible "no trespassing" signs, but this time the entrance was open as if to welcome visitors rather than scare them away like the old iron gate from the first cemetery. Still, I felt my stomach tighten and my senses become fully alert as I exited the truck and looked inside the cemetery. There was a full moon out, so I could see the cemetery quite well. I was a bit relieved by this, as I knew if I encountered any "ghosts" this time, I might be able to see them before they saw me! At least that's what I had hoped anyway.

Again, we grabbed our equipment and entered through the open gate of this cemetery and began taking photos and audio recordings. As we walked past the different headstones, I noticed this cemetery had quite a different feel to it from the other one. I felt very apprehensive and kept seeing movement out of the corner of my eyes. There were shadow figures that moved furtively about and suddenly I felt myself overcome with fear. I was sure I was going to have to go sit in the truck. It was at that point that I remembered my childhood fears, but I tried very hard to shut the memories out so I could be brave and remain in the cemetery. However, it became harder and harder to do so when I saw a shadowy figure move a bit closer to me. I found myself heading in the opposite direction hoping to get away from it. Here I was trying to capture evidence that ghosts existed; yet I was trying to escape them and run the other way. Of course it didn't make sense and seemed to defeat my purpose for being there, however I couldn't deny my fears and I was dealing with the situation the best way I knew how. If that meant I had to get away from them, then that was what I had to do.

I once heard if you went out looking for ghosts you would eventually find them or they would find you. That might have been perfect for the average ghost hunter, but it wasn't for someone like me who already had the ability to see them when they saw me. I told John about the things I was seeing and feeling and he told me to just stay by him and he would help keep me calm. He explained to me that he had read spirits could use your fear against you, if you let them. I wanted to tell him, "Too late!", but I tried to keep calm and let him know I was trying my best to be brave. I was so grateful to have such a fearless friend by my side. I felt if I just stayed behind him, they wouldn't be able find me as easily. Staying in his footsteps and only looking at his back instead of what was around me, I started to feel a bit better about being out there. However, I had forgotten about what could sneak up behind me. I remembered hearing footsteps behind us earlier, so I decided walking behind him wasn't such a great idea after all. Instead, I chose to walk beside him and stay close by his side.

As we continued our investigation, I heard a few different voices, mostly from disembodied ghosts, which were curious as to what we were doing there in the cemetery. A few times that night, I felt a woman come close by me, but I didn't know who she was or what she wanted. I didn't really care to know what she wanted either. I just wanted to hurry up and finish our investigation so we could go home. I had no problem admitting I was spooked. That night, the ghosts in this cemetery had gotten the better of me!

During our beginning stages of this investigation, we asked a lot of questions hoping to record some EVPs. I found it to be a bit strange to talk to the open air in hopes of capturing voices I could not hear at the time, but that was supposedly how many paranormal investigators collected them. Towards the end of our investigation, when we had decided to wrap up, we started walking back towards the entrance gate when my friend asked, "Is there anyone here who would like to say anything to us before we leave?" It was at that moment we both heard footsteps and rustling in the grass behind us. John turned to me and said; "Shine your light back there," referring to the area behind us where we had heard the footsteps and rustling sound. I immediately turned my flash light back behind us, but to our disappointment we saw nothing. We decided to call it a night so we gathered our equipment, loaded up in the truck and headed for home.

Once more, I was so glad and relieved that we were leaving. That cemetery, although small in size, had an intense amount of strange activity and if other places were just like this one, I really didn't know how I would be able to handle investigating on a regular basis. Yes, I had been very scared, but I also couldn't help but wonder what or whom those shadows were that I had seen. None of them looked like the 7-foot tall shadow man that my sister and I had seen that night in our living room, so what exactly were these shadows and whom should I ask? Were they ghosts or maybe demons? Some of these shadows resembled a human form, but some were just shadow masses.

We had heard footsteps behind us along with the rustling of the grass, but we saw no one. I couldn't help but wonder about how much control these entities actually had over physical properties. If they had no physical body, how were they able to control movement of physical properties here in this realm? I knew I had heard talking in the cemetery, so there had to be some form of "human" spirits there. Could they also take on different forms like such as a shadow, etc. and if so, why? Again, I had so many questions that I needed to find answers for and I wasn't sure where I would be able to find the information I needed.

We got back to my house and were so excited about what we had experienced with the footsteps and the rustling of the grass that we decided to stay up longer and review our audio recordings. We both felt confident we had recorded some EVPs, especially towards the end when we heard the footsteps and rustling. We wanted to look through the pictures we had taken from that evening, but we had used a 35mm camera at that time. Neither of us could afford a digital one as of yet. We knew that we would just have to wait until the next morning when we could have the film developed at a 1-hour photo developing center.

The night was already late, yet we settled down and turned on our audio recorder and listened attentively. After about an hour and a half of listening, we had nothing in the way of EVPs and we were getting really disappointed at the outcome. We were pretty sure that we would at least have something recorded from that evening. How could we have not gotten anything recorded when we had such an active night? Maybe we just weren't investigating the right way or maybe gathering positive recorded evidence was harder than we had originally thought.

We only had 2 minutes remaining on the tape, which was about the time when we had heard the footsteps. We listened even closer to the audio, sure that if we were going to get an EVP recorded, this would be the perfect moment. On the recorded audio, we heard John say, "If there's anyone here who has anything to say, now's the time to say it since we are getting ready to leave." A few seconds later, we heard a woman's voice say, "Hi, I'm Samantha." Next on the recording was when you could hear us commenting about hearing footsteps and rustling in the leaves. We were so excited that we played the EVP back and listened to it several times. We knew the woman's voice did not belong to me and we knew that I had never spoken those words during that time. We were both extremely excited about our first EVP. We couldn't believe it! We were just glad that our hard work and perseverance had finally paid off. It made the whole night worth our time and effort.

Another question came to me. Why could our audio recorder pick up a voice, but our own ears didn't physically hear it? Later, I would learn it had to do with the frequency limits the human ear was capable of hearing.

We met the next morning and headed to the 1-hour photo center. If we were able to record an EVP from this cemetery, then we should have been able to capture an image or something on camera-- at least that was our thoughts on the matter. As we drove, we talked about the investigation and again about the EVP we had recorded. We arrived at the store, submitted our film for development and browsed around the store's departments until our 1-hour wait was finished. I wanted to look at the pictures before we paid for them, so I immediately opened the envelopes and began browsing through the photographs. We had taken five rolls of 27-exposure 35-mm film, so I had quite a bit of photos to go through. I began to get a bit discouraged after the first three rolls when nothing appeared in the photographs; however the last 2 rolls revealed a few hidden treasures. A few of the photographs had shown mists in them and I began getting excited.

There were two photographs that showed strange shaped light anomalies that we had no explanation for. One of these light anomalies looked like a large bright white flame next to a headstone, which appeared to be about 3 feet in height.

The other one showed a big solid light about 4 feet long with white balls of light shooting out the right side of it. I stared at the pictures in amazement and was baffled at how these balls of light or "orbs" seemed to be shooting out of what looked like a 4-foot lighted doorway or opening of some type.

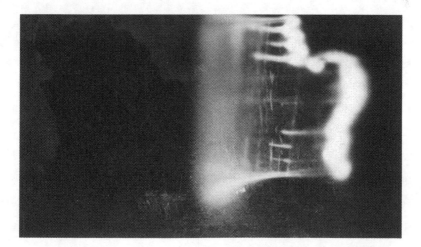

We both looked at the photos and shared the same excitement. We appeared to have captured paranormal oddities in photos as well as in an audio recording. As one could imagine, this sparked our interest even more for the paranormal field and gave us a stronger desire and drive to investigate. We were now on a paranormal mission and could not wait for our next opportunity to investigate, so we could get back out there and do what we now loved to do. I was so intrigued that I knew I had to find a way to overcome my fears.

That next weekend, we decided to go back out to the cemetery where we had gotten the weird light anomaly photos from in an effort to see if we could somehow recreate the shots. When using 35mm film, you don't have the pleasure of seeing instant photos right after they are taken. This makes it a bit harder to recreate the photos. Nonetheless, we headed out there again and took more photos from approximately the same positions we were previously in, hoping that we would have more of the strange lights show up again. We also went over by the gated area and asked Samantha to say hello to us again, if she was still around.

Unlike our last trip, we didn't experience anything unusual. In fact, the cemetery seemed really calm and peaceful. I noticed I wasn't as scared as I had been the last time either, which for me ended up being a very good thing since I hadn't overcome my fears quite yet. I found it odd that this same cemetery now felt peaceful and I didn't see the strange shadows or hear the voices that I had previously heard. How could that be? How could a cemetery be haunted on one visit, but not another? Did this mean that ghosts could just wander in and out of places of their own free will? Could this free will and free choice be possible? I had heard that many people believed that ghosts were trapped in a specific location, which made them unable to leave a place, but I didn't know if I believed that since the cemetery seemed so different. We continued the investigation some more before wrapping up it up and calling it a night. We left the cemetery with our fingers crossed hoping for the same success we had last time.

We made it back to my house once again and were excited that we now had more evidence to review. We were really excited to see our pictures this time, because we were curious to know if our recreations had turned up any similarities from the previous photos we had taken. Once again, we knew we would have to wait until the next day.

We grabbed our headphones and listened carefully to our audio. We only had a couple of EVPs. One said, "Hello," and another said, "Forsaken." These one word EVPs, although whispery in nature, encouraged us to push ahead for more investigating. We began to research places we could go and conduct further investigations.

The next day arrived and it was off to the department store again to develop our photos for review. We were a bit discouraged when we got our photographs and they revealed nothing. However, we knew that was the chance an investigator took when investigating the paranormal, because in our research we learned hundreds of photographs could be taken in a supposedly haunted location without anything paranormal appearing in the photos. We considered ourselves extremely lucky to have been able to capture the ones that we had and realized just how valuable those photographs were.

For the next six months, John and I kept investigating cemeteries and learned a lot about orbs. We went quickly from liking them to disliking them. We had done some reading on the Internet and learned that orbs are mostly dust or air particles. If these air contaminants are within six inches of a camera's lens, they will show up as an orb. They would appear larger, the closer they were to the lens. Orbs that have color are usually light reflected from another surface within the area being photographed. We also learned that an orb was considered more legitimately paranormal if it had a streak or trail to it, but not always. This completely changed our way of thinking. Although it took away our enthusiasm for orbs, we at least had gained some valuable knowledge. However, we did learn there are some true orbs and, although there is no proof that they are paranormally related, many researchers believe they are linked and represent a lower energy source or appearance for spirits.

We were new to the paranormal field and had only investigated cemeteries at that point, so we were getting a bit bored with them. This was especially true since we were only discovering a small amount of recorded evidence primarily in the form of EVPs. We hadn't been able to obtain any further photographic evidence since that night in the cemetery when we captured the unexplainable light anomalies. We were really hoping to be able to investigate a home or a building soon, as it seemed like we had hit a roadblock.

I talked John into creating a website where we could present evidence from our investigations on the Internet in hopes it would help generate some leads for more investigations by request. It was at that point we decided to put a name to our 2-person team and thus P.I.C.O. (Paranormal Investigators of Central Oklahoma) was born in June of 2000. We continued looking online for any other Oklahoma paranormal teams and eventually found one who had just recently started. We began occasionally conversing with them through e-mail.

In June of 2000, I was working for the local county sheriff's department and had previously spoken with a few friends of mine about the paranormal research my friend and I had been doing and many of them seemed interested. Occasionally, I would bring pictures to work with me of different cemeteries that we had investigated and I would tell them about our experiences. As word began to spread at work about the paranormal investigating my friend and I were doing, I was approached by a co-worker of mine who asked if we would investigate his house.

My co-worker had been married with two children, but a couple of years earlier, his wife had started showing signs of depression and their marriage began to be fall apart. He broke down and cried as he described the death of his wife. He told me, "One lonely night in desperation she pulled out a gun, laid down on our bedroom floor and shot herself." My poor co-worker told me he was shocked when he came home and found her lying dead on the bedroom floor. He expressed how very guilty he felt and how he thought he could have been responsible for driving her to suicide since they were having marital problems. He also said he blamed himself for the past few years now, but was coping with it the best way he knew how. He then told me that ever since her death, he and his two children had been noticing strange things happening in their house and he had often wondered if it might be her. He expressed how he wished he could have been able to tell her he still loved her and he was sorry for everything. He stated that he was now at a point where he needed some answers, but mostly wanted to find out if it was his wife that was still there in spirit. He hoped that if we came out and investigated that we would be able to answer that question for him. He also hoped we would at least be able to get her voice recorded on audio or that she would show up in our photographs. I told him that we would be glad to come out and help him and explained that I would call him later to set up a date and time for us to come out.

I went home after work and got ahold of John by phone. I told him about the invitation to investigate my co-worker's home. John was ecstatic and we were both excited to be able to finally investigate a residential location. We felt like perhaps this would be a new beginning for us since we would finally get to experience a whole new level of investigating.

After arranging a date and time, we arrived at his house without really knowing what to expect or exactly how to investigate a residential location, but we kept an open-mind and were eager to obtain more knowledge and experience. My co-worker started telling us in depth about the type of activity he had been experiencing and so we began settings up our equipment in the areas he stated that were active.

For some strange reason, I felt drawn to the front bedroom. I went in there and just stood in the darkness for a few moments. I closed my eyes and concentrated on the stillness of the room. After just a few moments I heard a shrill scream of agony and a woman's voice say, "Help me!" I was a bit startled, so I quickly turned on the bedroom light and went to talk with my friend to let him know what I had just experienced. I asked my co-worker if he had ever experienced any activity in the front bedroom and he said only a time or two. He asked me why and if I was picking up on something in that room. I told him, "yes," and explained to him what I had experienced.

He broke down and started crying and told us that was the same room where his wife had committed suicide. He took us into the room, moved some boxes out of the way and showed us a bullet hole that had pierced the old wooden floor. He asked if I thought it was his wife that I had heard. I explained to him that I didn't really know, since I didn't know his wife, and she didn't tell me her name. I had no evidence at that point to back up what I had heard, but it could have been her. I explained to him that I would let him know what we got recorded as soon as I went over all of the data. I couldn't help but feel sorry for him. Although my gut instinct told me it was his wife, I was hesitant to tell him it was her until I was certain for myself, but I knew what I had heard. This was my first time using my abilities on a residential location and all I knew how to do was to listen to what was around me. Speaking out and talking to any spirits while I was psychically "in the zone," so-to-speak, was something I hadn't developed a talent for yet. I was still trying to overcome my own fears and I wasn't sure about striking-up a full conversation with any ghost, regardless of whose past loved ones they might have been. Doubt from my logical mind was there too. Had I truly heard the woman's voice? Was I sure it was not just my imagination that had caused me to think I had her heard? I had to put the doubt out of my mind and tell myself to trust my abilities and instincts.

A few hours later, we wrapped-up the investigation and headed for my house. John and I talked about the investigation and discussed my experience in that front bedroom. I couldn't wait to get back to my house and review my audio. I was disturbed by what I had heard that night and I started questioning where ghosts went after they left their physical body.

When I got home I listened to my audio and sure enough, my audio recorder picked up the same scream and voice I had heard, but it was very light and you could barely make it out. This struck me as being odd since I heard it so loud …or at least I thought I did. I had so many questions that came to mind and I only wished I had more answers. I knew researching the paranormal was now not just an interest and hobby, it was my new passion. Little did I realize I would find paranormal investigating a calling to reach out and help people, those alive and passed.

CHAPTER 3

"The Awakening"

After our first residential investigation, word-of-mouth began to spread even more about the type of work John and I were doing. We started getting a few more residential investigation requests. We had also updated our website and had been discovered more by the general public which in turn generated more investigation requests. We were thrilled that doors were opening up for us and we were getting the chance to investigate different places. It was during this time that we received a few membership requests for our group.

One particular woman, named Lynn, wrote an email to us asking about soul-rescue for those ghosts who were stuck and lingering Earthbound. She was curious to know if it was an area that we dealt with. To be quite honest, we hadn't even thought about that concept because we didn't know it existed nor did we know if soul-rescue could even be done. As a result of her email, the topic sparked my interest and I wanted to learn more about it. I talked to John about exploring that side of research. After a few more lengthy conversations with Lynn, she expressed her interest in helping us and becoming part of our team. After talking it over with John, we decided that Lynn might make a great addition to our team so we extended her a membership.

It wasn't long after Lynn joined us that we had a residential investigation set-up in the eastern part of our state. I was excited to have Lynn there with us, not only as a new team member, but also because Lynn had stated she was a psychic/medium. I was curious to see how her abilities worked.

The scientific side of paranormal research already interested me, but I was even more fascinated and intrigued by the spiritual side. I had little doubt that what I had experienced while growing up was real at the time. I believed in what I was experiencing even more since I had begun to officially investigate the paranormal. I had come to the conclusion that, yes, some things could be logically explained, but not of them could. I became more convinced that my experiences weren't simply created by my imagination. I knew I didn't quite understand it all yet and there were many questions that still remained unanswered. However, I felt the more I continued on with paranormal research, the closer I was getting to having some of my questions answered. Lynn seemed to have answers in an area that I needed to learn more about and I hoped she could help shed some light on those areas that were unclear to me.

The investigation went quite well. I watched Lynn as she told us some information she was getting in from spirit. I admired her for being so brave to actually speak with the spirits she encountered. I had so many questions for her yet I didn't want to bombard with my inquiries all at once. Before the night was through, I was able to ask her a few questions and I told her I definitely wanted to learn more about how to use my spiritual gifts and abilities. I let Lynn know we were glad that she had come to the investigation with us and we were looking forward to doing another one with her in the near future.

I spoke with my friend John on the way back home from this residential location about our investigation experiences with Lynn that night. John openly stated he didn't know if he really believed in psychics, but he would be willing to give Lynn a chance to prove herself. We had done a lot of research on the Internet and saw how some groups had chosen not to have a psychic on their team due to credibility issues, but there were some that did. John was worried about our credibility being hurt if word got out that we had a psychic on our team. I asked him if he trusted me with the things I had seen and heard. He said he did, so then I explained how I believed there were real psychics out there with true abilities since I had some of these abilities too but mine were just a bit underdeveloped. I expressed that I didn't' think it wouldn't be fair to immediately judge someone that we hadn't worked with just because the word "psychic" had been given a bad name throughout the years. He agreed and it was decided that Lynn would stay on as a member of our team. I never did quite realize that night just how much keeping Lynn on as a member would help me, nor did I realize just how much I would be learning from her. I was also unaware that soon I would need her help more so than ever.

We had arrived home from our residential investigation. It was a long drive back and the hour was already quite late. We knew at that point we were too tired to accurately review any of our recorded evidence. A few weeks prior to this, we had come across a little extra money and decided to purchase a digital camera. This digital camera was a Sony Mavica, which only took photos on 3.5-inch floppy disks with each disk holding approximately 25-30 pictures. We were very excited, because now we could actually view our photographs right after we took them. This was great for us, as it meant no more waiting to get them developed.

After using our new digital camera on a few different investigations, I had developed a bad habit of placing our used disks in my back pants pocket so I wouldn't get them mixed up with the new ones during our investigations. My hands were always full while investigating and I wasn't able to carry a tote bag around with me. My bad habit quickly came to an end one day though when I made the mistake of forgetting about a used photo disk when it was time for me to do my laundry. I had grabbed a big load of dirty clothes out of my hamper and threw them in the washing machine. It was a short time later when I discovered my jeans had spit them out and my washing machine had eaten them! Since that accident,

John made it his mission to remind me to remove the disks from my back pants pocket once we got back to my house so I wouldn't wash them again. My mistake also became a running joke for John who stated that he knew dryers had been known for notoriously eating socks but this was a first for a washing machine to claim the life of plastic 3.5 floppy disks!

I had come home late from this residential investigation and was given John's usual friendly reminder. I took the used disks out of my back pocket and placed them safely on top of an empty shelf in my bedroom. I woke up the next morning eager to get started with reviewing our recorded evidence. I decided I would look over our pictures first and went to get the disks from the shelf, but when I reached up to grab them, they were nowhere to be found. I called John and asked him if they had perhaps fallen out of my pocket while I was in his truck and thought I might have just imagined putting them on my shelf late the night before. John checked his truck and said they weren't in there and he didn't know where else they could be. Baffled by their disappearance, I began searching further for the stack of missing disks. After spending two to three hours looking all over the house, I finally gave up my search. I was not only dumbfounded at their disappearance, but also a bit irritated because I knew I hadn't misplaced them. I even checked the pockets of my pants as a last resort! John had come over to help in the search efforts. With no photos to review, we had only our audio left to review, so we plugged in our headphones and began the long hours of listening that awaited us.

That night I went to bed and couldn't shake the feeling I was being watched by something unseen. At times, it felt as if someone was standing right beside my bed. I managed to fall asleep even though I felt very uncomfortable. While I was asleep, I had a very strange dream. I found myself in a swamp-like place with tall trees that had long lowering branches that draped downwards. These trees were dead and the swamp looked ominous without any signs of life. There was a light fog that encompassed my feet and when I looked up, there was a man standing there staring at me with dark black void eyes. He was Caucasian with brown hair, pale skin and about forty years of age. Although his lips did not move, I heard him tell me his name was Gary. He stretched out his hand towards me and he asked me to take his hand and help him. I felt very afraid and did not know what to do, so I started backing away from him. Suddenly, I awoke from my dream.

As soon as I opened my eyes from the terrifying ordeal I had just experienced, I saw the same man standing next to my bed. I was so scared that I couldn't even open my mouth to scream. All I could think about in my mind was how I wanted him to be gone and leave me alone. Then all of a sudden he *was* gone… he had simply vanished into thin air.

I was so shook up that I called John and told him what had just happened. He asked me if I thought it was perhaps just a bad dream and I told him, "no," as I had seen this man again *after* I had woken up. He told me to just ignore this man and try to go back to sleep. I tried to follow his advice, however I found myself so restless and scared that I didn't know if I could go back to sleep. My mind couldn't shut off and I wanted some answers for why this man had come to me and had asked me for help when I didn't have any clue what to do in order to help him.

Seeing him in my dreams and then beside my bed had reminded me of the encounter I had with the shadow man when I was a teenager. It was a similar dream and encounter where a shadow man was chasing me and ended up standing beside my bedside when I woke up. I didn't like the feeling the shadow man had given me back then and I didn't like the feeling the man had just given me with this recent encounter. I wasn't sure where he came from, but wondered if he could have followed us home from the residential investigation we had conducted in Muskogee the night before. Were ghosts able to follow a person home? After about an hour, I had finally calmed down enough to fall back asleep and I just hoped that I wouldn't encounter him again.

The next day came and went and it was time for bed once again. I was hoping everything would be quiet this night, so I could sleep normally again. Nothing unusual took place during the day other than just a couple of moments when I felt like I was being watched once again. I lie down in bed and quickly fell asleep. I wasn't sure just how long I had been sleeping, however I began to dream again and found myself standing in the same swamp area with the same spooky looking dead bare trees with the fog rolling in all around my ankles. It was the same nightmare all over again and I wanted to wake up. I knew what was going to happen next, but no matter how hard I tried I couldn't wake myself up. When I looked up, I saw the same man standing in front of me with his hands stretched out and his voice replaying his same plea for help. This time instead of backing away from him, I told him that I did not know how to help him and he needed to leave me alone.

I saw his facial expressions turn angry as he glared at me with his black empty eyes. Again, like before, I suddenly woke up and saw this same man standing beside my bed, but instead of a calm appearance he appeared angry. I started to say something to him, but before I could he was gone. I decided not to wake up John again with a phone call. I figured he would give me the same advice to ignore him and try to go back to sleep. I planned on letting him know first thing that next morning though. I knew I had a good imagination for some things, but after experiencing this two nights in a row, there was no way any logical part of me could convince the rest of me that this was my imagination playing tricks on me. This ghost, named Gary, was real. He was so real that he was scaring me out of my wits! If I had to deal with ghosts like this on a regular basis, then I didn't want to deal with ghosts any more.

I laid in bed with questions going through my mind again. Why had this man come back again to ask me for help and why was he so sure that I could help him? Why was he so angry with me for telling him that I couldn't help him? I was still so new to the paranormal field and I had never yet had a spirit ask me for help until this incident. I honestly had no idea how to give him any help. My mind kept searching for answers, but no answers were coming to me. I thought of our new friend and team member, Lynn, and I just knew I had to talk to her about this and ask her my questions. After all, she had said that she was able to communicate with ghosts and had even mentioned helping them, so I figured she would be able to help provide me with some answers.

It wasn't until after I spoke with Lynn that I would learn about spirit visitation. I learned even more in the months to follow when I began researching dream interpretation and spirit visitation within dreams. After talking to Lynn, it was confirmed that this man really was trying to ask me for help. The swamp, fog and dead trees represented a place where this man felt like he was trapped. It was a place of hopelessness and emptiness and he wanted to escape. He was considered a lost soul looking for help. He knew that I had the ability to see and hear him; therefore he felt I should automatically know how to perform a "soul rescue" and help him. Since I was brand new with using my abilities, I didn't know how to help him. I guess he wasn't aware of that or expected my help regardless.

I had been working the graveyard shift at the sheriff's department, so I had to sleep a bit during the day. My daughter, who had just turned six, was attending the afternoon kindergarten class and would normally come into my room to wake me up once my alarm clock had gone off. I heard my alarm go off and right afterwards I heard a loud thud and cracking sound coming from my bathroom. My daughter then came running into my room. She was very scared and climbed up into bed with me. She asked me if I had heard the loud sound coming from the bathroom. I told her I did and I asked her if she knew what it was. She told me that she was using the toilet in my bathroom and was holding our cat Darla. She said all the sudden something had yanked the cat upward and out of her arms and then she said she saw and heard the bathroom mirror brake. That's when she came running into my bedroom.

I told Sarah-Ann to stay there in my bed. I got up out of bed and carefully opened the bathroom door. I stood in the doorway for a moment, shocked as I looked at my bathroom mirror. It was cracked and shattered from the lower left-hand side upwards. It looked as if someone had taken a fist and punched it but how could that be when no one else was in the house except for Sarah-Ann and I? I began thinking of ways the mirror could have cracked and I tried to logically analyze it. I checked the clips on the mirror to make sure they were secure and of course they were nice and tight. I looked around to see if there was anything that might have fallen or something that might have accidentally slammed against the mirror causing it to crack and shatter. I couldn't find any logical explanation for why it was broken. I asked Sarah-Ann if she had done it and she told me no. It would be out of character for her to break something, especially a large mirror like this anyway but I had to cover all possibilities.

Freaked out, I called John at work and told him what had happened and he was baffled by it as well. He asked me to take a picture of the mirror and send it to him in an email. So I did. We had recently made friends with some other people in the paranormal field. John suggested I e-mail the picture to them as well and see what they thought about it. I felt a bit odd sending this photo out, but I explained to our paranormal friends the circumstances of what had happened. Not too long after I had sent the e-mails, I received a response back telling me to take a closer look at the photograph because in the mirror, they had seen a man's face. I hadn't noticed this before but of course I wasn't analyzing it for anything paranormal, just looking at it for the cracks in the mirror. Nonetheless I was very excited and immediately looked at the photo in depth and sure enough… there was a man's face in the upper right hand corner of the photo. As I looked even closer at it, I was shocked when this man happened to resemble this Gary guy that had visited me in my dreams. I used a photo-editing program and highlighted a box around the face of this strange ghostly man so his face could be more easily seen. Was this just strange pixilation in the photo or had I actually captured the face of the ghost who had been tormenting my dreams lately?

I really started wondering if this ghost Gary was the one responsible for cracking my mirror. Did he do it because he was mad at me for my refusal to help him and for telling him to go away? If this was true and he did in fact break my mirror, did he do out of revenge? If so, did that mean that ghosts could really harm a person? How much control over physical things did they really have? While the photograph intrigued me, it also raised more questions in my mind. I knew I had no choice but to talk to Lynn, but first I had to do something to make peace with Gary.

After speaking with Lynn, she told me that this ghost, Gary, was probably acting out because I had refused to help him. She told me that ghosts were able to manipulate physical properties if they had been on "the other side" for a while and had learned how to use energy to move objects. She told me that I needed to try to talk to him and see if I could explain to him why I couldn't help and that I was not familiar with soul rescue.

Later on that evening when I had some alone time, I went into my bedroom, closed my door and called Gary's name out loud a couple of times. I had no idea if he could hear me or if he was there listening, but I knew that I needed to try to get things settled with him so my haunting would stop. After waiting for a few minutes, I began talking out loud to Gary. I felt very silly talking to open air, however I didn't know of any other way to do it. I told him I sincerely apologized if I had made him angry by not agreeing to help him, but I was truthful when I stated I did not know how to help him. I explained to him that I was very new at dealing with the spirit realm and I did not know what I was supposed to do or I would have already helped him. I also told him that he had scared me and I didn't know how to deal with spirits that scared me. I explained that I did not like his anger and would appreciate it if he would move on and try to find someone else that could really help him. Finally, I informed him I did not want him to stay at my house.

I finished my conversation and hoped that it had worked. That following night I was given my confirmation, as I didn't dream about Gary nor did I ever encounter him again. I also ended up finding my photo disks a couple of days after I gave Gary my message. I was cleaning my master bathroom and began tidying up a few of the shelves that hadn't been straightened in a while. I moved a stack of magazines that I had sitting on my bathroom shelf and there, under the stack of magazines, lay my missing disks. I knew I hadn't moved them there, so I called John and asked them if there was a chance he had placed them there when he was over my house; even though I didn't think he had. He told me he didn't put them there and he found it odd for them to be under a stack of magazines that hadn't been looked at in roughly three months.

Again, another unsolved mystery and more questions that I had about the other side. Could ghosts really move objects and relocate them somewhere else? Lynn had told me they could, but my logical mind couldn't fathom this. But what other explanation could there be? My daughter rarely ever used my bathroom and she couldn't even reach the shelf where I had found the disks. Slowly but surely, I was becoming more of a believer!

I called Lynn and told her about the incident. Over the next few weeks, Lynn and I talked nearly every day and started developing a very close friendship. We would talk about many things including the paranormal and she became someone I trusted very much. At that time, she lived in Northeastern, Oklahoma, and I lived just a few miles out of the Oklahoma City metro area. Whenever I had some spare time though, I would drive up to visit her. I didn't mind the drive as it only took about one and a half hours. It was worth it to me as I enjoyed her company and friendship.

As I began getting to know Lynn better, the fountain of knowledge that she possessed fascinated me. I told her about my experiences as a child and the recent experiences I had been having since I started investigating and researching the paranormal. I explained every time I did an investigation I seemed to experience more and more things, odd things, I couldn't explain, especially since each time the incidents seemed to get stranger than the one before. I confided in her and told her that I didn't quite understand what was happening to me and after the incident with my disks, the mirror and with the ghost named Gary, I was very concerned about what was going on. Why were all these different ghosts coming to me like this? Lynn knew she was in for a long night and poured herself a glass of wine as she sat down to explain things in return to me.

She started off by telling me that ghosts are attracted to those who they know can help them. She had me picture myself in a dark room with a few other people. Each of us had candles and once lit, some were brighter than others. The better the candle, the brighter it shone. Also, in the same room there were moths that were attracted to the candlelight. She had me picture the moths going towards the light of the candles that were brightest. The stronger the light, the more moths the light attracted. She explained that those people with gifts and abilities were like those holding the candles and the ghosts were like the moths, which naturally flocked to the light. She explained that I was clearly one of those people holding a bright candle and with each investigation my abilities were strengthening. Therefore, I was attracting more ghosts to me. She further explained that this was what had happened with Gary. He had seen the light of my candle and was attracted to it because the light represented help. She said that spirits had a way of knowing things and they chose whom they wanted to come to. She told me that I needed to prepare myself, because I would be having others like Gary come to me in the near future. Also, I needed to learn about my gifts and abilities in order to know how to utilize them correctly.

I sat there taking in everything Lynn was telling me; however I did not know how I could make my gifts stronger or exactly what I needed to do to use them correctly. I began asking more questions and I'm sure Lynn felt a bit overwhelmed that evening. I thanked her for our talk at the conclusion of that evening, but I was not quite sure if she ever fully understood just how much she helped me that night. She had turned out to be such a great friend and such a great teacher.

Since that time, we had other extensive conversations. She once had asked me exactly how I saw ghosts. I told her that sometimes they would just suddenly appear in front of my eyes, but most times I would see them in my mind. I explained sometimes they would appear to move slowly, but they were usually fast. Sometimes they would allow me to see what they were doing. Other times they would simply stand there in front of me. I continued to explain that sometimes I would get flashes of different scenes or things and I didn't always understand what the images were. I told her I couldn't always tell if I was really seeing these ghosts with my physical eyes or if it was just with my mind's eye. Other times I would see them as if I were watching portions of a movie. I could see things happening to the spirits, but often it was only bits and pieces of information. I would see them in different scenes. Lynn just chuckled and told me that was how it usually worked when ghosts want to show themselves to us. It is often much easier for them to reveal themselves to us on a spiritual plane rather than a physical one. It felt like a light bulb had just turned on inside my head and it suddenly all made sense to me. Now I understood the visions I had seen in the past and why they sometimes appeared to be so confusing.

Lynn then asked me how I heard the ghosts talk to me. I explained occasionally I would hear them audibly, but sometimes I would hear words spoken in my head or I would see words and sentences in my mind. She told me that that was also the way they often communicated. Again, it made sense to me.

Lynn asked how I felt when I was around different ghosts. I told her that it varied with each situation, but there were many times that I was very afraid because I was uncertain if something bad would happen or if I would see something bad. I told her sometimes I would suddenly experience strange emotions that were not my own and I had no idea where they were coming from. Lynn explained sometimes if a ghost wanted to show us how they were feeling, they could impose emotional energy upon us allowing us to experience what they were feeling.

I was asked if I had ever experienced having a feeling about something random, if there were things I sensed about others, or myself or if I had experienced things like premonitions that later came true. I told her yes to all of it and how I found some information to be very odd since I had no idea where it came from. I told her most of the time after receiving spiritual information, I would feel it was valid information because of an overwhelming strong gut feeling that I would have about it. She explained sometimes spirits will give us information in the form of strong emotional impressions and if the feeling was strong enough, chances are it was a valid message.

Lynn asked me if I understood the different types of gifts I had and I admitted that I didn't. She then named the different types of psychic abilities and explained what each one was. She described clairaudient as the ability to hear spirits, clairvoyant as the ability to see spirits, and clairsensitive as the ability to feel spirits. She told me that she believed I had all three of these gifts and I needed to decide was if I was prepared to accept my gifts and learn how to use them. She advised if I decided to accept them that along my spiritual path I would encounter many strange things, some good and some bad. Most importantly, once I had opened up my spiritual mind or "door," it would be very hard to ever close it. Only I could determine just how wide I wanted to open that door. She said that I needed to find a level at which I would feel comfortable with my gifts and when I came to that point I would know.

Lynn described her first few experiences dealing with the spirit world and how she had learned to deal with her gifts. She was able to learn how to utilize her gifts safely and effectively. I thought about what she had told me and I was excited. I loved the paranormal field and wanted to learn all areas within it, especially the spiritual side since it already seemed to be a part of me. I knew I didn't have much experience, but I was confident I had the patience, dedication and passion it would take to commit to paranormal research. After talking with Lynn, I knew I wanted to learn how to use my gifts. I wanted to open up my spiritual doorway even further and awaken the abilities that I had buried inside me. Little did I know the decision I made that night would change my life forever.

CHAPTER 4

"Spiritual Attachments"

Time quickly passed and before I knew it, I had been researching and investigating the paranormal for two years. I noticed there seemed to be a paranormal frenzy taking place all over Oklahoma, because there were a lot of new groups that seemed to be popping up from all over the place. We were having contact with more and more groups and became pretty good friends with some of them, especially another group based out of the local metro area. This one particular paranormal group was unique because they had their own location to conduct their research at. This location was an old abandoned hospital built around the turn of the 20th century. As an exchange for research privileges, this group maintained the old building and the grounds upon which it sat.

The old hospital was nick-named, "The Lady," by the research team out of respect for the old building and the activity that took place there. It first served as a Catholic hospital ran by an ordained priest and nuns. Later, it became a county hospital until the late 1970's when a newer hospital was built in another location. Since that time, its rooms had remained empty and its hallways abandoned until the research team heard about its haunted legends and decided to adopt the building as their own.

The team members would get together every Saturday night and conduct experiments, investigate and exchange fellowship with one another. Back then, it was a dream of most paranormal investigators to visit "The Lady" and to conduct an investigation, since word had gotten out about her extensive amount of paranormal occurrences. Teams had actually witnessed some of this activity while sitting outside the building as small rocks were thrown at them and their vehicles amongst other things. Those who visited the old hospital would see shadows and apparitions roaming about its empty halls and hear audible noises and voices. The inside of the old hospital was quite active and teams who investigated there experienced all sorts of strange activity. One of its more infamous haunting stories involved the old nuns who were thought to be guarding the hospital. Visitors to the old hospital would occasionally see them on the property.

I had a chance to investigate "The Lady" and remember different occasions where I personally saw figures walking the halls, heard strange disembodied voices, was touched, saw things moving and objects that were thrown at us from an unknown source. One particular time, a threaded screw was thrown and our thermal imaging camera captured it showing the screw as red in color, indicating it was warmer than its surroundings. Within a few moments, the thermal camera revealed the red color screw had changed to black, indicating that the heat source was no longer present.

Back in the summer of 2002, my group and I were invited to conduct the usual weekend research at "The Lady" with the other team. We were ecstatic to have had the invitation extended to us. I had only been to the hospital a couple of different times prior to this invitation, so I was really excited about doing continuous weekend research there. I also felt like this would help me to fine tune my gifts. I knew if I investigated every weekend, it would definitely help me develop the skills I needed to improve my abilities.

I had been trying my hardest to develop my abilities for a while now, and so far it seemed to be working. I also noticed a few times I would get overwhelmed with messages from spirit. For some reason, everything seemed to be happening so fast for me. It was as if I had opened my spiritual door, or spiritual eye as some call it, really wide and I had all sorts of things coming at me all at once. I hadn't paced myself in opening that door just a little bit at a time. I would soon learn that that mistake would cost me in the long run. I had let my fascination and excitement get the better of me by rushing head on into things head first instead of first learning self-protection measures. I was like a sponge absorbing everything I could, however it didn't take me long to learn this was not a good way to approach the spiritual realm.

I wasn't fully prepared for what was about to happen on one Saturday night while we were investigating the old hospital. We were doing what we call our "investigative sweeps." During these sweeps, we took different types of readings throughout the rooms/areas. We record baseline readings for temperature and Electromagnetic Fields (EMF) and document the basic description for each room/area. We took photographs and conducted audio recordings to gather any other information about the location.

On this particular Saturday evening, we were up on the third floor in the hallway by the south elevator shaft doing our "sweeps." The hallways were about eight to ten feet wide. I happened to be standing with my back about two feet away from a wall while taking photographs. Right after I had snapped a photo, the camera flashed and I saw a woman who came running out of the opposite wall right towards me. She passed through my right side and disappeared into the wall behind me. I was shocked by what just happened, but even more at her horrifying appearance. She appeared to be young with dark brown matted hair and dark eyes. Her skin was not only pale and pasty, but also showed signs of rot and decay with small portions of her flesh slowly peeling away. I didn't know what to think right after it happened, but it scared me so badly I had jumped back against a wall that was two feet away. If the hospital wall had been made of sheetrock instead of concrete, I would have made a hole with the silhouette of my body pressed into it.

A couple of the other team's investigators had seen my sudden reaction and asked me what had just happened. It looked like I had just seen a ghost! I told them I had and explained what had just transpired. I gave them my description of her and told them this female ghost closely resembled the possessed little girl in the movie, *"The Exorcist"* with the actress Linda Blair. One of the other investigators spoke up to say, during the same time I had fallen back up against the wall, he thought he had seen a figure run across the hall, but he wasn't sure. It happened so quickly and he was several feet away from where I was standing. I assured him that he was correct in his assumption and it had to be the same ghost girl I had just encountered.

We continued our sweeps, but I was still pretty shaken and couldn't really concentrate on doing any more of the investigation. I couldn't get the horrible image of that woman out of my head. Why did she come running out at me like that and why did she look so awful? All I knew was she had scared me badly and I didn't want to encounter her ever again.

I pushed myself to continue the investigation with my peers until finally our sweeps were complete, so we took a break. If the weather was nice outside we would normally take our break out by the hospital's old ER doors, but if the weather was bad we would gather in the old ambulance shelter just outside of the hospital. This particular night we were sitting outside the ER doors when I heard my name called. I looked around at the others to see if anyone else had heard the same thing. It was apparent by the look on everyone's faces no one had heard the voice. I waited a few minutes longer. I wasn't brave enough at that time to ask if anyone had heard it too and I didn't want anyone to think my mind was playing tricks on me. I refocused my attention on the group's conversation and started to make a comment when I had to stop because I had heard my name being called again. I no longer cared what the others in the group would think, so I asked everyone if they had heard my name being called. Everyone responded with a "no," so I sat there puzzled wondering why my name was being called out and why I was the only one that was able to hear it? I couldn't determine if a male or female spirit was calling my name, since the voice sounded a bit whispery. My mind couldn't help but wonder if it was the same creepy ghost woman I had seen upstairs.

A little while later, we went back inside the building to conduct our last phase of the investigation we call a "sit-down." This is where we find a spot to sit quietly, watch and wait for any activity to take place all while monitoring the room with EMF meters and infrared (IR) night vision video cameras. If our stationary EMF meters were to illuminate its LED lights, we would start snapping pictures in hopes of capturing an image of whatever might have caused the increase in the electro-magnetic field.

I had developed a routine for practicing my gifts more since we had started coming to the old hospital every Saturday evening to conduct investigative research. I would pay close attention to what was around me and try to clear my mind and view what was really there on a spiritual level. There weren't a lot of distractions during sit-downs, so it was easy for me to concentrate. I had developed the technique of picturing in my mind a wooden door in front of me. On the other side of this door was the other realm where spirits lingered and when I wanted to see or hear them better, I would open that door and wait. This was my own technique and it seemed to work well for me. I had to find a way in my learning stages to connect with the other side so I came up with this technique.

On this particular night, I found a place to sit quietly for the sit-down. Once everything was still and quiet, I began concentrating and picturing my spiritual wooden door. I opened it up and within seconds this same woman came rushing right through and got right up in my face. She snarled at me and shot me a look as if she was daring me to fight her. I found myself trying to get her out of my face, so I swatted the empty air in front of me and told her to back off and leave me alone. She disappeared just as John pointed his flashlight towards my face and asked if I was okay. I told him I had just had another encounter with the ghost woman from upstairs and she was just trying to scare me again. Otherwise, I was okay. Truthfully, I was scared to death once again and I didn't know why this woman was spiritually attacking me like this. What did she want and why was she targeting me? I had done nothing to her, so why was she being so mean?

We finally ended the investigation and went home, but that night had changed me and I didn't feel the same afterwards. I had never had that happen to me before and I was concerned I would never be the same nor would I ever look at ghost hunting the same again. All my initial fears had come flooding back to me. This investigation at the old hospital was worse than any other encounter I had ever had with any spirit! I felt mentally and physically exhausted and I was glad to be going home and getting away from the hospital and that dreadful woman.

Another week had rolled by and it was Saturday evening again. It was time to go back out to the hospital. My mind could not help but wonder if I was going to encounter this woman again or not. The only thing I hoped was perhaps this dreadful ghost woman wouldn't be there. I hoped she was a wandering spirit and not one who was stationary to the hospital, because if she was I didn't think I could continue investigating that location every weekend.

My team and I arrived at the hospital and I entered with caution. I kept my eyes peeled praying I wouldn't see the angry woman. Our investigation began and we were on the second floor conducting our sweeps. I happened to be taking photographs down a long hallway when suddenly and seemingly out of nowhere, she appeared at a distance down the hall from me. She began walking towards me with twisted and contorted arms and legs as if they were broken. Her movements were short and choppy appearing as if she were limping and dragging her limbs. My whole body froze in fear and I could only assume she had done this to scare me even more. She snarled at me again and then started laughing before suddenly disappearing. I made sure to stay close to the group for the rest of the evening, as I didn't know what she might do next or how I would handle her again.

It came time to do another sit-down and I wasn't sure if I could open my spiritual door again. I was scared she would come right up to my face again. I didn't want to stop using my abilities and I didn't want to have to stop opening up my spiritual door just because of her. I decided I would just be careful and open my door slowly to make sure the coast was clear and that she would not surprise me again like that.

I tried to relax and prepared myself to connect with the other side again. I prayed she wouldn't show herself again. I pictured my wooden door and slowly opened it up, but only a couple of inches at a time. With each inch, I was feeling a little better and I was starting to think she wasn't going to show up after all. My door was now about halfway open when out of nowhere there she was, right up in my face again. This time she gritted her jagged teeth at me and growled. I pushed her back again and slammed the door shut. I sat there very angry. Why was she doing this to me? I hadn't done anything to justify her acting like this.

I didn't open my spiritual door for the rest of the sit-down. On the drive back I spoke with John about what had happened, but he didn't quite know what to say or how to help me since this was an area of investigating that was totally out of his scope of expertise. Lynn wasn't able to make it down every weekend to investigate the old hospital with us. I knew I had already bugged her to death with a million questions, so I thought I might figure this one out on my own. I figured if I could do this by myself, it would be a great learning and growing experience for me. I knew I needed to start figuring out how to deal with spirit independently, because I wasn't always going to have someone there holding my hand to help me.

For the next two nights, I had horrible nightmares and could not get a good night's rest. I started noticing small minor changes taking place at my house. My things would end up disappearing and re-appearing somewhere else and I would hear strange sounds and saw quick shadows move out of the corner of my eye. I also felt a change in my mood and I seemed to be quite irritable at times.

For the next few weeks, I kept my spiritual door closed at the old hospital. This was because each time I allowed spirit to communicate, the ghost woman continued to come right up to my face and scare me. I was getting tired of dealing with her and the activity kept increasing at my house; including the nightmares I was having. I would lie down in bed and would feel like she was right there hovering over me. By this time, I had learned to recognize her energy pattern, so I could tell when she was around.

I remember one night I had gone to bed and was alone in my bedroom. My daughter, Sarah-Ann, was fast asleep in her own room. I thought about how I was so glad this deranged ghost hadn't bothered her the whole entire time that she had been haunting me. As I lay there on my back, I closed my eyes and tried to fall asleep, but I couldn't. I felt her presence there with me once again. I opened my eyes and found her floating there above me, staring at me with her dark angry eyes. She was only about eighteen inches away and was doing her usual snarl and scare tactics. I knew I wasn't supposed to show her my fear, so I told her she needed to leave me alone. I then covered up my head and tried to go to sleep. I was finally able to fall asleep, but only to continue my nightmares about her. I could have a normal dream but she always found a way to enter my dreams and appear as her nasty self. I knew she was the cause of the nightmares, even though the situations would vary and change with each dream, but she always appeared in them. She continued to do this to me for many nights and I was beginning to lose sleep. Sometimes, I couldn't sleep at all. This was really hard on me because my sleep was already limited with working two jobs in order to make ends meet.

It was another Saturday night and time for our usual investigation at the hospital. I had decided to pull my two spiritual friends, Lynn and Maggie, aside and tell them what had been taking place. After telling them, they both suggested that I try to talk to her to see what she wanted and if there was any way that I could possibly help her. They told me that sometimes ghosts acted out in a negative manner because they needed help. Since I hadn't tried to offer her any help, it could have been the reason she was sticking around and haunting me. Personally, I didn't care to help her at all, especially after how horrible she had been to me for the past 3 months. In an attempt to end my haunting, I decided to try to talk with her during our sit-down phase of the investigation at the old hospital that evening.

We completed our sweeps phase and took a break before preparing for our sit-down. It was the part of the evening that I dreaded, because I knew she was going to come just as soon as I opened my door. It had been a few weeks since I had even tried to use my spiritual gifts, because no matter where I went, even outside of the old hospital, she would show up. I knew she was aware of her success in scaring me, so at this point I had no other option but face her head-on and at least offer her my help. I had to stand up to her and let her know I wasn't going to run away from her anymore. I wasn't going to take her bullying any more either. She could accept my offer for help and stop haunting me or not, but either way I was determined to get rid of her once and for all.

Everyone was seated for the sit-down. I stayed on the end farthest from where most of the group settled. This was so I could concentrate without added distractions. I dreaded what I was about to do, but I knew it had to be done. I took a deep breath, cleared my mind and pictured my little wooden door again. I immediately opened it and waited for a few moments. Amazingly, this nasty ghost never showed up. I couldn't believe it, but I thought maybe she had given up on me ever opening my door again since I had kept it closed for so long. I decided to do something brave, so I called her and asked her to come talk with me. Within seconds of calling her, she was there in front of my face again.

The moment of truth had arrived. Her jagged teeth were showing and she produced a snarl from deep within her throat as if to say, "How dare you disturb me!" Her eyes appeared to be full of anger once again as she glared hatefully at me. I tried to hide my fear as I mustarded up the courage to look her straight in the eye. I told her I wanted to help her and I asked her what I could do to help her out. She didn't answer. She just stood there looking at me as if she was surprised I was being nice to her and not slamming my wooden door on her face. I asked for her name and she reluctantly told me it was Pamela. I asked her why she was so angry, but instead of simply telling me, she showed me through a vision in my mind's eye of her own memories.

I saw her as a beautiful nineteen-year-old woman who was around 7 months pregnant, so not quite at full term. She did not appear to be feeling well. The next image I saw was of her in a hospital room. There were several doctors and nurses around her with machines as they began rushing her to a surgical room. They laid her on an operating table and then everything went black for her. She never knew what had happened afterward. When she blacked-out, she never woke back up. I could only assume that she had died on the operating table and she never knew why or what had really happened to her or her baby. The only thing she knew was she is now dead, her baby was missing, and she was furious. After she showed this to me, she suddenly disappeared. Even though she had put me through so much torment already, I kind of felt a bit sorry for her. I better understood her and why she was so angry at the whole world. It still didn't explain why she was still targeting me as an individual though. Maybe she wouldn't do it anymore since I had tried to help her. Maybe all she wanted was someone to hear her story. I thought perhaps my troubles with her were over and I wouldn't have to deal with her again. I didn't see her anymore that night.

The next three nights were wonderful. I slept in peace and did not see any signs of Pamela around me. I was happy and thought perhaps I had actually helped her by simply taking the time to listen to her story. Saturday rolled around again and it was time to go back out to the old hospital. I was excited and couldn't wait to meet up with everyone and tell them how nice and quiet everything had been on my end. Earlier that morning, I had to work so I ended up coming home to take a nap before heading out to the hospital. Normally John and I would ride out to the hospital together, but he had left an hour earlier that evening. He had a new experiment he planned to try out and wanted to arrive early to set it up. Our plan was to meet at the old hospital and he would show me this new experiment.

I got up out of bed and switched on my bedroom light. The days had been getting shorter since it was now fall. With less daylight, the house would get darker faster towards the evening time. I had overslept and was running about fifteen minutes behind my set schedule. I quickly changed my clothes and started to go into the living room to get my shoes when my eyes saw something that stopped me dead in my tracks. I had a long hallway that led straight into my living room where a reclining chair rested. There, in the recliner, I saw Pamela. She was sitting straight up with her back against the seat and her head looking forward. Her legs were hanging down and her arms were resting on the armrests. I started to hear her wicked laugh as she slowly turned her head to look at me. Her face looked worse than before and the way she smirked and growled at me sent chills down my spine.

I ran back to my bedroom, grabbed the remainder of my things and prepared to leave. I wasn't staying in the house any longer than I had to; since she was hanging around. I turned on all the lights I could and grabbed the keys to my truck. I only had one problem. In order for me to leave, I had to go through the living room and pass right by where Pamela was sitting. I opened my bedroom door, looked up the hallway towards the direction of the recliner and was relieved when I did not see her. I couldn't help but wonder where she went but regardless, I was glad she was gone. I had to get out of the house and head to the old hospital. I was baffled at why she was back and I didn't know why she had returned. I thought I had helped her and had given her some peace. She was obviously still angry and by the sound of the laugh I heard coming from her, she was not done tormenting me.

I headed down the hallway and slowly crept into the living room. I looked all around me but there was still no sign of her. I made it to the front door where luckily, I found my shoes lying where I had taken them off earlier that afternoon. I bent over to put my shoes on and suddenly felt someone behind me. It was almost as if I were in some Hollywood thriller movie where just as the victim is about to escape, some wicked ghost shows up and gets them right at the last minute. I slowly stood up, looked behind me and there she was. She stared at me with the same look on her face and the same hatred showing in her eyes. I yelled at her to leave me alone, hoping that she would. I ran out my front door, barely closing the door behind me, let alone locking it. I quickly got into my car and sped out of my driveway hoping to put as many miles between Pamela and I.

I had about a forty-five minute drive ahead of me before I would arrive at the hospital. I knew I wouldn't be able to get there fast enough. I was still shaking a bit from the scare that Pamela had given me at my house. My mind was blown away as to why she had come back. I thought I had made her happy by listening to her and offering her my help, but she obviously didn't want it, so why was she still hanging around bugging me? Why wouldn't she just leave me alone? Did I not help her correctly? I had followed the advice Lynn and Maggie had given me. I knew I wasn't able to help her anymore the last time I had tried, because she disappeared and I didn't see her the rest of that night. I couldn't logically understand what her overall purpose was for haunting me and quite frankly, I didn't know at that point how I was going to be able to handle her anymore. I was already drained from fighting her off in the past.

I felt very uncomfortable driving and I couldn't wait until I got to the hospital. I looked in my rear view mirror several times expecting to see her sitting in my back seat, but thankfully, I never saw her there. I figured I would see her at some point, because that is the way it seemed to always happen in the movies. I just kept my fingers crossed, hoping she hadn't followed me to the car. I had always heard ghosts couldn't just magically appear in a moving vehicle, but I wasn't sure if that was true and I really didn't want to find out at that particular point. I still felt nervous, like she was watching me, but I just attributed it to my encounter with her at my house.

I had been driving for about thirty minutes and was finally able to calm down a bit. I didn't have much farther to go, so I decided to put on my lipstick and give my hair another quick brushing before I arrived. I quickly glanced down inside my bag to find my lipstick and hairbrush. When I looked up, Pamela was sitting there beside me in the passenger's seat. Her quick appearance scared me so much that I almost ran off the road. It also angered me to the point that I rolled down my windows and yelled at her to get out of my truck and leave me the hell alone. She just snarled at me and laughed before disappearing.

I was so angry for the rest of my short drive there. What was this woman's problem? I felt like she just didn't know when the game was up and when it was time for her to quit. She might not have known it then, but she caused me to declare a sort of "spiritual war" on her. It had been three months now since I had first encountered her and, quite frankly, I was tired of her scaring me and getting away with it. I knew I had to put a stop to this. It was time for me to somehow fight back and give her a dose of her own medicine.

I finally arrived at the hospital and decided to talk to Lynn and Maggie again. I was able to pull them away from the group and fill them in on what had just happened. I explained that obviously my efforts to talk to Pamela the other night had not helped. I told them I felt she was only out to torment and scare me and I was tired of it and didn't want to deal with her anymore. I asked them why they thought she was targeting me and what purpose did this hold for her?

Lynn and Maggie both told me she must have been attracted to my energy for some reason and I came off as an easy target, because I didn't know about spiritual self-protection. They asked if I had been unusually tired since I had encountered Pamela the first time and I replied with a "yes." It was true that I hadn't been sleeping well at night due to her appearances beside my bed and the horrible nightmares she had given me. They explained she was the reason for my fatigue and the act of draining my energy through scaring me was only an added bonus, because she took pleasure out of it.

I understood what they were telling me, so I told them I would fight fire with fire. I planned to find her weakness and force her to leave me alone. Lynn and Maggie both warned that finding her weakness was not the way to spiritually fight her. They told me the best thing I could do was to find my spiritual weakness in which she was targeting and strengthen it. It would be only then that she would lose her interest and stop haunting me.

I felt a bit like a child in school, but I knew that Lynn and Maggie were both knowledgeable and experienced in the spiritual realm. I knew they could really help me. I couldn't think of what my spiritual weakness was, so I asked them how I could discover it. They explained that my weakness was my spiritual protection and without it, I could not properly protect myself against negative energies that were out there. They told me that along my spiritual path I would encounter many negative entities like Pamela. They would try to attach themselves to me for various reasons, but I had to prevent that from happening or I would encounter many instances like I was currently experiencing.

I couldn't help but think of a bible scripture that I had learned growing up in church:

> *Ephesians 6:12—"For we wrestle not against flesh and blood, but against principalities, against powers, against the rulers of the darkness of this world, against spiritual wickedness in high places."*

This made perfect sense and went right along with the spiritual protection that Maggie and Lynn were telling me about. After all, this scripture was talking about putting on the full armor of God when you deal with things of a spiritual nature. Now, I only had to learn how to spiritually protect myself. They assured me there were many different methods. I just had to find the one that worked best for me.

I told Lynn and Maggie how I felt about this whole spiritual journey and how discouraging it had been for me so far. Lynn reminded me of our conversation when she had told me that if I had decided to accept my gifts, I would have to accept the good with the bad. She told me it was all a part of universal balance and you couldn't have one without the other. I was beginning to understand there was way more involved in working with the spiritual field than what I had initially realized.

I felt like I was on a merry-go-round. Here I was again, trying to find something that would work best for me for spiritual protection. I didn't have the slightest clue what I needed to look for. I was beginning to think all this spiritual stuff was just too much work. If I would have to keep encountering mean ghosts like Pamela, I didn't know if I wanted to continue doing this. I knew there was a lot involved on the spiritual side of things, but I didn't quite realize just how much, until I got more involved with my spiritual journey. Pamela had definitely been a wakeup call for me.

I also didn't understand why my head would hurt whenever I encountered stronger spirits. It's almost a bad migraine headache, but in the front of my forehead and behind my eyes. I asked Lynn and Maggie about this and Maggie told me that it was my "third eye" causing the trouble. She said it was because my mind was trying to process spirit message and to do so, my brain had to speed up in order to process the information coming in at such a higher spectrum. She explained that spirits operated on a higher frequency and she used a ceiling fan as an example. A ceiling fan has three speeds. The highest speed was the spiritual realm or plane that spirits reside and operate on. The lowest speed was the Earthly plane that we reside and operate on and in order for an individual with gifts to communicate with spirits; they had to raise their vibration levels to meet that ghost half way in the middle. Since raising vibration levels caused our physical brains to speed up and change levels, it could also create headaches. Again, this made sense to me.

I thanked Maggie for the explanation on the spiritual headaches. Lynn then began telling me about her experiences when she first started learning her spiritual protection. She told me she found that a good way to start by imagining a protective force field around her. She explained it almost looked like a force field you would see in Star Wars Movies or Star Trek TV shows. If your shields were up then nothing could come near you or harm you unless you allowed them to, but at the same time, you had to be mentally strong to project this outward. She further explained it would take a lot of practice to get the mental image perfected, but eventually I would be able to do it automatically; without first having to concentrate and think about what I was doing. I told her I didn't care how much practice it took, just as long as I was able to keep negative ghosts like Pamela away from me.

I asked what I could do to make Pamela go away. Lynn told me not to worry any more about Pamela, as she had plans to help me get rid of her once and for all. She had previously made plans to come stay with me for the remainder of the weekend. I couldn't wait for her to do whatever it was she needed to do in order to get rid of Pamela. I fully trusted Lynn and figured she had to know what she was doing since she was so experienced in the spiritual realm. Perhaps Pamela wouldn't bother me at the house with Lynn close by; as she was a lot more powerful on the spiritual side of things than I was.

We joined the investigation late because of our conversation outside in the hospital parking lot, but I didn't mind since I needed some guidance. I now had so much to think about that I decided I wouldn't open up my door that evening. I had already had too much excitement and was finished with my spiritual fight for the night. My physical and mental state was exhausted. I stayed close by Lynn's side during the sit-down and I practiced putting up my protective shields like Lynn had told me too, just in case Pamela decided to show up again. I was feeling pretty relieved knowing I wouldn't have too much stress that evening. If I could get my shields in place correctly, I wouldn't have to worry about Pamela bothering me anymore. Little did I know, Lynn would be Pamela's next target.

Lynn didn't say much on the way home other than to let me know she had encountered Pamela for herself that night in the hospital. She described her to me and told me that she was indeed a nasty spirit who needed to go. We made it back to my house and Lynn and I decided to go right to bed since we were very tired from the long night we had just had. Lynn stayed in my daughter's room since my daughter was out with her dad for the weekend. My daughter's dad and I were divorced, but he was pretty well with following through with his visitations on the weekends. Feeling exhausted, I went to bed.

The next morning I woke up and made some coffee and poured Lynn a cup. She was just waking up and told me she was very tired and hadn't slept well at all. She told me she had seen Pamela floating above her bed and she tried to scare her by twisting and contorting her body all while showing her jagged teeth and growling in order to scare her. She described how Pamela was getting louder and louder with her snarling and growling. Lynn tried to ignore her, but Pamela persisted. I could relate to Lynn on what she had experienced. Sometimes Pamela's growling sounded like an angry cat warning someone to stay away. The growls could even be low, guttural and drawn out. Lynn said she asked Pamela *"Is that all you've got? You're going to have to do better than that to scare me, so why don't you just go on and leave and quit bothering Christy too!"* She said that Pamela acted like she didn't want to leave, so she had to tell her a second time. She threatened her and told her that she was going to leave or face the consequences. What those consequences were, she never told me, however I guess that Pamela took her seriously, because she quit bothering her and left my house all together.

That morning Lynn and I burnt sage throughout my house. She scattered some seat salt around the perimeter of my home and instructed me to repeat the same rituals once in a while. She explained that burning sage would help clear the air within my home of negative energy and reapplying the sea salt created a barrier that they cannot penetrate. Even though I was still somewhat new to the paranormal field, with only three years under my belt, I had heard about different people burning sage to ward off bad spirits, especially the Native Americans who kept this as part of their traditions. At this time I hadn't even thought about resorting to my roots and using the power of prayer to ward off bad spirits. This should have been my first line of defense however. Perhaps if I had tried this first, Pamela wouldn't have lingered around as long as she did.

Lynn told me to keep a close watch on the house and to always take notice of any energy changes in order to make sure my house stayed clear of any spirits or negative energy. She told me if I ever felt an unwanted spirit or a negative energy come into my house, I should direct all my energy towards it, tell it that it wasn't welcome, then demand that it leave right then and there. Again, using the power of prayer would have come in handy here. I found throughout my experience of dealing with spirits that fervent Godly prayer should always be number one.

Lynn also told me to remember something very important. She said not to think about Pamela or speak her name out loud because if I did, there would be a chance she could come back and my haunting would start all over again. Lynn told me there was a theory that some spirits could be called back if they thought they were missed, if they were being thought of too hard, or if they knew they were needed. I told her she had nothing to worry about, because Pamela would be the farthest thing from my mind. I asked her what I should do if I encountered Pamela at the hospital again. She told me to block her and keep my protective shields up and she was confident that if I did that, she wouldn't bother me anymore, especially now that she knew I would no longer tolerate her torment.

The weekend was over and I had to believe that Pamela was gone. I kept practicing my protective shield, held it up at all times showing that I had no fear, even though that was still a bit hard for me. For the next week, things seemed to stay quiet around my house and luckily I didn't have another encounter with Pamela in my home again. I was a bit nervous about what might happen once I visited the old hospital again. I tried to tell myself just to stay protected and keep faith that Pamela would stay away from me for good.

Saturday rolled around again and I went to the hospital as usual. Sure enough, I saw Pamela again. This time was different though because not only did I have my spiritual shields going, I also had the attitude that she would no longer able to scare or bother me and nothing she could try would bother me. I watched her for a minute. I knew she had seen me too, but instead of coming over to taunt me, she just looked at me sadly, turned and walked away in the opposite direction before finally disappearing.

I was so happy. I felt like I had learned a new lesson and my efforts towards building spiritual protection had worked. I was even happier, because there would be no more Pamela and I was finally free of my awful spiritual attachment. I had learned so much from this. From that point forward, I never left home without saying a prayer and putting my spiritual protection shields up.

CHAPTER 5

"Learning to Overcome Roadblocks"

Time had passed by quickly and I had finally learned to master the technique of spiritually protecting myself. Lynn had also taught me about meditation and had given me some insight on the different types of meditation techniques. She told me to find one that worked best for me. I tried all sorts of methods for beginning meditation, but finally discovered using the flame of a candle was the easiest for me. I became very serious and dedicated to my new cause, so much that I didn't realize just how fast and strongly my gifts were coming back to me.

We continued to conduct our investigations. Even though we investigated using the routines, I set aside a bit of time for myself to observe and listen to things around me. I wasn't completely aware at this point that I was capable of doing the same type of spiritual work that Lynn did. Even though I was starting to understand and use my gifts and abilities more, I felt like I was nowhere near the level that Lynn was, because she had been doing spiritual work for many years and I had only just began my spiritual path. I also had a lot of doubt that would creep in when I was on investigations. I was told by Lynn that I had to learn how to overcome my insecurities and not be afraid of who might come to see in spirit or what I might see or hear in spirit. I decided to take her up on that advice one night when we were doing a residential investigation.

Another woman I had worked with at the sheriff's department, named Angela, told me she had some very strange things happening at her house and she felt like she was going crazy. She stated her children felt completely afraid and one of her daughters would no longer sleep in her bedroom. She also stated she would have things moved around in the house and they would see shadows from the corners of their eyes, but when they looked, no one was there. She asked us to come out and investigate and let her know if she was losing her mind or if there was something really there.

Lynn was unable to make this investigation and I felt lost without her, however we were taking along our friends from the other local metro paranormal group to help us investigate this location. The house wasn't too big, four bedrooms with one living room, kitchen and dining room. We finished our sweeps and ended up having a few EMF spikes in one of the bedrooms and in the kitchen area. During the investigation, I was in the dining room when suddenly, I saw a young boy's face come through the wall and then go back in again. He appeared to be around the age of fifteen and had brown hair and brown eyes. I thought that it was very odd and I couldn't help but wonder who he was. After the wall incident, I kept periodically seeing him, but he would never come over and talk to me. He would just disappear. We decided to do a sit-down and I thought I would try to see who this young boy was.

I sat down in the living room for a moment and concentrated as I put up my protective shields. I asked him to come and talk to me. I knew he was there, because I had seen him. At first, he didn't want to come over and talk. He eventually snuck around the corner and told me his name was Caleb. He told me he liked to play practical jokes on people and from the reports my friend Angela had told me, I figured he was the culprit.

Normally, when our group would conduct a sit-down, the members of our team would call out the things they were experiencing, feeling or seeing. I was very nervous and a bit scared to verbally announce anything I might have been picking up on as I normally just kept what information I received to myself. I did this because I was afraid I might be incorrect in what I was sensing, since I was so new to using my abilities for investigating the paranormal. I never wanted to mess up and give out the wrong information to my team if I had accidentally misinterpreted a spiritual message. I was so new to this field of work that I was not fully confident with my gifts. I was afraid that there might be someone in the group that might accuse me of faking my abilities if I was wrong with interpreting spirit messages, even though I would never intentionally do anything to deceive anyone.

I decided to put the negative thinking out of my head and just go with whatever information I received from spirit. I knew I had to start trusting myself more in order for my gifts to start getting stronger. I thought in times like these, it would be helpful to have another gifted person around to observe what spirit was saying. Then the two of us could compare notes afterwards to see what matched. The best way to do this would be for both of us to write down what information we were getting for comparison later. Since there was no other psychic present with us this evening, I just had to be brave and do what I needed to do.

We had audio and video recording going on during this time, like usual. Later on, when the audio and video were reviewed, we found we had recorded Caleb's voice. During the time I was talking to Caleb, the audio from the video camera confirmed the things I was sensing psychically and relaying back to the group.

I asked him if his name was Caleb because I felt that's what his name was. A few seconds after I asked him this, you could hear him say, *"Caleb"* on the audio recordings. During the same conversation, I asked him again if his name was Caleb and in my head I heard him say, "And what if it is?" I then repeated his statement back to the group during the investigation and sure enough, the audio recording had picked up on his voice also saying,

"And what if it is" in response to my question. I was so excited to have actually collected confirmation of the things I heard psychically. It gave my confidence a much-needed boost. I think it also let the group know that I wasn't full of bologna and that I really was seeing and hearing the things that I had described. I thought perhaps I could do this after all, as long as I kept humble and not haughty with my gifts.

As the night went on, I began to pick up on more spirit messages. There was also the ghost of an elderly woman in this home whose name was Marjorie. She was there because of the homeowner and her children. She died shortly after her husband. In death, however, she longed to see her husband again and had set out on a journey to find him. Her search had not yet led her to her husband, but rather to the home of Angela and her family. Marjorie had been passing through when she stumbled onto the family. She immediately felt the need to help them, since they reminded her of her own family.

Caleb had ended up being an aggravation to Marjorie, as he would antagonize her every chance he got. Marjorie had refused to give into Caleb's annoying whelms, especially since he was still a child at the age of fifteen. Marjorie told me there were times when she became fed-up with Caleb's pranks, so she had developed her own way of handling him. Although she never revealed her method to me, she stated it usually worked because Caleb would back off and leave her alone for a while. In addition to aggravating Marjorie, Caleb also liked to bother and scare the homeowners. He admitted he was the one that kept moving things around in the house and was also responsible for scaring the girls. He said he did these things because he thought they were amusing. This could be typical thinking for a teenage ghost who had nothing better to do.

We weren't able to get any recorded evidence of Marjorie's presence, however I felt like I had accomplished a great deal by getting correlating evidence to back up what I was sensing psychically with Caleb. That correlation also helped me to take the next step in using and trusting my abilities and gifts. I also felt more confident towards relaying the information to my investigative associates, since they also heard the audio and were with me when I got Caleb's message. I felt better knowing they had more confidence and trust in my abilities. I truly felt this particular night and investigation allowed me to grow stronger and gain a new confidence and strength, which was something I really needed. My lack of self-confidence was beginning to fade and I found I was able to overcome another roadblock.

My religious upbringing and fear of relaying spirit message to others were not the only roadblocks I had to overcome during my spiritual growth. I was growing spiritually but didn't know how to label my abilities. I didn't want to say "psychic" because that was such a bad title. I thought of the title "intuitive" and thought maybe that would sound better for now. Over time, I was able to work a lot with Lynn who helped me correlate and confirm some of the spirit messages I was receiving. I wanted to make sure what I was sensing was interpreted correctly. She helped me to overcome my self-doubt by building up my confidence. Writing down what we were getting on investigations instead of always speaking it out loud and comparing notes afterwards was a method that helped me to learn to trust myself with the spiritual information that I was getting. It kept me from trying to fight my own consciousness. I had a habit of telling myself it was all part of my imagination. When our notes had a lot of the same information, it boosted my confidence and trust in myself, giving me the validation I needed. I figured the reason I was conflicted over most of the spirit message I received was due to the teachings of my religious upbringing. I was still battling with religious beliefs about paranormal research and if this was the right thing for me to be doing.

I grew to love and trust Lynn and I really enjoyed working with her on investigations. However, I found out later that not all people who are gifted could work together like Lynn and I, because it seemed there were a lot of other gifted people out there who had issues working with other gifted individuals. I didn't quite understand this at the time, but I found out later that a lot of it had to do with jealousy and competition between psychics. I also believed it was because of a fear of being told by other psychics that their impressions or interpretations were wrong because they did not receive the same information. Any experienced psychic knows and understands that not all of us will receive the same information. It all depends on how the individual connects with the other side and how they interpret the information they receive. Most often, a psychic connects with spirit through different frequency levels. Psychics pick up on and receive messages from these different frequencies. It is similar to tuning into a different radio station.

Overcoming those with closed minds that assume one psychic fits all was another roadblock to conquer. I've previously mentioned my struggle with religion and the paranormal. One of the reasons for this personal conflict was due to the state of Oklahoma's strong religious affiliation with Christianity. This was also the state where I have lived my whole life. It has been nearly impossible to investigate some places using logical explanations in our state due to the strong religious views and opinions of some clients. I remember one specific investigation we had conducted back in 2004. A woman contacted us to come out and investigate her place of employment. She worked at a historical library in a small town in southwestern Oklahoma and had gotten permission from the library's director for us to investigate. She was also a believer in the paranormal. Both women had stated they had encountered strange experiences while working there.

The employees had reported seeing and hearing a couple of children run through the aisles of the bookcases. They also saw them playing in the children's reading center. They reported on many occasions the staff would tidy up the entire library before heading home at night, but upon opening back up in the morning, they would discover the children's area messed up again with books and small toys lying about. They also stated sometimes they would hear children laughing and talking off in the distance while working late at night. A few of the workers also reported seeing a tall man often seen by the book cases in the back of the library for a few seconds before he vanished.

This case sounded intriguing to us, so we accepted the invitation to investigate the historical library. A date was set and on the day we were scheduled to arrive, I received a phone call from our client. She informed me she had to cancel the investigation at her library. When I asked her why, she told me it was because there was a strong opposition to our investigation voiced by Baptists who sat on the town's city council. Their concerns were that we would be performing witchcraft and conjuring up demons and unruly spirits and they did not want that to happen in their library or their town. We were also told one of the Baptists stated if they saw any of us "Ghostbusters," they would "run us out of town."

This was a disappointment to us, not only because we couldn't investigate the library, but because of the negative attitudes, lack of knowledge and the passing of judgment on who we are and what we did. There are many common misconceptions that people have about what is involved with paranormal research. It is understandable that many groups investigate differently; however it does not mean all groups are involved in witchcraft or use Ouija boards or conjure up spirits with séances. We would like to think that every group or paranormal investigator researched and gathered correct information when it comes to paranormal investigating. The truth however is that no one has all he correct answers or methods. Investigating the paranormal is a learning process. The reputation of each specific group can also be tainted if they do not follow certain protocols that the majority of seasoned paranormal investigators use but it doesn't mean their different methods are wrong. Some paranormal investigators can be unfair in passing judgment on others and the same applies to those outside of paranormal investigating who pass unfair judgment on those who do. It has been said that people fear what they do not understand, but that fear could be diffused if individuals would take the time to understand the details and get the facts involved before jumping to outlandish conclusions.

I remember a case that we did in southeastern Oklahoma. We were invited by another team to come in and investigate this location with them. There would also be another third party investigative team there as well. I had some unique experiences here but was very concerned about working with other investigators outside of my team that I didn't know very well. I knew some of these other investigators had heard about my gifts and abilities but since they had never worked with me before, I also knew they would probably be skeptical.

We had nicknamed this investigation, "The Lost Church" because of its history and since it had been abandoned for years remaining vacant. This church was built around 1901. It remained a church until it was abandoned in the 1920's due to the death of the pastor. This church was an African American church during a time of racial segregation. It is located in a country area, miles off any main road and after it's abandonment, it became lost and forgotten. There isn't much more background information on this church other than a list of members who are all now deceased. Our team spoke to the previous owner of this church and we learned a few stories about its past. We were told the pastor of this church was very strict on his congregation. The preacher was known to use belts to discipline the children within this church if they acted out during service. One Sunday while at church, the aging preacher had a heart attack and died within the isles of the church. It is believed that this same preacher, along with some of his congregation still visit the church in spirit.

When we arrived at this location, I was shocked by the small size of this place. When I learned we were investigating a church, I expected it to be a little larger in size. This one however reminded me of one of the small, picturesque country church that you would see on a calendar or advertisement page, just with some age added to it. When I walked inside this old church, it looked very typical of a small church. Its old wooden pews were all still there, just covered by bird droppings and some a little out of place. The stage was barely raised up to a foot in height where the pastor would give his sermon from the old pulpit and the choir would sing off in the corner. The main entrance to the church was inaccessible since the floors and ceilings were giving way to age. I could however picture how this little lost church looked in its glory days. The church had a heavy energy feeling too and while there, I felt like I was not alone but accompanied by many in spirit who were watching my every move.

We had been told by that this location was very active and the array of paranormal activity occurred here and ranged from loud footsteps, knocking coming from within the walls, talking, laughing, church hymnals being sung, the sound of horses being heard galloping next to the church, flashlights coming off and on by themselves and much more. One of the other investigators who had previously investigated this location told me that this church was also nicknamed, "Church of the potty mouth" because through recorded evp, they heard a man's voice spouting occasional curse words. They assumed this was the deceased preacher since he was the one rumored to haunt the location. I was very excited about checking this location out and I hoped my first night there would prove to be as active as everyone else had claimed it was for them.

I was sitting off to the right side of the church on one of the wooden benches. I felt a heavy presence of a male spirit sitting close beside me to my left. I didn't know who he was but I knew he was there observing what we were doing. I didn't tell anyone I felt he was there because again, I was nervous about other investigators not believing what I told them since they didn't know me well. I decided to just remain silent for the moment and see how events of the evening played out.

I never try to speak ill of others, but this particular night there was an older female investigator there who continuously talked and spouted out her opinions. She also addressed the spirits there in a bit of a disrespectful manner, which was something my team and I would never do. A few others and myself were getting tired of hearing her constant chatter. We were under the assumption that she was trying to be a "superhero" investigator since she was fairly new to paranormal investigating. It was almost as if she had to prove herself to her fellow investigators. I didn't want to offend anyone but as she was addressing some of the spirits there, I heard the male spirit sitting beside me call her a "bitch." I immediately grabbed my camera and took several pictures one right after the other. I just had the feeling that I had captured something in my photos. I called out to the other investigators and told them what I had heard and I didn't feel like I was taken very seriously.

Upon review of my photos, I found I had captured three photos that were amazing! In the first photo, there was a bright cluster of light there on the pew next to me. The bright light form looked similar to a cluster of grapes. In the second photo, the bright light cluster is larger but still in the same position. In the fourth photo, the bright cluster of light was still there and there were strange lights above and around it, almost in a circular shaped pattern. To me, it honestly looked like a person sitting there in the pew with their head bent down as if in prayer.

I remember how nervous I was when I decided to call out what I had heard that night to the other investigators but I was glad I did. It was very hard for me but I overcame another roadblock and learned that I should never be afraid to just speak what I felt was coming through spiritually. I also think I gained the respect of some of the other investigators that night too and that made me feel pretty good.

We concluded this investigation that night and found ourselves back investigating the site several more times after that. This investigation will always be a favorite of mine. It was always very active each time we went. I personally witnessed strange paranormal activity ranging from loud footsteps, knocking coming from within the walls, flashlights turning off an on by themselves, laughing from children, religious music and singing and disembodied voices. This will definitely be an investigation I will always remember.

Not only do paranormal investigators receive opposition oftentimes from fellow investigators but outside parties as well. There are some who also receive it from their family members as well. Some families disagree with the work members are doing and will not support their research endeavors. This was a very personal roadblock for me to overcome. It was very difficult got me since I had to deal with my family, their religious beliefs and my own personal religious convictions I had learned from my upbringing.

My dad's side of the family is Native American and my aunts have told me that their grandmother, my great grandmother, used to read tea leaves for people. My aunts also told me that my great grandmother just used to "know things" and she used her "knowledge" to help people she knew with her own "abilities." My dad's side of the family has always been open to the paranormal, but it was my mother's side that has never believed in the paranormal. It was my mother's side of the family whom I received the most opposition from. This included my mother, who had always said she wished I never had embarked upon the paranormal field. She said she constantly prayed for God to deliver me from it. If anything ghostly or paranormal came about in conversation with my mother, I learned it was better if we didn't approach or discuss the topic. I learned it is better not to try and convince someone to believe what you do about the paranormal field, especially if you know they have a different opinion on the subject. It would be the same scenario if you tried to convince a skeptic that ghosts were real. It just wouldn't work and it wouldn't matter what type of "evidence" you presented to them, if they did not believe in the cause, your "evidence" would hold no credibility with them.

I will say in my mother's defense that I can now understand where she was coming from because there are a lot of dangers associated with the spiritual realm. It took me a long time to realize my mother's point of view, but over the years I started growing spiritually while gaining an appreciation for things of a spiritual matter too. It was then that I was able to realize and fully understand my mother's concerns. I will say that I am very thankful for my mother who has always been a spiritual leader and a prayer warrior in my childhood home while growing up. To this day, if I ever need a spiritual prayer partner, I know my mother is only a phone call away and she would be on her knees in fervent prayer with me.

I do think there are a lot of Christians though who believe all things that are paranormal in nature are automatically evil and of hellish origins. It is my opinion however, that this is not the case. I believe that if more Christians would be open to thinking outside of the box, they could understand all aspects involved in the spiritual world. Yes, spirits are part of the spiritual world, but they don't make up the spiritual world in its entirety. There is so much more involved in the spiritual realm than what most people realize.

When it comes to roadblocks within the paranormal field, there have been many cases where investigators have feuded with each other over who is right and who is wrong about case evidence or theories out there within the paranormal field. There have been group rivalries, which have led to jealousy and competition in the field, which does nothing for the credibility of the field itself and for those of us who try to remain serious about our research. For some groups, learning to overcome their differences can be hard, but they should remind themselves about the true reason they began investigating the paranormal instead of feuding over minor things. Some researchers like to believe they have all of the answers, but they should realize it is okay to have different opinions, because no one will actually know the truth until they, themselves, are on the other side.

However, there are those of us who do support the efforts of like-minded people in this field. We believe in group cooperation and sharing of discoveries, since we all have the same goal to find out more about life after death. There have been times when my group and I have had to distance ourselves from various groups of people who call themselves paranormal investigators or teams, due to the unnecessary negativity they bring to the field. Remaining professional is a requirement at all times.

Our primary goal as investigators is to help our clients understand their potential haunting through recording, documenting and observing any paranormal activity that might be taking place. Other goals are to find out why ghosts remain Earthbound and if they need help reaching the other side. I couldn't help but wonder if ghosts somehow got lost or stuck while crossing-over to a place on the other side. What if they didn't cross over because they were afraid to? Maybe they feared judgment or felt too attached to loved ones or possessions here in our realm. What if they didn't realize they were dead? I had thought about so many different possibilities and how these questions intrigued me.

The questions seemed endless, but I at least knew I had finally reached a time in my life where I had began to trust myself. I had to believe in what I was doing or I could never completely reach my goals. I had to learn to put the negative thoughts behind me and ask myself why I was doing paranormal research. Was it for myself or for others? My answer was clear. I was doing it for myself to grow spiritually and to help others in need. If other investigators in the paranormal field did not agree with who I was or what my goal was, that was okay because I knew in my heart I was doing right despite what they thought. Most importantly, I had to be the one to learn to trust in myself and to find the truth that awaited me out there. I had already overcome so many road blocks and I knew, as time passed, I might encounter more, but the longer I did my paranormal research, the stronger I felt my calling to grow spiritually and to help others.

CHAPTER 6

"Emotional Spirits"

Time passed quickly once again, and we had really built up a good reputation for our group. We found ourselves getting more and more requests from different locations. Staying active with investigations was not a problem. It was such a change from when we first started and I was so glad our group had done so well. I found myself having to take over a lot of the group duties at this time, because John began losing interest in investigating. He wanted bigger and more exciting things to happen while we investigated. As any seasoned investigator would say, paranormal activity doesn't always happen when you want it to and it's not always as exciting as some might see on television. We had been getting investigation requests requiring us to travel longer distances. John was feeling discouraged when we would spend our personal funds to drive to a location to investigate and then have nothing happen in the way of personal experiences or recorded evidence. We ended up nicknaming these types of locations as a "dry run."

We did, however, have occasional requests come in to us for local investigations and one of these was for a very interesting house not too far from where I lived. The home was small but when a friend of mine contacted me about investigating this location, it sounded intriguing.

My friend told me she had other friends of hers living there who had just recently moved into the home and were experiencing strange events. This activity had become so intense they were planning to move out as soon as they could. When we spoke to the residents of this home, they expressed their confusion about the events taking place and wanted to know if we could help provide some answers as to what was happening. Arrangements were made for an initial investigation to be conducted on December 2, 2003. The residents had been renting the home since June of 2003 and knew very little history about the location. From what little history we could find on the location ahead of the investigation, we discovered the home had been built in the 1920's and had been home to a few different families. It was built on rural land, and had nothing else built around it at that time. It wasn't until the 1960's that developers came in and began building other homes on the vacant lots surrounding this old 1920's home.

Our initial investigation began at approximately 11:00pm. By 11:30pm, we conducted our walk-through of the home and then began our environmental sweeps by recording baseline EMF, basic photographs and various temperature readings throughout the home. During our sweeps, no anomalous EMF readings were found and the home appeared to be quite normal. It wasn't until we were setting up equipment in the kitchen area of the home when I saw an elderly woman by the kitchen sink cutting something on a cutting board with a knife. We asked her for her name and I heard her say, *"May."* Then I saw her clutch her chest and say, *"heart attack."* I wasn't sure if her name was truly May or if she had died from a heart attack in the month of May. After another team member conducted further research on the home, I was told there had been an elderly couple previously living in the home. An elderly woman had died of a heart attack in May of 2002, about 1 year prior to the current residents moving in and the year prior to our investigation.

Intrigued by the image of this woman, we decided to do an extensive investigation of the kitchen area and an hour of video and audio recording was completed. A couple of our team members noticed shadow movement by the front bedroom doorway. I had also noticed this shadow movement and heard a male's voice say, *"Mark."* I suggested having a sit-down and moving some equipment to this front bedroom. While setting up the equipment, the bedroom door slammed shut on us, but we could not verify whether this was caused from paranormal activity or the clothes hanging on the back of the door resulting in a possible weight imbalance. Strangely enough, however, right before I sat down in my chair to begin our sit-down, I felt this sharp stabbing pain in the upper right side of my back. Right then, I sensed a visual impression of a man that had been stabbed in the back. I immediately announced to my team that this man was stabbed in the back which resulting in his death.

Once all of our equipment was set up in the bedroom, I started to psychically connect with this man who identified himself as Mark. We had several EMF meters positioned in various areas of the room. When I began asking questions to Mark, there were several activations on our EMF meters as if in response to our questions. Within a few minutes, I found myself connected to this ghost and he began to tell me his story.

He told me he was twenty-seven years old and had been murdered. I began to see the room change its appearance right before my eyes. I felt like I was in some sort of strange time warp. The windows were open and the curtains were blowing inward with the breeze. I received a date of August, 1977. Suddenly, I saw Mark standing up by his bed stretching as if he was getting ready to lie down for a nap. I heard him say, *"I'm tired"* and watched as he was getting ready to climb into bed. All of a sudden, I saw a knife thrust into the upper right side of his back and then saw Mark lying on the bed in a puddle of blood with his right arm hanging off of the bed. While I was conveying this information to my teammates, they began asking questions towards Mark. Our EMF detectors were registering and activating as if in response to our questions as Mark was answering.

Movement caught my eye over by the bedroom door and when I looked, I saw a blonde headed toddler in a diaper, running past the bedroom door. At first I didn't know who this toddler was or why I was seeing him, however I later understood it was Mark's way of introducing me to his young son, brought forward from his past memories.

I then saw Mark standing, in spirit, outside of his body next to the bed. I saw his son with his big beautiful blue eyes enter the room and approach the bed where his father's body lay. The young boy began shaking his father's arm as if to wake him and I could faintly hear him calling out to his father saying, "Daddy, daddy!" At that time, I saw Mark in spirit, crying while reaching his arms out to hold his son. He kept trying over and over again to let his son know he was there. I heard him say repeatedly, "I'm not dead, I'm not dead! I'm alive and right here son! I'm right here!" It was at that moment when I felt all of the emotion's Mark had felt on that day of his death. All of a sudden, I started to cry uncontrollably. It was very hard for me to take in all of the emotions Mark was sending to me. Due to my intense and emotionally depressive state, the other investigators decided I needed a break and it was probably a good time to wrap-up the equipment and end the investigation. A couple of them led me out of the house, so I could regain control of my emotions.

I really didn't want to leave Mark there as I felt like he wasn't done telling me his story. I felt so compelled to help him. I didn't have the chance to find anything else out that night, but before I left, I thanked Mark for communicating with me and told him I would be back to help him. I felt like he was happy with our communication. I felt he believed me when I promised him I would keep my word and return again to help him.

I drove home that night in awe of what had happened. I had felt spirit emotions before, but never that much all at one time. My heart went out to Mark. I just wanted to be there to hug him and tell him I was sorry for what had happened to him and I would do everything in my power to help him. He was such a sweet spirit and he was hurting so badly. I knew this was one case I would never forget and one I couldn't just ignore.

When I reviewed the video footage from that night, I documented all of the meter activations that took place during the investigation. The majority of the EMF spikes were while I was communicating with Mark. The actual transcript from this sit-down session was unique and is detailed as follows:

Sit-down start time: 2:40 am

Location: Front East Bedroom

Date: November 2, 2003

Equipment was set up in bedroom and sit down began at 2:43.11 AM.

Gauss Meter & Electro Sensor Activation

Christy says "He was stabbed in the back."

2:43.53 - Team member notices cold spot near him

2:44.29 - Christy was talking about the feeling of being stabbed in the back.

Gauss Meter Activation

2:45.12 - Silence

Gauss Meter & Electro Sensor Activation

2:48.08 - Question: "Mark will you make our meters go off it if was you I saw who was stabbed in the back?"

2:48.13 - Gauss Meter Activation

2:49.29 – Silence

Gauss Meter Activation

2:49.51 - Question: "Can you make those meters go off if you were killed in this room?"

2:49.54 - Gauss Meter & Electro Sensor Activation

2:53.21-32 - Christy's Impression "I'm getting open windows with a breeze coming through with the curtain's blowing. He's lying on the bed on his stomach."

2:53.33 - Gauss Meter Activation

2:55.31 - Question: "Mark are you the one who's been slamming the doors?"

2:55.35 - Gauss Meter Activation

2:56.00 – Group Question: "Are you slamming the doors because you want to be acknowledged?"

2:56.08 - Gauss Meter Activation

2:56.19-35 – Group Question: "Is there an older woman that stays here with you? The one who died in the kitchen? The one who died in the month of May? Is that correct?"

2:56.39 - Gauss Meter Activation

2:57.56-58 – Group Question: "Do you know who it was that killed you? If not, will you make the meters spike?"

2:58.03 - Gauss Meter Activation

3:06.31 - Silence

Gauss Meter Activation

3:06.41 - Silence

Gauss Meter Activation

3:08.00 - Christy was giving her description of what Mark looked like

3:08.10 - Gauss Meter Activation

3:08.40 - Christy was giving her description of Mark's hair color

3:08.50 - Gauss Meter Activation

3:08.56 – Question by Christy: "Was that you I was describing Mark?"

3:08.59 - Gauss Meter Activation

3:09.01 – Group Question: "Are you married Mark?"

3:09.07 - Gauss Meter Activation

3:13.34 - Silence

Gauss Meter Activation

3:13.50 - Christy was describing the toddler she had just seen.

3:14.02 - Gauss Meter Activation

3:14.38 – Group Question: "Did you have a son, Mark, with blue eyes?"

3:14.45 - Gauss Meter Activation

3:14.57 - Silence

Gauss Meter Activation

3:15.19 – Question by Christy: "I don't know why you're telling me August of 77." Christy then hears & repeats Mark's response, "I was killed"

3:15.24 - Gauss Meter Activation

3:16.14 – Group Question: "Are you tired?"

3:16.16 - Gauss Meter Activation

3:16.19-30 - Group Question: "Were you going to go to sleep maybe when someone came up behind you and stabbed you in the back?"

3:16.32 - Gauss Meter Activation

3:16.38 - Gauss Meter Activation

3:17.08 - Christy describes the toddler she just saw.

3:17.13 - Electro Sensor Activation

3:17.24 - Christy says: "He saw the kid after he had passed. The kid came in here to get him."

3:17.45 - Gauss Meter Activation

3:18.26 - Christy says: "He sees himself lying there and his kid coming in and he can't, he can't do anything. He's upset."

3:18.36 - Gauss Meter Activation

3:18.38 - Christy says: "He's upset because the kid is by himself and he can't reach out to hold his son. He wants his son to know that he's there." Christy gets upset and begins to cry.

3:18.40 - Gauss Meter Activation

3:20.00 - Christy is crying uncontrollably and is taken out of the house.

3:30.00 - Investigation is concluded.

Nearly a month had passed, but I kept my promise and had scheduled to go back out there for a follow-up investigation on January 6, 2004. I wanted to get out there sooner, but because it was December and the Christmas holiday season, I wasn't able to go. I had to prepare myself for what I might encounter with Mark again, but I didn't care what kind of information or emotions he might convey onto me. Even though Mark was a ghost, I had quickly learned to love Mark as a friend. I felt so connected to him that I had become compelled to help him.

We arrived at the house and I immediately went to the front East bedroom and took my equipment with me. I wanted to get started right away with helping Mark. I connected with him right away and he thanked me for coming back. He apologized for upsetting me on my last visit, but I told him not to apologize, as I was glad I could be there for him and understood his situation. I told him I wanted to help him; I just needed to know how. He told me where he was buried, but he said his son didn't know where his body had been laid to rest. What mattered to him most was for his son to know the truth about what had happened to him and to know where he was buried. He also stated he missed his son tremendously and wanted to see him again, but he didn't know where to find him. His wife and son moved out of the house right after his death, many years ago.

Mark was confused about some of the events that happened to him after he was murdered. He would have followed family if he knew where they had ended up moving at. He said he had been waiting there at this same house for all these years to see if they would come back to look for him. I told him I would do my best to find the information he needed. Then I asked him if he wanted me to find out who had murdered him. He told me he already knew as he found out shortly after his death. He said getting revenge on his murderer didn't matter to him anymore either, since he knew he would never be able to come back in his physical body to be with his family.

Next, he told me he needed to go for a bit because *she* was coming. I asked him who "she" was and he said *she* was the crazy girl down the street who had murdered him. He disappeared and a young woman appeared in front of me. Her name was Alicia and she was 19 years old. When she was alive, she had lived down the street from Mark and his family. Upon talking with her, I learned she knew Mark and she claimed to have loved him. When she and Mark were alive, she had told Mark she wanted him to leave his wife and child for her, but Mark wouldn't do it since he loved his wife and son and wasn't interested in her. Her mental state seemed to be unstable and I watched her go from being very calm to very angry and then back to calm again. Alicia's behavior, words and actions indicated she might of had a of bi-polar disorder or schizophrenia disorder of some sorts. She told me she still loved Mark even though he refused to return her love back and that's why the accident happened to begin with.

She continued telling me her story and said, one day, she decided to go over to Mark's house and talk to him while his family was gone. She said she had quietly let herself into his house that day and she confronted Mark in the living room. He refused to talk to her, told her to leave and when she refused, he pushed her out the front door and closed it behind her. Alicia told me she stood there for a few moments on the front porch and felt herself getting angrier and angrier. She decided if she couldn't have Mark, then no one else would either. She ran home and grabbed a knife, slipped back into Mark's house through the same unlocked back door. She then entered his bedroom where she saw him standing by his bed, stretching. She crept up behind him and out of rage, she stabbed him in the back three times. She watched as Mark collapsed partially onto the bed. She found herself in a state of shock, because she couldn't believe what she had just done. She became very frightened and ran out of Mark's house. When it started to get dark, she buried the knife at the foot of an oak tree in one of her neighbor's yards.

A year had passed since Mark had died and the police hadn't suspected Alicia, nor did they have any evidence that linked her to his murder. Still, Alicia could not get over what she had done and she carried her guilt with her. She had loved Mark so much and now that he was dead, she missed him even more. She had thought about ways she could be with him again and since it wasn't physically possible, she decided she could reunite with him in spirit, if she was also dead. On the edge of insanity and in severe stages of depression and desperation, she overdosed on sleeping pills and committed suicide in her bedroom. She told me that now, even in death, she still comes over to see Mark, but he still turns her away leaving her eternally miserable.

I really felt bad for Alicia, but I was also angry with her for what she had done to Mark. Not only had she committed murder, but she had also taken Mark away from his wife and young son who needed him. While Alicia's story was sad, it was not as sad as the hurt she had caused Mark and his family or even the hurt he was still feeling in death. I couldn't explain to anyone just how I was feeling about this case and how Mark's emotions had touched me so deeply. It was one of those emotional stories that would stay with me forever.

I told Alicia she had done wrong and she needed to leave, because she was unwanted here. I honestly felt like she was responsible for causing some of the trouble for the homeowners by coming in and bothering Mark. She became very angry with me when I told her this and threatened to dig-up the knife and stab me too. I told her I wasn't scared of her and didn't want anything more to do with her. I told everyone we should wrap-up the investigation and call it a night.

We left after gathering our equipment, but I was still unsatisfied with this case. I knew I had to help Mark by finding out about the things he wanted me to check on. I checked with the town's local police department to see if there had been a murder that had taken place there in 1977. The officer informed me nothing from back then was stored on the computer, but the written case file would be in a box in the back storage area; however it wasn't open to the public. I also checked with the cemetery where Mark stated he was buried and found a couple of plots with his same name. So, I wrote a letter to the curator to get more information, since they didn't have a phone number I could call, and they never wrote back to me. The drive was too far for me to make to go do more research on my own. I thought about the old knife that Alicia said she buried by the old tree. I wanted to go over to the neighbor's yard and ask them if I could do some digging, but I didn't want to knock on a stranger's door and ask them such an unusual request, as they might think I was insane. Even if I were able to find the knife, what would I do with it? I'm sure the case has been closed for a long time now. What good could the weapon do at this point when both parties involved in the case were dead? There was no physical punishment that could be administered to Alicia.

I even searched the Internet looking for references on Mark and anything related to the town during that time, but I really couldn't find any useful information. I felt like I had reached a dead end. I went back later to tell Mark about my failed results. I apologized and said I wasn't able to uncover much information. He told me he understood and it was okay, since I was so nice to help him in the first place. I talked to Mark about crossing-over and advised him that he would be much happier. He agreed to do so now that the truth was known, but he would take his lingering regret of not seeing his son again with him. I reassured him if he crossed, he might have an easier time finding his son, because he would be at peace and would have spiritual help and guidance from people on the other side to assist him. I left that night with a heavy heart and knew I would miss Mark very much.

Since this case meant so much to me, I kept following up on the home and the activity there for a couple of years after our initial investigation. One day, I happened to run into the family who actually owned the home and rented it to the client we had worked with. They stated they had been told we did an investigation at the house. They were also told about our experiences and the recorded evidence we obtained during our investigation times there. They said that when they bought the home, they were informed there had been a murder of a young man that had taken place in the home back in the 1970's. They said they knew he had a wife and young son, but that was all the information they had. I thanked them and felt very glad I ran into them. They gave me validation for the information I had received spiritually and for the connection I had made with Mark.   Was it fate that I had accidentally bumped into them one day? I will never be convinced that it was just a coincidence.

Quite a while had passed, but I still found myself often wondering about Mark and if he found the peace he so desperately needed. I went by the house one last time to say a final goodbye. A friend of mine had informed me that a new owner had purchased the property and they were getting ready tear the house down so they could build a new home in its place. I couldn't help but wonder if Mark had moved on and he was no longer waiting in the home. I arrived and walked up to the front bedroom from the outside. I looked into the bedroom where I had first encountered him searching for Mark, but didn't find him. I felt relief and reassured that he had likely moved on and crossed over to the other side of this world. His memory, however, still weighed heavily on my mind. I suppose he knew somehow since a couple of days later, I had gone to bed and had a dream about him. In the dream, he came up to me, gave me a hug and told me he was doing fine. He also said he appreciated everything I had done for him and I didn't need to worry about him anymore, because he had found peace. I was so happy for him and told him even though I wouldn't worry anymore; I knew I still would never forget him. He smiled at me before he faded away. After that, I knew everything was okay. I knew his visit to me in my dreams was real. I was just so happy that he had thought enough of me to tell me goodbye.

Mark was not the only spirit I had encountered over time that had strong emotions conveyed onto me. Sometimes when a spirit has not crossed over, they can carry with them a variety of emotions. Their current state of mind depends on which emotions they will display. It's the same basic concept as living humans and their emotions. Mark was a very unique spirit as he not only displayed his sorrowful emotions to me, but he also expressed a lot of love. This is something that you don't always see with different ghosts and their personalities. I have come across some spirits that are just plain hateful or angry. Some are depressed or confused and some are very content and happy. It is difficult to deal with a spirit that is angry or controlling and sometimes you can only hope your communications with them will be beneficial in convincing them to stop acting out.

I remember a residential investigation I once completed in Southern Oklahoma. It stands out in my mind quite often because of the particular spirits that were there. The homeowners had contacted our group for help because they were seeing the ghost of a little girl and a man throughout their home. They also reported having things moved, feelings of being watched, hearing unseen voices, laughter and various other commonly reported paranormal activities. They fully believed their house was haunted.

This home was built in the early 1900's and a family of four, who were well known in the community, had occupied it. The great depression came were many were struggling to make ends meet, including this family who fell on hard times like so many others. The father was very concerned because he knew he was about to lose everything they had, including their home. His stress and worry nearly drove him to insanity. He tried to find a way to keep his family from suffering. Although his intentions were for the good, his actions were not.

We arrived at the residence and began setting up our equipment for the investigation. There weren't many strange things that happened, other than witnessing a tall plant shake while we investigated the dining room and when one of our meters was knocked-over by something unseen on the stairwell. It was during our investigation of one of the upstairs bedrooms that we started to receive some interesting information.

I was sitting on the bed conducting a small sit-down when my hair started to move on its own. I felt like someone or something was moving it. I then saw a little dark-haired girl around the age of 5. I began talking to her to try and figure out who she was. She revealed to me that she was part of a family who had lived there once. After speaking with her for a while, I asked her what had happened to them. She told me she couldn't talk about anything, because it would make her father angry and he would punish her. The little girl then disappeared. I was puzzled by this and had really wondered what had happened to this family.

In one of the other bedrooms, I felt drawn to an area in one of the closets that led up to the attic. I opened the attic door and kept hearing the screams of a woman. In between her screams, I heard her say, *"He killed us. He killed us!"* I started to talk to the woman, but this man suddenly appeared and was very angry. He told me we needed to leave and quit bothering his family. I told him we weren't there to bother them but rather there to help everyone if we could. He stated we couldn't help them and we just needed to leave them alone "...or else." I asked him why he was so angry and he wouldn't answer me. I repeated myself and he replied, *"Do you want to see why I'm so angry?"*

I felt myself getting irritated with him, but I knew I was feeling some of his anger and frustration through his emotions. I asked him what it was that he wanted to show me. He said, *"You'll see!"* I wasn't sure if I really wanted to see what he had to show me. I was leery of him, because I knew his emotional state was a bit unstable. Before I could think any more about it, I saw him quietly sitting in a chair. He was wearing a light blue shirt that had some blood splatter on it. He had a horrible look of depression on his face. He then raised a rifle up to his head and pulled the trigger. I was horrified as I watched the top part of his head and brain blow backwards hitting the wall decorating it red. I immediately shut my eyes and told him

I didn't want to see those types of images. He just laughed at me and said, *"You shouldn't ask to understand things if you don't want to know the truth."* I knew he had a point and I did not argue with him.

Although I didn't want to see any more graphic illustrations, I had to know what had happened to the family and I wanted to know why they were so scared of him. Careful how I worded my question to him, I asked him why his family appeared to be so afraid of him. I also asked what had happened to his family. He showed me an image of himself walking through his house toward one of his little girls as she was playing on the second floor. He told her to come downstairs and help him in the basement. Like an obedient child, she obeyed her father and followed him to the basement. Once they arrived, he then hit her on the back of her head with a large wooden board and tried to catch her before she hit the ground. I saw a white sheet spread out on the dirt floor as he laid her body upon it. I watched as he went back upstairs to get his youngest daughter and he repeated the same process with her. I noticed one of the little girl's head was bleeding and started to soil the white sheet.

Then he showed me what happened to his wife. He met her in the kitchen unaware and stabbed her with a kitchen knife in the stomach area. He then carried her body downstairs, wrapped it in a white sheet and laid her beside their two girls. He told me he called the local police to tell them what he had done, sat down in the chair and then took his own life. He explained to me he did not want to see his family suffer and lose everything they had during the depression that was taking place. To prevent that from happening, he did what he felt he had to do. He said he kept his family there with him in spirit so he could watch over them and take care of them, but in return all he got back was hate. His family wanted nothing to do with him for what he had done. He was angry because he could not make his family understand the reasoning for his actions. He wanted them to know it was for their own benefit but his family did not agree nor see his point of view. After listening to this desperate soul, I knew that his two children and wife were living a life of misery in the spirit world all because he was controlling and would not let their spirits go free, good intentions or not.

I tried letting him know what he was doing wasn't fair and by keeping his family there, they would never forgive him or accept his decisions. I asked him not to make his family stay there with him but he wouldn't listen to me or any other advice I had to give to him. He blatantly told me there was nothing that I could do or anyone else for that matter that would cause his family to be taken away from him. Knowing that I could do nothing else to help, we ended up wrapping-up the investigation. I couldn't help feeling sad about what I had seen and heard at this location. I had wished I could change things for this family so they wouldn't be stuck in the afterlife reliving misery. I wasn't sure how I could accomplish this either since I was still learning so many things about the paranormal realm. Nonetheless, it was still very hard for me to leave given the events that had taken place that evening. I knew this man's mental state was a bit unstable due to his past and present circumstances and I felt all of his emotions while I was there at this location. I could feel all of his depression, anxiety, anger and hopelessness. I could also feel the hurt, upset and hopelessness of this man's wife and two daughters. I knew this man was angry and I also knew that he would never find peace until he found forgiveness for himself first. I knew forgiveness wouldn't happen as long as his family felt the way did and as long as he kept them trapped there with him, but I didn't know how to help spirits who were unwilling to cooperate.

There are some spirits that can cause other spirits to remain Earthbound. At first, I didn't really understand this since everyone has free will and free choice while alive in the physical form. I assumed spirits would have the same free and free choice as well while in spirit form too. I learned later, if a spirit doesn't fully understand their freedoms, they could fall victim to other spirits who are controlling by nature. This was the case with this man who had control over his family and caused them to remain earthbound.

Sometimes, when emotions run high, it can cause a spirit to lose their clarity and they cannot see the real truth that is presented before them. Much like people who are alive in the physical form whose minds are plagued by alternate realities or people who choose to take their own lives due to depression and hopelessness. Spirits can also suffer the same delusions in death fueled by their own powerful emotions.

I have actually had a few strange encounters with spirits who were too caught up with their emotions to do right by themselves and others. We had a residential investigation once at a placed we called, "Elizabeth's Homestead." It was named for the spirit there who had gone insane during her life and promised revenge on anyone who tried to take her land from her. She told me in spirit her real name was Elizabeth Lawrence Sampson and the location we were investigating was the farmland she owned and lived on back in 1886. She was very angry, because she was murdered by some of the local Native American children that didn't live very far from her land. She went on to tell us she was once married and had several children of her own, but they all died of diphtheria and scarlet fever before the age of five. She said after her children died, she suffered from a deep depression that had affected her marriage. She went on to tell me about how her depression caused her husband to leave her. Before he left, he told Elizabeth that she had gone insane and he could no longer be married to her.

The Native American children who lived nearby deemed her as insane as well and they also called her a witch. Since these cruel children considered her to be a mean crazy witch, they felt she needed to die and they devised a plan to kill her. One day they snuck into her house and somehow poisoned some of her food. Unaware of the death that awaited her; she ate the food and shortly afterwards ended up losing her life. Now in death, she was angry, bitter and admitted she causes havoc for the homeowners. She also stated the land was hers and no one was taking it from her because it was all she had left. Even in spiritual death she was never able to find her children and reconnect with them again.

Elizabeth was also angry we were there and that we had seen her for whom she truly was. When she found out we were not afraid of her and would not back down from her attempts to scare us, she became angry and demanded that we leave. Our group ended up recording several EVPs from her. Some of these recorded evps said, *"Get out! You're aggravating me!"* and *"You're gonna get it!"*

I could feel all the emotions coming from Elizabeth. I also knew that underneath all of her negative emotions she was a sweet woman who was just pushed over the edge because of the death of her children. Most parents expect to die before their children. It is hard enough to loose one child let alone all of your children. Being a mother myself, I couldn't fathom loosing either of my children. Even though I couldn't relate totally to Elizabeth's heartbreak, I could feel what she was feeling. I felt very sorry for her. I only wanted to help her but because of her anger and bitterness, she refused any sort of help. After speaking with the homeowner about her haunting, she understood where Elizabeth was coming from too and she was no longer afraid of Elizabeth.

One last experience of an emotional spirit is one I encountered at a residential location with a woman whose sorrow deeply touched me. I first met her when we were investigating one of the bedrooms at the location and I smelled the scent of roses. I heard a woman's voice that was soft-spoken, yet I was unable to make out what she was saying. Then I sensed her name was Maggie Lou and suddenly I saw the image of a pink rose. I was then drawn to the bathroom of the home. I went into the bathroom and just stood inside for a while. Suddenly, I saw an image of this woman upset and crying next to the sink. I then saw the bathtub filled with water and there were pink rose petals floating up on the top of the water. These petals looked similar to potpourri or some scented bath mixture that you would place in your bath water.

Maggie Lou was standing in front of sink looking into the mirror. Still sobbing she asked, *"Why did he have to leave me? Why did he leave me?"* Then she grabbed a flat bladed razor and slowly cut the upper part of her forearm, almost as if she wanted to see how it would feel if she cut herself. I knew this woman was very upset over a failed relationship and I also knew she was severely depressed over loosing her significant other. I felt the strong sense of guilt that she was carrying. I knew she had a lot of regrets and was desperately wishing for her love to come back to her. I experienced all of her emotions ranging from depression, guilt and hopelessness.

I saw her take a drink of what appeared to be alcohol from a bottle and then, as she set it down, I saw her pick up the razor again. Only this time, I saw her slice both of her wrists. I watched horrified as droplets of blood filled the sink. I listened as she gasped with each cut she made. She placed herself inside the bathtub where she awaited death to take her. As I saw her lay there in the water, I watched as she cried and as she experienced brief moments of regret from her decision, realizing she was letting go of life as she knew it. Her pain was too much for her to bear. I kept watching as I saw her eyes get heavy as if she was falling into a deep sleep. Then, I saw death embrace her.

I felt so much sorrow and heartache from this woman that I sat down for a moment on the edge of the tub and quietly tried to place the images of her death out of my mind. I felt myself on the verge of tears as I had felt everything that this woman was feeling at the time of her death. It was then that I heard her soft voice speak, but when she spoke she sounded very weak, as if she was fighting to speak. I looked behind me and saw the bathtub fill with a black mass. I watched in confusion as I saw her start to take form and come up out of the tub. As I started to move away from the tub, I felt her touch me as she reached upwards trying to pull herself out of the bathtub. It was during this time that my audio recorder picked up a Class "C" EVP that I believe to be Maggie Lou saying, *"Wish I were like you, not dead."*

Since I had been in the bathroom for quite a while, some of the other investigators came into the bathroom to make sure I was okay. They told me they had asked me a question and when I did not respond, they grabbed my hand and led me out of the bathroom. My fellow investigators also told me that I seemed to be in an unresponsive state for about five minutes. The investigator who came to get me out of the bathroom told us they happened to glance into the tub for a brief moment and saw a black mass in the tub before it quickly disappeared. It was then that I told my co-investigators what I had just experienced.

I tried to continue with the investigation, but I kept seeing Maggie Lou and feeling her sorrowful emotions. It was as if she had decided to push her emotions on to me so I would know her pain was real, even though she was deceased. Towards the end of the investigation, I felt myself becoming overcome by her emotions again and I felt like she didn't want me to leave. I had to excuse myself from the rest of the investigation in order to break the connection with her. I felt that Maggie Lou's death did not happen in the home we investigated, but rather in another time and place. I felt she had followed one of the resident children home, because the child had underdeveloped abilities to see and hear her. Due to her miserable state, she was desperate for someone to acknowledge her. Instead of getting her message across to the child though, she scared him terribly. She also scared the rest of the family and as a result, the mother called our team to come out and investigate their home. The images and emotions I felt that night from Maggie Lou are some I will never forget. She is another perfect example of a spirit conveying their emotions on the living.

Some ghosts transfer their emotions on the living in order to let us know their story and what happened to them. Spirits also do this as a way to get people's attention so they can be helped. The longer a spirit remains earthbound, the more negative they can become because of heavy emotions they carry with them in death. Spirits can also sometimes feel ignored and therefore project their emotions on the living to cause havoc as a way to get revenge.

Throughout the years, I have had many people tell me they have moved into a place that is haunted and feel all sorts of weird emotions. Some of them report emotions such as abrupt anger, depression or sudden bouts of crying. Some say they feel a lot of tension in their home and they report their family does nothing but fight while they are together within the home, but not while outside the home. Some people who have experienced personal spirit attachments have reported feeling emotions that are not their own. Most report that these emotions will come upon them very rapidly and sometimes they leave rapidly too. It can be extremely hard on an individual receiving these emotions if they do not understand what is happening to them. One of the things my group and I began doing to help our clients, was to explain the emotional impact a spirit(s) can leave on an individual or family. Knowledge is an important key in recognizing what is taking place during a haunting where spirits are causing emotional upset.

Can an individual stop a spirit from transferring their emotions onto them? It might be hard, but the first step in accomplishing this is to recognize what is happening. Look for signs of a haunting. If there is strange activity taking place in a home or around a person, chances are there might be a spirit present. If this is happening and a individual starts experiencing strange emotions that aren't typical of their personality, or if there is a lot of sudden tension in a home between family members, the spirit could be portraying emotions on that individual and essentially be the one causing all of the trouble. The next step in these cases are to recognize they are not normal emotions and stop them by consciously switching the emotion to something different in order to reverse what the ghost is trying to project on the individual. If a person is feeling angry, they need to switch their emotion to being happy. An individual can also demand that the spirit stop causing them problems by pushing their emotions on to them. As always an individual can say a prayer and ask God to help deliver them from the troubled spirit. Eventually, if this process is repeated enough, a spirit can be deterred from causing the issues.

Can those of us with abilities stop the emotions of a spirit from affecting us? That would depend on one's level of sensitivity. Unfortunately, even most people who are strongly gifted cannot fully stop the emotions of spirit from coming through, especially if we are in communication with them. However, applying the same technique of differentiating spirit emotion from one's personal emotions and changing the negative emotion to a positive one is vital in stopping the spirit from affecting us. By doing this technique, a sensitive individual should be able to block a spirit's negative emotions from bothering them. If a sensitive individual is in communication with a spirit, they need to learn how to block any unwanted negative emotions. Communication with a spirit will allow a sensitive individual to feel the emotions of a spirit, but they also must learn how to discontinue the projected emotions when they are done with the communication. This is not usually accomplished overnight, but rather through years of practice and experience in dealing with spirit communication.

CHAPTER 7

"Spirit Dreams and Visitations"

Three and a half years had passed since I started researching and investigating the paranormal. The inevitable finally happened and my friend, John, finally lost his interest in the paranormal and decided he did not want to investigate or research the paranormal field anymore. As life would also have it, our close friendship started to drift apart. We weren't spending much time together since I was investigating the paranormal without him. Due to all factors involved, we disbanded our group, PICO, as it was a name we had both worked under together. The disbanding wasn't too bad on our team at that time, because it was small consisting of myself, John and one other part time member. About 6 months prior to this, Lynn had resigned from our group due to her inability to do the extra traveling, but since she enjoyed investigating, she decided to start her own local team in the area where she lived.

I knew I had to come up with a new team name for my group. Out of respect for John, I didn't want to continue using the PICO name, even though he told me I could. I had decided to rebuild a new group from the ground up and make it strong, continuing where PICO left off. This time however, I wanted to make an even better group. I finally came up with a new name, O.K.P.R.I., which stood for Oklahoma Paranormal Research and Investigations.

It wasn't long before I made the new team name public and published a new website. Shortly afterward, there were even more investigation requests rolling into my new group than what we had when I worked under the name PICO. I ended up accepting some new members into my group. Any group leader will tell you it's hard to find good help. I had some members start only to be to let go shortly after joining and this process repeated for a while until I was eventually able to establish a decent team.

Without warning, tragedy hit my family two days before Thanksgiving in 2004 when I received a call from my mother letting me know that my step-dad, Howard, had finally lost his two-month battle with cancer. I felt horrible that I was not there in the hospital with my family when he passed. At the time, I was in California on vacation. I arrived back home shortly after hearing the news and spent a few days with my family and attended Howard's funeral. During the memorial ceremony, I watched as family and friends mourned. I didn't want to tell my mother at the time, but I briefly saw Howard's spirit at the funeral. I watched as he walked up beside my mother and put his hand on her shoulder for a short moment before suddenly disappearing. I didn't know if he saw me or not, because he did not acknowledge me during that brief moment but I knew it was him.

During the next two weeks, my daughter, Sarah-Ann, who was now nine years old at the time, was having a hard time coping with Howard's death. She felt bad, because of the last words she had said to him while he was alive. She was visiting my mother and Howard and had gotten into trouble for something minor. Howard was the one to correct her behavior. My daughter has never taken authority well, so she told Howard that she hated him and was mad at him. After Howard's death, my daughter told me she felt so bad and wished she could go back in time and take back her mean words. She said she wished she could have seen Howard one more time, so she could tell him she really didn't mean it and she really did love him. I tried to comfort her by telling her I was sure Howard knew how she really felt and she shouldn't carry that guilt around with her. Despite my attempts of comforting words, it wasn't enough help my daughter feel the peace she so desired.

About two weeks after Howard's death, my daughter and I had both gone to bed one night and we both had a similar dream. In our dreams, Howard came to visit us and told us he loved us. Sarah-Ann said she wanted to talk to him in her dream, however she found herself unable to speak. Howard told her that he had to go away, but he would always love her. Sarah woke up crying and again wishing she could have talked to him.

I, on the other hand, was able to talk to Howard in my dream. I apologized to him for not being able to be there in the hospital when he passed. He told me he understood and that it was okay. He also said he wanted to apologize to me. I asked him why and he replied, "For not believing you." I didn't understand what he was talking about, so I asked him and he said, "For not believing you about the paranormal, the existence of 'the other side' and the work that you do. I understand it all now." His comment made me feel humbled and I was very happy he was appreciative of what I was doing. It made me feel that the work I was doing in the paranormal field was not futile. I thanked him and told him I only wished my mother could also understand it the same way he did. He chuckled and told me told me, "We both know better. You know as well as I do that she won't believe or understand it until she passes too." I laughed and told him I understood and I wasn't going to try to convince her any time soon either. I thanked him again for understanding and told him that we would miss him. He assured me he would check in on us from time to time but he also knew we would all be okay. I wasn't surprised that he didn't have a message for me to give to my mom. We both knew she wouldn't be receptive to any spirit message from him nor would she believe me if I told her anyway.

When I woke up, I felt a bit sad because I knew Howard was really gone, but then a part of me was happy, because I got to visit with him again and say a proper goodbye. I had felt so bad about not being able to be in the hospital when he had passed. I thought perhaps that might have been why he stopped in to say goodbye and give me the message that he had. Shortly after waking from my dream, my daughter Sarah-Ann also woke and immediately told me she had a strange dream about papa Howard. After she told me about her dream, I also revealed to her the dream I had about Howard. We were both in awe that Howard had come to the both of us like he did. Sarah-Ann asked me why papa Howard had come to her in her dream instead of just coming to her when she was awake where she could talk to him. I explained most of the time our loved ones chose to come visit us while we are asleep, because we can hear them better. I further explained that our minds could pay closer attention to them in a dream state. She didn't quite understand how that was possible, but she knew I was telling her the truth. She accepted my answer for the time being and agreed with my explanation. She did ask me if I thought Howard would come back and visit with us again. I told her maybe he would but until then we would just have to keep our eyes and ears open and pay attention to our dreams. Sure enough, we received a couple more visits from Howard over the next few upcoming months.

Previous to this, I also had been curious why ghosts chose to visit some of us in our dreams. I had heard many people say they had very vivid dreams of a passed loved one or close friend. They told me when they awoke they couldn't stop thinking about their dream, because it had all seemed so real. Other people I knew had reported dreaming of certain people and then upon waking, they would find them standing beside their bed. I found this to be true with my personal experiences.

There were many nights I had gone to sleep and would have a strange dream about someone. I've had "visitors" that would show me places important to them or things that had happened to them. On many occasions, I would awaken with them standing beside my bed. While it was startling at first, I eventually got used to it. I think the hardest ones to accept were the ones who presented themselves in the image they were at the time of their death, if they had died tragically.

There is a reason why information is passed to a living person in the way that it is communicated. Usually spirit has a personal reason for coming to a particular living individual and conveying a specific message. If nothing else, sometimes spirit just wants a certain person to know they are with them.

My interest with spirit visitation and dreams began to increase and I started doing more in-depth research into this area. The main question I had was why spirits choose to come to us during our sleep? I consulted many sources, including a PhD professor I had in a college psychology course. I learned when our bodies are asleep we are very relaxed, so much that we are at the closest point of death we can ever be without physically dying. It is also during this time that our subconscious minds are wide open and we are more receptive to our surroundings and to any information our brain may receive. The brain goes through different sleep stages, beta, alpha, theta and delta. I'll go more into detail about this a bit later however, since our bodies are so relaxed and our subconscious minds open, we seem to be able to be more aware of a spirit visitor when they are in our presence.

When we sleep our mind does what I call a "psychological brain dump." This is when your brain tries to refresh itself in an attempt to "wipe clean" the events of the day. It puts certain thoughts into memory as it prepares to ready itself to receive new information the next day. Our brain is much like a computer when you defrag it, all of the files go back into their proper place and the memory space is prepared and ready for its next use. Sometimes with each refresh cycle, the brain will also bring forward to the surface some of your fears or worries that you haven't quite dealt with. It does have a way to remind you that there are psychological issues you still need to work through. During this whole process, your brain can still receive information. This is why it is good for us to have silence while we sleep, so our brains can properly refresh themselves.

Many of us have fallen asleep with the TV on and have found ourselves dreaming about something we were watching before we fell asleep. The reason for this is because while our brain is trying to refresh, it still has to process the information coming in around us and the media around us can influence our thoughts and enter our dreams. This is the reason it is better to not have any distractions while an individual sleeps.

The subject of psychology intrigued me, so I pursued a degree in psychology and received my associate's from Oklahoma City Community College. With my increased knowledge, I began to conduct further literary research into areas such as dream interpretation. Many people had asked me how they could tell a casual dream from a true spirit visitation dream. In order to do this, one has to be familiar with both the physical and spiritual aspects of dreaming in order to properly understand the difference between these two types of dreams. There are some differences in actual spirit visitation dreams and there are symptoms our physical body and mind produce for a casual dream. I'll explain the physical first, which covers sleep paralysis.

I wrote an article called, *"Sleep Paralysis (AKA: The Old Hag Syndrome) Is It Really Connected To the Paranormal Realm?"* I did a lot of research on this after I had quite a few people come to me and tell me about how they thought an "evil ghost" had held them down while they were sleeping or "on the verge of waking up." At first, I was fascinated by their stories until I did my research.

As I've previously stated, I've had several people, including one of my former group members, who shared a weird experience with me. It was similar to other accounts, which stated their experience usually occurred at night, or in the early morning hours when they were coming into full wakefulness. When talking to one of our group members about this, he described his experience as being a bit frightful. After waking up from sleep, he couldn't move stating it felt as if someone or something was holding him down. He also reported feeling an unpleasant presence standing close by him and stated he heard a "hum" or "buzz" type of sound. He said he was totally aware of what was going on around him and that he felt fine with the exception of the inability to move his body.

So what exactly is "Sleep Paralysis?" According to Moturi and Matta in their 2013 publication on Recurrent Isolated Sleep Paralysis (RISP), it is when the mind has awakened from the deepest REM (rapid eye movement) dream state of sleep only to discover that the body is still in a state of paralysis. The body has a safety mechanism that is activated when we are dreaming. The body will shut down larger muscle groups to protect us from potential harm. Without this muscle atonia, we would be physically acting out our dreams and potentially hurting ourselves. In this state, we are not able to move our head, neck and limbs, but we may still be able to open our eyes and breathe. Studies have also shown that when the brain is in the sleep paralysis state, it can also cause the person to have auditory and visual hallucinations that can cause the person to see and hear things that are not actually there.

So what does Sleep Paralysis have to do with the "Old Hag Syndrome?" The name of the phenomenon comes from the superstitious belief that a witch or an old hag sits or rides the chest of the victims, rendering them immobile. Although that explanation isn't taken very seriously in current days, the perplexing and often very frightening nature of the phenomenon leads many people to believe that there are supernatural forces at work, especially evil ghosts or demons.

This condition has been around and reported for hundreds of years by men and women. A systematic review of thirty-five studies by two Penn State Psychology professors reveal sleep paralysis is relatively common in the general population with 7.6% having experienced at least one episode in their lifetime. They reveal that 28.3% of students have experienced this parasomnic episode while a staggering 34.6% of psychiatric patients with a diagnosed panic disorder have experienced at least one episode of sleep paralysis in their lifetime. This indicates that sleep deprivation, stress, anxiety and panic disorders are some factors that contribute to the episodes. Minorities over Caucasians are potentially at a higher risk for experiencing a sleep paralysis episode and another study showed a familial connection to this experience passed down genetically among family members without having any psychiatric disorder connected to the experience.

There is essentially dissociation between alertness of wakefulness and the muscle paralysis of deep REM sleep. A case report also suggests a disconnect between the state of mind as well as the physical paralysis involved with sleep paralysis that can explain the auditory and visual hallucinations that can occur with such an experience.

So is "Sleep Paralysis" really connected to the spirit realm? Well, that would depend on whose opinion you decide to believe. Medical professionals are certain sleep paralysis is not paranormally related. On the other hand, experts who study metaphysics state their case studies have shown a high percentage of those who have experienced sleep paralysis have no psychological condition that would predispose them to a sleep paralysis episode. They believe a sleep paralysis state may be connected to out-of-body experiences (OBE). A global survey on the OBE conducted by the International Academy of Consciousness (IAC), a leading research organization on out-of-body experience and paranormal phenomena, revealed that 52.57% percent of individuals who have had an OBE claim to have experienced sleep paralysis in association with this phenomenon. The individuals who reported having had OBE's also attested to having no known existing health condition that would trigger sleep paralysis.

There is a way to test and control sleep paralysis and the range of psychic phenomena that is said to be associated with the dreaming and out-of-body experiences. Subjects are advised to use techniques for relaxation and concentration on controlling body movement, such as breathing more deeply or concentration on moving a finger or the tongue. The ability to be able to master one's own subtle energies is know as bio-energy, chi or prana by those who study metaphysics and this strange phenomenon.

For most of us who have studied Psychology in depth, we know there are several stages involved in sleep ranging from the highest brain wave activity to the lowest. These are the stages I mentioned earlier, known as Beta, Alpha, Theta & Delta. In the Beta stage, the brainwave frequency ranges between 15-40 cycles per second, which indicates a strong, active and engaged mind. An example of this would be someone who is lying in bed and thinking about all of the day's events or perhaps what it is that they have to do the next day or maybe lying in bed engaged in conversation with their spouse.

In the Alpha stage, brain waves are slower with the cycles being 9-14 per second, which indicate a person's state as being more relaxed, and calm. A good example of this could also be someone who is in a meditative state.

In the Theta state, the brainwaves are even slower with the cycles being 5-8 seconds a cycle. This stage is also one where a lot of creative ideas are formed. A good example of this would be a person who is daydreaming.

In the last stage, the Delta stage, the brainwaves are at their slowest, ranging from 1.5-4 seconds a cycle. The cycles can't go down to zero because if they did a person would be brain dead.

Researchers and scientists have divided non-REM (rapid eye movement) sleep into different stages, which accounts for about 75% of total sleep. In each stage, brain waves become progressively larger and slower, and sleep becomes deeper. After reaching stage 4, the deepest period, the pattern reverses, and sleep becomes progressively lighter until full REM sleep, the most active period. Dreams mainly occur when a person is in this deepest sleep cycle where the body's breathing, heart rate and brainwave activity increase.

Sleep studies have shown most people dream in ninety-minute cycles and can have several different dreams in any one given sleep period, even though they may not remember all of the dreams they have had. Dreams are stored in the short-term memory area of our brain, so if a person does not recall their dream within the first five minutes of waking, it will be removed from their short-term memory causing them to forget their dreams.

The treatment for psychiatric conditions, including sleep paralysis and other parasomnias, often positively affects sleep cycles through inducing some desired change in sleep habits. For example, antidepressants like Prozac usually quicken sleep onset and lengthen REM stages. People who take antidepressants often benefit from the effects they have on the quality and length of their sleep cycles.

So what really occurs in the REM stage of sleep? Our brain releases a chemical called a neurotransmitter to communicate information from our brain to the rest of our body. This neurotransmitter gives our brain the ability to voluntarily move our muscles. When our brain goes into a REM cycle, it stops secreting this chemical to our muscles causing a temporary paralysis. This is meant to prevent our body from acting out our dreams during sleep. This stage of sleep has also been known as paradoxical sleep. The first period of REM cycle typically lasts ten minutes with each recurring REM stage lengthening to the final one lasting for about one hour.

So is the sleep paralysis state harmful? It is often associated with narcolepsy, a neurological condition in which the person has uncontrollable naps. However, there are many people who experience sleep paralysis without having a sleep disorder such as narcolepsy. Sometimes sleep paralysis can be genetic. It is not harmful to the person who experiences it, however many people report feeling terrified, as they do not necessarily understand what is happening. The fear is short lived since it's only a matter of minutes when they are able to move again. A sound, voice or a light touch on their body often terminates this paralyzed state.

According to research, there are some cases where hypnologic hallucinations are present during a sleep paralysis episode. This is when people experiencing this phenomenon feel as if someone is in the room with them. During a sleep paralysis episode, one is waking before they leave their dream state, so along with the continued paralysis from certain neurotransmitters comes the experience of seeing people and images from their dreams as if they are in the room with them. Some experience the feeling that someone or something is sitting on their chest giving them a feeling of impending death by suffocation. That is where the nickname "Hag Phenomena" originated. The depiction of the "Old Hag" was created and passed down with each generation of people who have experienced this strange and scary phenomenon, when in fact it is the sensation of the weight of your body in it's relaxed state felt by the non-voluntary muscles in your chest. Although this weird experience may cause emotional distress, anxiety and sometimes terror, ultimately there is no threat of physical harm from a sleep paralysis episode and people are able to continue breathing as they would in a normal REM sleep cycle.

So who does sleep paralysis affect? The answer is quite simple. Those who suffer from the above mentioned narcolepsy, those who aren't getting enough sleep over a lengthy period of time, those who have irregular sleep patterns/habits, and those who are diagnosed with anxiety, panic disorders, clinical depression, and bi-polar disorder. Dr. Otto, a psychology professor at Boston University, published an article in the Journal of Anxiety disorders in 2006 stating research revealed rates of sleep paralysis are elevated to 20% in those diagnosed with panic disorder and 22% for social phobia over individuals diagnosed with generalized anxiety disorder. Even those who sleep on their back, entering into puberty and those who experience consistently high levels of stress are at risk for experiencing at least one episode of sleep paralysis in their lifetime.

Over all, the process of waking might seem quite simple to some, but it is a complex process involving many physiological changes. One of these is the reversal of the paralysis. People experience sleep paralysis when the brain does not submit neurotransmitters to begin communicating motion to voluntary muscles again once they wake-up. If they are lying on their backs, the weight of their own body can feel as if someone is sitting on their chest. Eventually, the paralysis resolves in minutes or with light stimulation and normal function is restored.

Now that I've explained a bit about sleep paralysis and the different sleep stages according to medical science, let's take a look at it in a spiritual aspect. When our brains are in the most relaxed point of the delta stage of sleep, it would be understandable that this would be when we are most open to receiving our "dream visitors." No one can be certain, however this is the common theory believed by most on the spiritualistic side of the debate.

How do we tell the difference between a regular dream and a true spirit visitation? This took me a long time to figure out, as I wasn't completely sure myself, so I started documenting my own dreams in a journal and continued researching theories about dreams. I came to the conclusion that you are the only one that can truly tell the difference between your regular dreams and true spirit visitation. The reason is because only you know how the dream has truly affected you. Chances are you might have had an actual spirit visitor if your dream was about a passed friend, loved one, or someone you don't know personally.

Remember that most dreams are stored in our short-term memory and if not recalled within the first five minutes after waking, they are forgotten. Usually spirit visitors leave you remembering details all day long, even months or years later, so the dream stays with you. Spirit visitation in dreams can also be troubling or could produce information that deeply affects you for some time. The most important thing to remember is spirit visitations during sleep are very vivid and not like actual dreams that can be easily forgotten. Spirit visitations have some meaning to them, even though the meaning is not always clear to the dreamer right away.

I have also had spirits come to me and give me information that I didn't know what to do with. Spirit has asked for help when I don't know how to help them. For example, one night I went to sleep and met a young six-year-old boy, named Billy, who asked for help. He showed me his body, which had been buried in a field full of tall, dead grass. He wanted me to tell his parents where he was so they could come get him. He didn't show me any other landmarks, nor did he tell me a town, city or state where they could find him. I had no idea how to help him since I had no other information to go on. I woke up feeling very sad, because there was nothing I could do to help him. I wondered why he had not given me more details that could have helped me find him, but I came to the conclusion he might not have known where his body was buried, other than it was in an open field with tall, dead grass. Sometimes spirits will relay information to you from their viewpoint and, like in the case with Billy. He couldn't give much more information to me, because he didn't know all of the information himself. He probably didn't know who took him, how he died or exactly where his body had been laid to rest.

Another example of a dream visitor I had was one from a spirit named Alice. Her story was very vivid and had many details, yet I didn't know exactly what she wanted from me or how I could help her. She was seventeen years old in physical years, however her mind was that of about a twelve year old. She showed me where she lived, which was by the foothill of a mountain, and showed me the house where she stayed with her aunt and uncle. Her parents had died in a car accident when she was quite young and her aunt and uncle had taken her in. They also had a barn out back behind their house. This was a special place for Alice as she had her own special area picked out and fixed up amongst some of the hay bales. She showed me around the barn and the little area she had set up as her "special place." She wanted to tell me a secret, but made me promise not to tell anyone. She didn't want her aunt and uncle to find out because they would be upset with her. After promising to keep her secret, she told me she was a few weeks pregnant by her boyfriend and was worried about her aunt and uncle finding out.

The scene went from happy to tragic when she showed me what had happened to her. She showed me herself sitting in the barn reading a book with an older man who looked to be at least twenty plus years older than her. He was Caucasian with light salt and pepper hair and was clean-shaven. I asked her if this was her boyfriend. She shook her head, no, and told me to watch. I continued watching as she sat there among the hay bales in her secret hiding place, reading this book to her male visitor. Then suddenly, I saw this man on top of Alice threatening to choke her into submission. She gasped, begging him not to choke her and offered herself sexually to him by raising her dress and exposing herself in exchange for him to let go of her. Then I saw the man turn Alice over and I watched in horror as he raped her from behind. When he was finished, he began choking Alice again until her body was finally lifeless. The man took Alice's limp body and dumped it in a fast moving river close by. I watched as her body drifted downstream and away from everything in life she had ever known.

The scene changed again and I watched as a couple of men pulled Alice's soaked and bloated body out of the river. I suddenly woke up and was very disturbed by what I had seen. I couldn't understand why Alice had come to me and had shown me these things, unless she just wanted someone to know the truth about what had happened to her.

I felt a bit helpless because I didn't know what I could do for her. The dream bothered me for days afterward. I didn't know if Alice would come back to me later with more information about how I could help her, but until then I had no choice but to wait with the horrifying images remaining in my head. Time had passed and she never showed up in my dreams again. I just assumed she didn't need my help but maybe just wanted me to know her story. I figured if she wanted some help, she would ask for it the next time she came if she ever decided to visit me again.

There are also spirits that come to you with a specific purpose or message. Usually, those spirits come through so strongly they don't leave any unanswered questions or need for piecing the information together, because their message is very bold and straightforward. Sometimes these spirits can cause havoc for you by being mischievous until you either listen to them or help them in the way they want to be helped. Some spirits actually come to you with a plea of desperation and you feel so compelled to help, because you can feel their sorrowful emotions, especially when it involves a child spirit.

One night after an extensive investigation at an old abandoned school in northeastern Oklahoma, I found myself visited by a little girl from that very school. This location has a unique history, some known and some unknown. The owner of the building told us a gruesome story about its past. When this building was first constructed, its original use was for a church, but the construction was never fully completed due to lack of funds. Later in 1930, the building was sold and turned into a local school. Years later, the building was then sold to individuals who converted the old church/school into a home. The home was occupied for many years until its history turned tragic. One of its residents was mysteriously murdered.

Our investigation there proved very interesting in the way of personal experiences and recorded evidence. One experience I had there was intriguing to say the least. There was no electricity at this location whatsoever since the building had not been used in several years. While in the main room area of the building, we had some of our emf meters activate off and on. A few of us commented about how we felt watched and how the energy in the building felt very heavy. At times it almost felt as if numerous unseen spirits surrounded us. As we were leaving the main area of the building and heading down a small hallway, lights in the main room suddenly began to flicker off and on. The lights were as quick as blinking strobe lights and the light source came from the ceiling area. The lights lit up the entire room for the brief seconds they were on. It was almost as if someone was turning the lights off and on very quickly.

I was at the tail end of the group while we were walking out into the hall area. The sudden flickering lights had caught my attention so I quickly turned around to look back into the main room area. A couple of the other investigators had also seen the flickering lights and had turned around to see what was going on. As we looked in the main room, the lights began to flicker off and on again a couple more times and then they stopped. We were surrounded by darkness again. I called for the other investigators who were already in the other room at the end of the hall. They immediately came and joined me in the search for trying to recreate the flickering light phenomenon. I flipped off and on the light switch on one wall and another investigator flipped the light off and on on the other side of the room's wall. Neither of us could get the lights to come on. One of the light fixtures also did not have a bulb in it. I knew that spirits could manipulate electricity but how were they able to do it when there was no electricity present and on at a location?

Regardless of our efforts to recreate the lights coming on and off, we were not able to recreate this occurrence. After about 20-30 minutes, we decided to continue on with our investigation. I still could not shake the feeling that we were being closely watched. There was a set of stairs inside the main building area that led up to another room. I felt like I was being watched by something unseen from under the stairs. I took my camera out and began taking pictures. I did not notice this right way, but later when I was analyzing my photos, I realized I had captured a partial apparition of what appears to be a man with dark hair under the stairs. Was this possibly the man who was supposedly murdered at this location? In the photo there also appeared to be another fleshly looking image beside this man but I couldn't make out the details of this "other spirit." To those who may be doubters, there was no living person under the stairs either when I took the photo.

There appeared to be many spirits present that had taken up residency here at this location, including the murdered relative, a few adults and some children. One specific child was a dark-haired young five-year-old girl, named Betty. I had encountered her during our investigation, however she was a bit shy and did not come through to me very strongly during the investigation. I assumed it was because of a fear she might have had with us being there.

The investigation concluded and all members went home. I fell asleep that night in my bed and began dreaming. In my dream, I found myself in a large empty room that had one door. I was sitting in a chair in the far corner of the room when all of a sudden this door came flying open and there was this young dark haired girl that came running towards me then suddenly jumped in my lap. She began begging me to help her and stated, "Don't let him get me please!" I recognized the little girl as the one from the school investigation earlier that night. Realizing the fear from this little girl, I told her I would protect her and that I wouldn't let him get her. I didn't know exactly who was after her, but I knew that she was really frightened and I needed to help.

Without warning, there was a large gust of wind that carried in a very large tumbleweed, which floated in mid-air right in front of me. In the center of the tumbleweed was a hideous looking man's face. This man appeared very angry and when he opened his mouth to speak, he had large teeth and looked like the mouth of a lion. He demanded that I give him the girl. I told him no, he wasn't going to get her and he needed to leave. He became angrier and kept insisting that I turn the girl over to him. I kept refusing, holding my ground until he finally he became so angry, that he left the room in a large gust of wind. When he left, the whole room seemed to shake and both Betty and I felt a cold rush of wind go right through us. I sensed this man had been a child molester in his physical life and he still chose to terrorize children like Betty, even now in death. I told Betty she would now be safe and encouraged her to cross over to the other side where the bad man could never find or hurt her anymore. Betty must have felt truth in my words because she nodded her head and in an instant, Betty was gone.

I suddenly woke from my dream to find my bed's headboard violently shaking above me. My headboard was quite tall and wobbled so a couple of days prior to my dream, I had nailed it to the wall. I didn't want it to fall forward on me in my sleep one night. I'm glad I had nailed it down and made it sturdy or else it would have fallen on top of me as I awoke from this dream. There was no doubt in my mind this angry male ghost from my dream had caused my headboard to violently shake. I knew this was his way of acting out to let me know he was angry with me.

Strangely enough, a few days later, Betty came back and visited me in my dreams again. She thanked me for helping her and told me she was finally able to find some peace from the bad man who had been chasing her for quite some time now. I was just happy she had chosen to come to me for help and I was very glad that I was able to help her. I finally understood why Betty had been so shy about coming forward that night during our investigation there. It wasn't because she was afraid of us, but rather the angry ghost who was chasing her.

Another strange spirit visitation I encountered was one that occurred in 2006. My group and I had done an investigation in a rural location in Northern Oklahoma. By this time in my paranormal career, I had learned how to do soul rescue and was helping as many souls as I could to cross over. After our investigation at this location, I agreed to help do a soul rescue of some innocent ghosts that were stuck at this particular location. The rescue was a success and the controlling ghost, who had been keeping the other ghosts prisoner, was whisked away by an angel that I often have around me. I have seen my angel three times, but have been told by other various investigators that they have also seen my angel around me on a few different occasions too. I never found out where my angel took this possessive spirit, but I figured if they wanted me to know they would have told me. All I saw was a large bright white pillar of light that flew upwards and out of sight. It was at that point that I knew this controlling spirit was gone and would no longer bother any other spirits.

It wasn't until a few nights later, when I had gone to sleep; I had an unusual spirit visitation from about forty different spirits. I dreamed I was in an old 1800's single-room, wooden church. I was standing up at the pulpit and found myself looking out at a congregation of about forty people. These people were dressed in 1800's period clothing and were all looking up at me. The vision was in color, however when I looked at the people in the congregation, they were all in sepia color. The peoples' faces were void of expression, but all of their eyes were big, black and looked empty. There was one man that stood out to me more than the others. He was sitting closer to the front and I had chills run up and down my arms from his deep, blank stare. I suddenly remember feeling very uncomfortable and I remember wanting to run as far away from there as I possible could. Then suddenly, I woke up.

The dream visitation was so vivid and troublesome to me, because I couldn't figure out how to interpret it. A week had passed and I still didn't know the meaning of the dream. I found myself becoming very ill. Three weeks had passed when I had enough of being sick and putting-up with the haunting activity that had been taking place in my home. I had all sorts of things happening. Things were disappearing and moving on their own. My daughter and I were hearing strange voices and music that seemed to stop when we went looking for its source. We would see shadows and felt like we were being watched on a constant basis. I just had a feeling our haunting was caused by the church people from my dream.

The more time that passed, the sicker I got. Out of desperation, I contacted a friend of mine from the East coast for help. I needed to know what the dream meant and what these people wanted from me. My friend was pretty good at dream interpretation, so I figured she would be able to help me.

She told me she thought the dream was a plea for help by this large group of church people. She said that word had probably gotten out to the other side about the soul rescue I was doing. These spirits likely needed help, so they sought me out since I lived in an area close to where they had once lived. She said they looked up to me as someone who could help save them and used the analogy of a preacher standing at the pulpit in front of a congregation. The preacher delivers sermons of saving grace and help to his congregation and in turn the congregation looks up to the preacher for words of help, encouragement and a way to find eternal salvation through Jesus Christ.

I asked my friend about the sepia color and the dark blank eyes of the congregation of people. She told me the sepia color represented the stuck stale state the people were in and their dark blank eyes represented the empty, void and hopeless feelings they were experiencing. It all suddenly made sense to me and I could see why the group of people were getting frustrated with me for not being able to help them. My East coast friend also did spiritual work, so she was familiar with spirits and told me that she was assuming this group of people initially brought on my sickness. The longer they stayed around me, the sicker I became, because my immune system was in a weaker state and more vulnerable to illness.

I asked my friend how to soul rescue a large group of people, since I had never crossed over such a large number of souls all at once. Later on and with her help, we were able to finally get the church people to crossover. Afterward, my haunting finally stopped and I was able to find some peace in my home once again. However, I was still very sick and it only grew worse.

I started running a fever of 105 degrees Fahrenheit and had ended up contracting pneumonia. I was so sick one night; I couldn't even drive myself to the emergency room to be examined. My family lived about an hour a way, so I didn't want to ask them to take me. I promised myself I would muster the strength to take myself to go to a doctor in the morning, after I had gotten some sleep and if I couldn't break my fever. I put myself to bed with a washcloth on my forehead, hoping it would help reduce my fever along with the Tylenol I had recently taken. I fell asleep and had another spirit visitation, but this one was a little different because it wasn't the usual troubled spirit that had visited me. This time it was my angel.

I don't know how long I had been asleep, but at some point in the night, a beautiful white bright glowing angel awakened me. I had previously heard angels are supposed to be unisex, but this one had long white flowing hair and looked to be female. She took me by my hand and helped to raise me out of bed. Once I was standing up, I turned, looked at my bed and saw myself lying there asleep with the washcloth still on my forehead.

Next, the angel led me through my bedroom wall. As we passed through, I saw flashing of colored light resembling sparklers. The colors were a vibrant red, blue, yellow and green. The next thing I knew, we came into a place that was beautiful. I didn't recognize where we were, but the place was very peaceful and very bright white as far as the eye could see. In one area, I saw an even brighter white, arched, and open doorway. There was a shorthaired angel standing there on the inside of the doorway guarding the entrance. My angel told me to stay where I was and she walked over to speak with this other angel. The shorthaired angel looked over at me, then back at my angel and they began talking.

While I waited, I leaned over to my right some so I could see inside the arched doorway. I saw pure white souls in the form of people all looking at me. They were smiling and waving at me and motioning for me to come in the area with them. There was one man in particular who was wearing a hat and was standing out in front of all the other people. Even though I didn't recognize any of these people, they all still felt familiar to me. I remember feeling I wanted to go in there and be with them. It was almost as if I felt I belonged in there with them. At this point, nothing in my physical life mattered, because all I could think about was going into this beautiful area. It was if a strong magnet was pulling my soul there.

My angel came back over to me and told me we had to go back. I told her I didn't want to leave. I wanted to go through the doorway and be with the other people. She shook her head, no, took me by the hand and told me I had to go back because it wasn't my time. She also told me I still had a lot of work to do and a lot of people to help. Then before I knew it, I was back in my room standing in front of my body again. I still appeared to be sleeping peacefully with the washcloth on top of my head. I don't know how I got back in my body, because one minute I was outside of myself and the next minute I found myself awake and sitting straight up in bed. I still felt sick but my fever had finally broken. I was puzzled by the experience and it took me a while before I was finally able to fall back to sleep.

I awoke the next morning with another high fever, so I went into the emergency room to receive medical attention. I know the angel and what I had experienced wasn't a hallucination. I had heard about "of out of body experiences" and "near death experiences" and was fully convinced what I went through was a near death experience related to my pneumonia. I also believed this because of the angel that took me to the other side. I felt so peaceful and saw so many other transcended souls. Since I had this experience, I had no doubt in my mind when it is my time to go, later on in my lifetime, I will cross over and not stay earthbound. I didn't want to leave when I was on the other side with the angel, so I know I will cross over later when I leave my physical body in death.

Some time had passed since I had the near death experience and I began noticing my gifts and abilities had gotten stronger. I figured it was because I had been given the rare opportunity to touch the other side and come back to tell about it. It was an experience I will never forget. I remember my grandfather telling me as a child about his experience with dying. He had a heart attack while on the operating table. He saw himself floating above his body as the doctors and nurses were trying to bring him back to life. He then found himself in a beautiful and very peaceful place. He said he heard beautiful music and saw beautiful rolling hills and flowers. My experience wasn't exactly like his, but I am pretty sure we experienced similar things. Many people have talked about seeing a tunnel of light when they died while others have reported seeing angels and being in a beautiful and peaceful place. Whatever the case may be, I believe those who have died and come back have specific purposes to be here and alive in the physical body. We all will know the truth about the other side one day when it's our turn to experience Heaven.

Many people have unique experiences from spirits and angels who visit them in their dreams. Not everyone understands why he or she may have been chosen to receive a specific spirit message or what that message might be, but in time the truth will be revealed. Some spirit visitations in dreams are given to us as a way to help warn of impending danger or as a plea for help from that particular spirit. Other times, they are given to us as a gift of spiritual insight into the other side. Once an individual is able to recognize spirit visitations, they are better able to understand how the process works. There are some of us who have spiritual gifts and some who don't, but not everyone has to have abilities and gifts in order to receive a spirit visitation in their dreams. I have had countless people tell me throughout the years about their own ghostly visitors at night in their dreams. Spirits have a unique way of communicating with all of us, including when we sleep and dream. They know who will be more receptive to them and who won't, so they choose whom to come to. All we have to do is be able to recognize the times they visit us and pay attention to the messages they have to offer us.

CHAPTER 8

"Can Our Minds Really Create a Ghost?"

Throughout the years I have heard many paranormal investigators debate whether our human minds can actually create a ghost if we believe strongly enough. Some new and old homes, even buildings new and old, claim to have resident ghosts whom never leave. More and more people are accepting the existence of ghosts and the paranormal; especially with the ghost hunting shows that air all over T.V. these days. Due to this acceptance, some locations that have resident ghosts are becoming more and more of a tourist attraction for those seeking the evidence of ghosts or those who wish to have their own ghostly encounters. Paranormal enthusiasts flock to these haunted places in hopes of capturing any recorded evidence of a spirit. Some of these well-known locations have infamous ghosts who have specific names and, throughout the years, have become part of the location's legendary ghost tales. These ghost stories most often originate from a true historical tragedy or death connected to the location. Some result from urban legend or local folklore told about a specific place. Like any good ghost story, it is passed down through the years and retold over and over again. It is here that specific details or parts of a story can be misconstrued and exchanged with fictitious details.

I cannot ridicule paranormal enthusiasts or investigators who visit these places to satisfy personal curiosities, as I too have visited a few of them in my past. Many people who visit these haunted locations initially believe they have better chances of seeing one of these legendary ghosts, since so many others report frequent sightings or encounters. The cold hard truth, however, is most do not end up seeing these ghosts, nor are they able to experience anything paranormal. This can be a huge disappointment for most, but for those few who are lucky enough to experience something paranormal, they tell of their encounters and the ghostly legends of the location continue.

In my experience, I have noticed some of the more haunted and well-known places have less paranormal activity than those places that are undiscovered or unknown. My paranormal investigation group, called Oklahoma Paranormal Research and Investigations (OKPRI), and I have spent a lot of time and have done a lot of footwork to find undiscovered and discovered locations to investigate. There are other teams who do not appear to spend hours and hours of investigating or conducting historical research to discover a truly haunted location. It seems they wait for another team to do the hard work of investigating only to attempt to later wedge their way into the location to experience those findings for themselves. This has caused some animosity and hostility between certain teams resulting in an inability to collaborate on discoveries for the good of the field. While some teams become territorial over certain locations, it may be for good reason since some of these locations end up being a gold mine for paranormal activity and require a certain level of protection from exploitation.

When an investigative research team has thoroughly investigated a location and has published their work/findings on the web, paranormal enthusiasts then flock to these locations requesting permission for access. Some of these investigators or enthusiasts then conduct their own paranormal investigation and often do not have personal experiences or are able to obtain the same type or amount of recorded evidence as an experienced team had. They ultimately conclude and publically report the location as "not haunted" after only one visit. Those that do capture what they believe to be evidence of a haunting, however, are the ones that help keep the haunted legend stories alive.

Although this method has caused some rivalry among different teams, there is a positive side to this because legit paranormal teams can verify true paranormal activity in conjunction with other teams. It is true that paranormal activity doesn't always happen when people expect it and if a place is haunted, evidence of the haunting may not be seen each time. There have been many locations my team has investigated where nothing out of the ordinary has happened on our initial visit, but turned out to be quite active a second or third visit. Often times, the opposite has occurred. This is why investigating a location multiple times results in a more conclusive report of the evidence and factual conclusions can be made.

All of this desire of the public to seek out their own experiences had lead me to wonder if someone believed strongly enough in ghosts, could they actually create one with their mind and cause the ghost to physically manifest? Many experienced paranormal investigators have asked this same question and have wondered if certain locations have ghosts because so many people have believed in them over the years. This theory could explain the phenomenon of legendary ghosts in locations that may or may not have ties to the location itself. If this theory is true about our minds having the capability to create a ghost, how easily can it be done? One of the bonuses for investigating unknown locations is that there are no well-known ghosts to influence an investigator's mind. This leaves the mind free and clear and doesn't allow an investigator to create a specific ghost or look for a specific or stereotypical ghost.

We do know there are places that can be haunted by legendary ghosts. Some of these locations have unique stories, but are these infamous ghosts real or were they created out of the mind of those who deeply wanted them to be there?

One such infamous haunted location is Myrtles Plantation, located in Saint Francisville, Louisiana, near Baton Rouge. This old plantation was originally named Laurel Grove and has many ghost stories attached to it. One legend states the plantation was built on top of an old Tunica Indian burial ground, so restless Native American spirits are said to haunt the grounds. The most infamous ghost at the Myrtles Plantaion is of Chloe, an African slave who supposedly lived and died there back in the 1800's. Guests have reported seeing Chloe in a green turban, along with 2 young girls and all dressed in white 1800's period clothing.

Myrtles Plantation

General David Bradford built the plantation in 1794 and lived there with his wife Elizabeth and their five children until his death in 1808. Clark Woodrooff married Bradford's daughter, Sara, on November 19, 1817 and lived there with their 3 children, Cornelia Gale, James, and Maggie Octavia. The legend says the Woodrooff family had many slaves. One in particular was a house slave, named Chloe.

There are different versions of this ghost story. One is that Woodrooff was having an affair with Chloe. When he no longer chose to carry on with the affair, he threatened to put Chloe out into the fields to work. No slave wanted to work out in the fields, because it was supposed to be one of the worst types of labor a slave could have endured. Fearing such a fate, Chloe began eavesdropping in on family conversations and business. After Woodrooff caught her listening to a private conversation, he ordered for her left ear to be cut off in order to teach her a lesson. The legend states from that day forward, Chloe always wore a green turban around her head to hide the scars where her ear once was.

The other version of this story is that no affair occurred between Woodrooff and Chloe, but simply states that Chloe was nosey and always tried to listen in on family conversations and business. The legend continues from there with the same story about being caught eavesdropping and her ear was cut off as punishment. Woodrooff was so upset at Chloe for what she had done, he threatened to put her out in the field to work but placed her in the kitchen instead. The kitchen was not an area Chloe wanted to work in either. After this point the legendary ghost story stays pretty consistent.

Chloe wanted to remain a house slave so she devised a plan that would help her regain her original position back. It was supposedly the eldest daughter's birthday, so Chloe made a cake for the celebration. Some say Chloe's plan was to poison the cake with crushed oleander leaves so she could help nurse the family back to health to show her worth. Oleander leaves are said to carry the same properties as strychnine if ingested in larger amounts. Other's say that Chloe's motive was to murder the Woodrooff family to gain revenge and her freedom.

As the story continues, Chloe served the cake to the family who sat down to celebrate the daughter's birthday. Mr. Woodrooff had previously not been feeling well and therefore did not eat any of the cake along with the youngest child, who was already in bed for the evening. Unfortunately, it was Sara and two of her children who ate the poisoned cake and had become deathly sick before the end of the evening. All three died a short time afterwards, despite Chloe's efforts to render aid and attention to their needs.

The legend has two different but similar endings. One version is after the death of Sara and the two children, the other plantation slaves feared that they would be punished for Chloe's actions if Woodrooff found out what she had done. To protect themselves, they dragged Chloe out of her room one night and hung her in a nearby tree. After she was dead, the slaves cut her down, weighted her body down with rope and rocks and threw her body into the Mississippi river.

The other version of this ending is that Woodrooff accused Chloe of poisoning the cake and killing his wife and two of his children. In a rage, he had Chloe hung in a tree in the front yard. After her death, he had her cut down and had her body weighted down with rope and rocks and thrown into the Mississippi river.

Another part of the legend said Woodrooff was not the type to have an affair and was very devoted to his wife, Sara. This is believed since he never remarried after her death.

Historical records reveal Sara wasn't poisoned, but rather died of yellow fever on July 21, 1823. Their only son, James, also died of yellow fever nearly a year later on July 15, 1824. Tragedy would strike the family again, because two month's after James' death, their daughter Cornelia Gail fell victim to the same epidemic. Historical records show the last child, Maggie Octavia, lived well into adulthood.

In 1831, Woodruff and Sarah moved to Covington, Louisiana, leaving a caretaker to look after the plantation. By 1834, Woodrooff had sold the plantation to Ruffin Gray Stirling. Clark Woodrooff died in New Orleans in 1851. Stirling and his wife began remodeling the plantation and made it twice as large as it once was. They also changed its name from Lauren Grove to Myrtles Plantation. The Stirling's had nine children, but five of them died before they were of marrying age. Mr. Stirling died in 1854 of consumption, leaving the plantation to his wife.

So is the legend of Chloe really true? There has been research done on Myrtles Plantation and no records of Chloe have ever been found, but this is because in the 1800's, slaves were not listed as individuals with names on census records. They were documented much like cattle, receiving only a headcount for them. There were no identities such as names assigned to them. There are records of the Woodrooff's having slaves despite what some people have thought when researching the history of Myrtles Plantation. In fact, the 1920 Federal Census showed Woodrooff owned 5 slaves that year. By 1830 (6 and 7 years after Sarah, James and Cornelia had died of yellow fever) Woodrooff had increased his ownership to 32 slaves.

Since the Woodrooff family had slaves, there is a possibility that Chloe could have existed. One of the things to think about however, is that if Chloe did exist and if she did the things she was alleged to do while she worked for the Woodrooff family, why was the legend or story of Chloe started in the 1950's instead of being told and passed on through the generations after her death in the 1800's? Most incidents that greatly impact a family leave families telling stories year after year. This doesn't appear to be the case since the legend of Chloe was started in the 1950's with reports of sightings of a woman seen in a green turban type hat. Another thing to consider in this ghostly legend is if Chloe had poisoned two of the Woodrooff children, Cornelia Gale and James, and Clark's wife, Sara, then why are their historical records showing they died of yellow fever?

Legend states that in 1834, Clark Woodrooff sold the plantation, land and slaves. After checking the 1840 Federal census for the new owner, Ruffin Gray Stirling, it shows that Stirling owned 141 slaves on the plantation. By 1860, 29% of Louisiana families owned slaves and 49% of the population were slaves. That's almost one in three families. One would think that if the legend of Chloe were really true, then Woodrooff himself would have passed on the tragic stories of his family to Stirling when he sold the plantation and land to him. There have also been rumors that Myrtles Plantation had ten murders on its property, however historical documents show that only one murder took place there and an additional eleven deaths were illness-related.

A man named William Winters was hired in 1865 by Ms. Stirling (also known as Maggie Cobb) to be her attorney and agent. Winters fell in love with Maggie's daughter, Sarah Stirling. They eventually married and had a total of six children, all who lived to adulthood except for one daughter, named Kate, who died of typhoid fever at the age of three.

On January 26, 1871, William Winters was said to be teaching a Sunday school lesson in the house when he heard someone approaching on horseback. The stranger on the horse called out to him saying he had some business with him. Winter went out onto the side gallery of the house where he was shot and immediately collapsed dead on the porch. Those in the house heard the gun shot and hurried outside only to hear a retreating horse and found William Winter dead. Legend says William Winter climbed up to the 17th stair where he died in the arms of his wife on the staircase. This is not true since it is documented that he died on the front porch of the house.

Winter was buried the next day at Grace Church Cemetery. The newspaper reported a man, named E.S. Webber, would stand trial for the murder of Winter, but there are no records of a murder trial ever taking place. It appears that Winter's killer still remains unidentified and unpunished even to this day.

So how did the legendary story of Chloe get started? It was in the 1950's when Chloe's story began being told. The acreage of Myrtles Plantation was split and divided by the Williams' heirs and the plantation itself was sold to a woman named Marjorie Munson. At some point, Marjorie had started to notice strange paranormal-type phenomenon taking place within the home. She then began asking around to find out if the old plantation was possibly haunted. She also spoke with one of the Williams' granddaughters who recalled stories told by her aunts about seeing an older woman in a green hat. Marjorie was credited with starting the story that a lady in a green "beret" haunted Myrtles plantation.

The plantation changed ownership a few times over the next two decades. Arlin Dease and Mr. and Mrs. Robert F. Ward owned it in the 1970's. By this time, the legend of Chloe had been well established to include details of the affair Woodroof had with Chloe, the story about her ear being cut off and her plot for revenge by poisoning the birthday cake. The latest story added to the legend was about Chloe's death by hanging from a tree on the Myrtles property. It is speculated that with each new owner, the stories and ghostly accounts were greatly embellished, making the legend what it is today. Media eventually became involved in the stories of the Myrtles Plantation and other details such as multiple murders were also added to the ghost stories.

The current owners of the plantation John & Teeta Moss purchased the home sometime in 1995. Before purchasing the home, Teeta was out surveying the property and took photos of the house, outside buildings and grounds. One of the photos she took of the side of the house showed an image of what appears to be a woman leaning up against the side of the house. This ghostly woman was dressed in what appeared to be old slave attire with a turban type hat on her head. The photo was taken in black and white so just looking at the photo colors cannot properly be identified. When the photo is blown up and examined, a woman's image can however be seen and uniquely enough, the wood siding of the home can be seen through her body. Is this photo proof that Chloe is real or could a ghost's energy have been created out of the many imaginative minds that believe in in the legend of Chloe? Albert Einstein theorized that energy cannot be created nor destroyed, only transferred elsewhere. So can our minds really create a ghost like Chloe?

Teeta Moss had given a statement that she and her family had also had ghostly encounters while living at the old plantation. One particular night, her two-year-old son was in bed and awaked to find a little ghost girl sitting on the chandelier hanging from the ceiling. He described her as having blonde hair and wearing a white dress. A child at the age of two can describe images that they have seen with their eyes, but they have not developed the skills to describe things in detail such as they can with things that come strictly from their imagination.

Visitors who have been to Myrtles Plantation have also reported seeing a woman and two young children. Some have reported seeing a young black woman who wears a turban. She has been seen holding a candle while leaning over the bed of guests. What if Chloe existed, but her story was just exaggerated? Maybe she was hanged on the property for other reasons besides the poisoning, so her restless spirit remains earthbound and wanders around the plantation as a result. Maybe Chloe isn't really the ghost of the former slave, but rather a transient spirit who has taken on the personality and traits of Chloe so they could be recognized and acknowledged. It may be possible that some of the ghosts from the Plantation's past have come back to haunt it, but how can Chloe be there if she never existed... or did she?

The Stone Lion Inn

Another infamous location, one found right here in Oklahoma, is one that my paranormal research group and I are very familiar with. It is called The Stone Lion Inn and its located in Guthrie, Oklahoma. Our group has done extensive investigations and historical research on this location. While researching its history, we found out many interesting things. Let me first give credit and thanks to our group's current researcher and historian, Kathryn Wickham, for all the help she has given me in this section about the Stone Lion Inn. She was a great help to the OKPRI team and I with discovering further historical details about this location.

Without her accurate and thorough research, we wouldn't have been able to discover everything we have revealed about this historic location.

The town of Guthrie was established in the 1800's and, for a short while, it was also the capital of Oklahoma. Like most emerging towns, Guthrie started growing with the expansion of railroads in the 1800's which added to the increased population of this frontier town. Frederick Ernest Houghton was a prominent figure in Guthrie and was the founder of Cotton Oil Company, which allowed the Houghton family to be very wealthy during his time.

Fred Houghton was born in Lancaster, PA on March 18, 1854. He married Carrie M. McKisson on Nov. 15, 1874 in LaSalle County, Illinois. Their first daughter, Maude Lee Maggie Houghton, was born in April 1877. They eventually moved to Kansas where Grace Helena was born in July 1885. It is believed he and his wife divorced before 1890, a rare event of that time.

Fred participated in the Oklahoma land run of 1889 with his two daughters. He is next found in West Guthrie on the 1890 Territorial Census of Oklahoma along with both Maude and Grace. The next records reveal Fred married a second wife, Bertha Beatrice Killough, on Aug 29, 1890, in Guthrie, OK. She was about twenty years younger than he was. Fred and Bertha began having children and historical records reveal they had seven children from 1892 until 1906. Coralee Augusta (b. Sept 1892), Gladys Margurite (b. June 1894), William Jennings (b. Aug. 17, 1896), Alma Gertrude (b. Sep 1897), Frank Ernest (b. July 4, 1899), Adolph Theodore (b. 1902), and Dorothea Vernon (b. Sep 1906).

It is important to note William Jennings is not listed in any of the family censuses. He is only mentioned in a newspaper birth announcement. There is also a newspaper article that sends condolences to Fred and Bertha for the death of a son, but no name of the child is given and the date does not match with other records. One can only assume that Fred and Bertha lost William at a very young infant age.

The family started out in a little house that once sat on the vacant lot next door to the east of today's inn. This little house is no longer there, except for the outline and steps of the foundation. The Houghton's lived there until they had their seventh child. That's when they decided they needed more living space.

In 1906 they began construction on their new home eventually completing it in 1907 at a cost of $11,900. That was a great deal of money since the average home at that time was built for a cost between $800 and $1200. In 1907, the Houghton's new home was the most expensive house in Guthrie totaling around 8,000 square feet. The home is three stories plus a basement making it 4,748 square feet in living space.

A few years after moving into the new house, the 1910 census revealed the Houghton's had three more children. These children are Russell Beverly (b. Apr 1908), Marjorie Louise (b. Apr 15, 1910) and Gordon Summer (b. Oct. 1911). All of the 12 Houghton children survived childhood except for one son, William.

William was born on August 17, 1896 according to a newspaper birth announcement. Further research reveals a newspaper article from the fraternal benefit society, Woodmen of the World, in which F. E. Houghton was a member expressing the group's sympathies to the Houghton's for the loss of their infant son who died Nov. 15, 1896. It is suspected this loss was the child that Mrs. Houghton claims in her census data in 1900 and 1910. The child would have been nearly three months old at his passing, however records for a Frank Houghton (not to be confused with Frank Ernest Houghton (1899-1971) are on file at Guthrie's Summit View Cemetery with a birth year of 1895 and a death year of 1896. The data for the birth year at the cemetery conflicts with the birth announcement in the newspaper. Also, the name Frank with the death year 1896 in cemetery records matches the year of death with the newspaper article, but there is no name mentioned in the article. This would indicate that perhaps Frank's baptismal name was William Jennings. Death records are also not available for the year 1896 in Logan County. It is not known by the city where these records have gone. It was also not required to keep birth and death records in Oklahoma Territory until statehood in 1907. Even then, vital records have remained missing until about the years 1910-1912. The cause of death for this Houghton son in 1896 remains a mystery.

The Houghton family moved to Enid in 1929 and rented the Stone Lion Inn to Ray and Rachel Smith, who co-founded the Smith-Gooch Funeral Home. Gooch only stayed with the funeral home business for four months. In 1936, the Smith's moved their funeral home to 220 N. 1st Street in Guthrie where the business is still conducted today under the name Smith and Gallo.

The Stone Lion Inn remained vacant for a while before it was deeded to Fred and Bertha Houghton's daughter, Dorothea. It remained unoccupied for an unknown amount of time between the years 1936 and 1940 when the next census was written. The house had been heavily remodeled and turned into apartments during this time. Each resident at 1016 W. Warner Av. in 1940 was listed as head of household indicating separate living units existed within the home.

In early February of 1943, not long after returning to his home in Guthrie, Fred Houghton has suffered a stroke. He was sent to Cimarron Valley Wesley Hospital for treatment. He returned to his home on February 14 at his own request and passed away at 4:00 am on February 22, 1943 from acute pulmonary congestion (F. E. Houghton certificate of death & The Guthrie Daily Leader Feb. 22, 1943, pg. 1).

Sadly enough, Fred and Bertha's daughter, Dorothea, also passed away on Monday Dec. 17, 1945, returning ownership of the home to her mother, Bertha, by inheritance (Homes of Historic Guthrie, 1987). Her obituary is printed in The Guthrie Daily Leader on Dec. 19, 1945.

Alma Suddeth had lived in the home at one point while her mother, Bertha, had ownership. Bertha Beatrice Killough Houghton passed away in her home on Sunday May 1, 1958. Upon her death, the home was willed to her daughter, Marjorie L. Bates. Marjorie then sold the home to Mr. and Mrs. Joseph T. Walker in May of 1961 (Homes of Historic Guthrie, 1987). The Walkers had the home restored to its original condition while they operated an antique shop from the basement. Rebecca Luker, the current owner of the Stone Lion Inn, bought the home in October of 1986 and developed the bed and breakfast that it is known to be today.

The Stone Lion Inn has a very long history and a lot of interesting ghost stories attached to it as well. I have extensively investigated this location numerous times and became good friends with its owner, Rebecca "Becky" Luker. I have interviewed her about the Stone Lion Inn's past on several occasions. She reveals that when she first purchased the Stone Lion Inn, she and her two sons lived in the home for a while during the remodeling process and even some years after the remodeling was completed. She spoke about some of the interesting things she found inside the inn including an old embalming table left from the old funeral home. She told me she and her boys used to sleep up on the third (top) floor and one day her son opened up his closet door and saw a young ghost girl sitting in there playing with his toys. Becky said she had never discussed the topic of ghosts with her children, so when her son mentioned seeing the ghost girl in his closet she was shocked.

Becky and her children witnessed several strange things while living at the Stone Lion Inn. They heard footsteps, witnessed things move, heard voices and saw apparitions. Becky said they lived there for a long time, but when she started spending more and more time there by herself, she felt she needed to move. She stated she didn't feel comfortable in the house alone anymore, so she purchased another residence and moved. From that point forward, the Stone Lion Inn became strictly a bed and breakfast with murder mystery dinners conducted every Friday and Saturday evenings.

In my exclusive interviews with Becky, she revealed that not too long after she had purchased the Stone Lion Inn, she had spoken to an elderly lady who worked at the Guthrie Historical Society. Becky was trying to learn more about the history of Guthrie and also about the strange occurrences she and her boys had been experiencing while living there at the Stone Lion Inn. The elderly woman told her that she personally knew the Houghton family and that they had lost a little girl whom she thought was named Augusta. Supposedly, Augusta was around 7-8 years old when she contracted whooping cough and was accidentally overmedicated with cough syrup by the maid and died. Cough syrup in the early 1900's contained opium, a narcotic drug that has morphine and codeine, and it was also used for pain relief. Opium is fatal if taken in high doses, especially for a child, but not many people were aware of the dangers of overdosing at that time.

Not long after Becky had purchased the Stone Lion Inn, she was contacted by some of the remaining Houghton children who asked to hold a family reunion in their childhood home. When they gathered for their event, many childhood memories and stories were shared with Becky. Out of curiosity, Becky asked if they had a sister who died around the age of seven or eight from an overdose of cough syrup to treat whooping cough. The siblings at this time were quite elderly, but thought they remembered having a sister who passed around the age of seven from an illness, but confessed they were all quite young when it had occurred.

The Houghton siblings recalled fond memories and shared one story with Becky of a time from their childhood. They stated their parents were usually in bed on the second floor by 10:00 pm. Once their parents were fast asleep, they made a habit of sneaking up to the third floor, pulling their toys out of their closet and playing for a while before going back downstairs to go to bed. Strangely enough, their toy closest was the same large walk-in closet where Becky's son had seen a ghost playing in it when they lived there.

When the Stone Lion Inn was turned into a bed and breakfast, Becky stated that many of her guests reported seeing, hearing and experiencing the same things she and her sons did when they lived there. There have been guests who have reported seeing a young woman, an older gray-headed woman, and a man in a gray suit with a hat and a young girl during their stay. Some of these guests have been so frightened that they have refused to spend the night and some have even left in the middle of the night. Guests have most commonly reported seeing and hearing a little girl playing on the second and third floors bouncing a ball or playing with a doll. This little girl has also been known to pull blankets up to cover guests who stay overnight in the Cordial Suite.

So who is this little girl? Is she the little Houghton girl who truly was overmedicated and died or was this story false and she just became the figment of people's imaginations after hearing the legend about a little girl who died at the Stone Lion Inn? Becky also has a few employees who assist with the bed and breakfast and murder mystery business. They too have reported experiencing strange activity while working at the Stone Lion Inn. The staff have reported seeing some of the same ghosts: the ghost of a man in a gray suit and derby top type hat and a younger woman with long dark hair up in the wedding suite. Other sightings have included an older gray-headed woman and a young girl.

One of her assistants does not like to stay overnight in the Stone Lion Inn because of a personal encounter she had with an older gentleman apparition she saw on the first floor. She previously had worked late after a murder mystery and decided to stay over night in one of the rooms on the first floor. It was there that she saw a man in a gray suit walk past the mirrored armoire.

Another one of Becky's assistants also refuses to stay overnight at the Inn because one evening, after a busy murder mystery weekend, she stayed overnight on the third floor. Lying in a bed in one of the alcoves, she heard footsteps on the stairwell leading up to the third floor. She heard the door open and close and then heard footsteps coming towards her bed. Next, she felt someone get into bed with her. Terrified, she covered her head with the blankets, too scared to look, in hopes the ghostly visitor would go away. She eventually went to sleep and dreamed about a man in a gray suit reading a newspaper down in the basement. The next morning she awoke, went down into the basement to grab a mop bucket and there she saw the same man in a gray suit reading a newspaper. He looked up at her and simply disappeared.

This "legendary ghost girl of the Stone Lion Inn" has been described in countless newspaper and magazine articles and at least seven television news stories have been reported on her, but does she really exist? Our OKPRI group has also done filming with local news stations throughout the years, and even appeared on a national cable network show in 2006 with TAPS (The Atlantic Paranormal Society, as seen on SyFy's show, "Ghost Hunters") and again in 2012 with A&E's "My Ghost Story" about the legendary haunting of the Stone Lion Inn.

The media mainly focuses on the legend of the little Houghton girl, but is the ghost of this little girl really the deceased daughter of the Houghton family that was supposedly over medicated by the family maid? Who are the other ghosts that allegedly haunt the Stone Lion Inn? Could they be the ghosts from the time when the Stone Lion Inn was Smith's funeral home? Do those who visit the Stone Lion Inn go in with the belief the little girl is there and assume they will see her? Again, were their minds able to create not only the Houghton girl ghost, but the other ghosts as well? There have been people who have investigated the Stone Lion Inn who have recorded EVPs (electronic voice phenomena also known as "voices of the dead") with a little girl's voice and other voices not of this world. Does this prove the little ghost girl and others really exist or have people believed in them so much that they were able to create her out of a strong belief and record evidence?

Separating Fact from Fiction

Intrigued by the history of the Stone Lion Inn and the legendary ghost stories told about it over the years, my group and I have continued our investigations and research at the historic location. Through our historical research, we learned the Houghton family had two hired servants at the Stone Lion Inn, one male and one female. The male was a coachman, named Asbury C. Cooper, listed on the 1910 Federal Census as a mulatto male age 47. The cook was Lucinda Cooper, a black female age 41. Both of them were originally from Alabama and did not appear in any other Houghton family records.

We also discovered that Augusta Houghton was not the little girl who was overmedicated by the maid as the legend was originally told. Perhaps this rumor developed because she was seen on the 1900 Federal Census with the family at age seven. Then she disappears off the family censes by 1910. Other records reveal she, in fact, lived well on into adulthood. She is listed in the 1910 census as a student at Mount Carmel Academy in Wichita, KS, at the age of eighteen. A copy of her marriage license reveals she married Wilburn Waller Houser on Christmas Eve in 1914 when she was twenty-two years old. His father was a local cream dealer on Noble Avenue. The Guthrie City Directory lists her as a student at Methodist University in 1915. By 1935, she and her husband lived at 218 E. Madison St. in Harlingen, TX, and had two sons, Fred H. and James S. Wilburn was a real estate salesman and she sold cosmetics. According to some records, Augusta went by her first name, Coralee or "Cora", later into her adulthood. She was eventually widowed (according to her death certificate) and passed away in a Harlingen, TX, hospital from heart failure at the age of eighty-one years old.

Others think the poisoned child might be a daughter named Irene, since she appears as a newborn on the 1910 census, but an extensive search does not show her in any other records. The date this census was taken was on April 26, 1910. There is record of a daughter born on April 15, 1910, by the name Marjorie Louise. It is highly likely that the "Irene" mentioned in the census is actually Marjorie. This would mean she was 11 days old when the census taker visited the home. Dr. Vella, genealogist for the Houghton Project (the world's largest compilation of Houghton family records), confirms that many children had different names (or no name) on census records than their actual names. This was likely before they received a legal name on a birth certificate or their baptismal names.

Oklahoma Territorial Museum records do not include any birth records for that year. There are many years where records are misplaced for Logan County. Also, records were only kept if a physician or midwife attended a birth. Many births in that time occurred at home with the assistance of family and were not recorded.

There is another child in the Houghton family that may have gone by a different name than their baptismal name. Newspaper records reveal a birth announcement for a boy born to F. E. Houghton who was baptized as William Jennings. His birth date was Aug. 7, 1896. No other record exists with this name however; this male child does not fit the description of a little ghost girl seen there at the Stone Lion Inn. The only written evidence of a Houghton child death is documented in early census records. The number of total births and of living children was routinely assessed and records reveal only one child in the family had died before 1910. This is likely the boy, William Jennings.

So if the Stone Lion Inn is truly haunted by a little girl and she isn't Augusta or Irene, then who is she? Is there a chance the Houghton family did have a female child whose birth and death was not recorded? Is the legend true according to the elderly historian at the historical society and the elder Houghton children? One would think the death of a child, even accidental, would be recorded in local newspapers, especially since the Houghton family was well known in Guthrie at that time.

What if the Houghton family covered for their African-American maid who caused the accidental overdosing? With hardly any rights for Black Americans in the early 1900's, perhaps the Houghton family was afraid she'd be given an unfair trial or that she might be lynched for her carelessness and wanted to protect her by covering-up her mistake.

What if the little girl that so many have claimed to see is actually a child that had been brought into the Stone Lion Inn during the time it was a funeral home? What if she was truly one of the Houghton children who lived and died there so long ago? Our group believes there are at least 4 ghosts there at the Stone Lion Inn. We believe that three of these ghosts are there from the time when the inn was used as a funeral home. These three ghosts are the man in the gray suit and hat, the young woman with long dark hair, the older gray-haired woman. Our group knows there is a female child spirit there, but as of now, we don't know her exact origins.

I personally have had numerous encounters with the man in the gray suit and hat. I first encountered him down in the basement. He told me his name was Edward and he had died of lung cancer. He stated his body had been brought in there to the Stone Lion Inn for funeral arrangements. He liked the old place and decided not to leave. He still loved the smell of cigars, which were his weakness. He asked me if I had one I would give him. On my following visits, I would occasionally bring a cigar for Edward. I have found this male spirit to be a bit of a prankster and found he also likes to pick on females. One particular night I was sitting in the study by myself while some of the other investigators were upstairs investigating. The hour was late, around 3am so I closed my eye to rest for just a moment. I suddenly felt like someone was standing right over me. I opened my eyes to find Edward there grinning at me and then he disappeared. The study area is known to be one of Edwards popular hang out. Cigar smoke is often reported to be seen as wispy smoke and is also smelled by guests. One night while investigating in this area, I captured a photo of a ball of light in movement. It was during a time when we had smelled the cigar smoke and our emf meters were showing high activations. Some have debated this photo to just be dust in motion but others who have looked at it believe it to be a true light anomaly.

Edward pulled a similar stunt on me in the kitchen area too. I was writing in our investigation log when all the sudden I heard, "Boo," in my left ear. I turned my head and there stood Edward smiling at me for a brief moment before he disappeared again. One will never known when and where Edward will appear and disappear at within the Stone Lion Inn.

The long dark-haired woman remains somewhat of a mystery. She always appears very sad, depressed and is often times seen looking out from the balcony windows. She is most commonly seen in the wedding suite and bordello room. One night just before I entered the wedding suite, I saw her sitting on the bed with the moonlight illuminating her silhouette. I wasn't expecting to see her there like that and it caught me off guard and scared me a bit. Then after I entered the room, she disappeared.

The older gray-haired woman is kind of a grumpy spirit. She does look after the house but also acts-out when she doesn't get her way about something. She is also very vocal about things taking place in the house. We have gotten EVPs recorded of both her and Edward in conversations with each other and apart. We have also gotten evps recorded of the younger woman with long dark hair.

While investigating the Stone Lion Inn, our group was able to record all 3 forms of recorded evidence: photos, video and evp. Evps and video cannot obviously be shown in a book but a couple of the photos we got from there were quite interesting. While investigating one evening in the Bordello room, we started noticing temperature changes within 10 degrees from our original recorded baseline. One of our investigators also stated she felt like something was around her and she felt coldness around her so we started checking the temperature. I also began taking photographs in the direction of the investigator and there was two photos in particular that showed a strange light anomaly around the seated investigator who made the claims. After taking each photo, I noticed the strange light anomalies in the viewfinder. Recreation attempts were made without success. Evps were also recorded during this time as well.

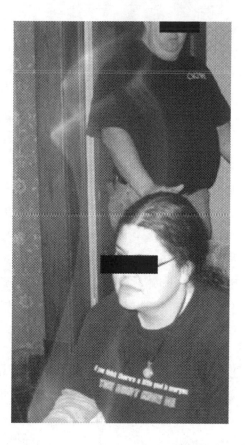

Our group has been able to verify some of the haunting claims that have taken place at the Stone Lion Inn. On our very first initial visit back in 2002 and while touring the Stone Lion, I personally witnessed a door slam shut on its own while we were up on the 3rd floor. I also have this event recorded on audio. Throughout the years we witnessed a few other doors open and close on their own. We have heard disembodied voices; have seen things move on their own, we have heard footsteps and so much more. One particular evening while on the 2nd floor, myself and another investigator we chased by the sound of fast footsteps, which followed us all the way up to the 3rd floor where we were conducting a sit-down with our group. Shadows are frequently seen at Stone Lion Inn too and there are times when you just don't feel alone and I have always stated that I would never feel comfortable spending the night alone there by myself. While in the kitchen area one night, our group was able to record on video, a straw moving around and around in a cup by itself. When people ask me what location in Oklahoma is one of the most haunted, I will always stand by my answer of, "The Stone Lion Inn."

Then there is the question of the infamous little ghost girl. I have personally seen her while investigating at the Stone Lion Inn. She looks to be about the age of six to eight years old and has long brown hair about to the middle of her back. I have seen her wearing a little light colored dress. She can be somewhat shy, she likes to play hide and seek and likes to giggle. I can't deny that she is there, even though the only thing we have in the way of evidence is through EVP. In the many years I have been investigating the Stone Lion Inn, I have never been able to get her to announce her name and get it recorded on my audio recorder either. Our group and others have been able to record her voice but we haven't been able to get any further recorded evidence of whom she truly is.

A theory is that people who have grown old and died can at some point, return in spirit to places they loved the most at times when they were the happiest. What if this little girl is a Houghton child who has returned in spirit as a child to the Stone Lion Inn since she had her happiest times were likely while she was a child living in the home?

No one really knows for sure if this same ghost girl often seen at the Stone Lion Inn is indeed the spirit of the Houghton child or if the legend of the Houghton child dying from accidental poison is true. Much of what people have to refer to for information is speculation from ghost stories passed down throughout the generations. Much like the Myrtles Plantation case with Chloe, could this ghost girl just be another transient spirit who's taken on the identity of a Houghton child to get acknowledgement for her existence? Were these ghosts created because people believed enough in the legendary stories and caused them to exist?

The Phillip Experiment

One day when I was doing some research to see if it was possible for our minds to create a ghost, I came across an interesting article called, "The Phillip Experiment." The subject of this experiment was to see if a fictitious historical character created by those doing this experiment, could in fact manifest itself through group efforts of concentration and false data. This experiment was conducted in the 1970's by a group of people from the Toronto Society of Psychical Research."

Believe it or not, the Phillip Experiment was successful and the TSPR group was able to get the ghost of "Phillip" to appear. To give you some history on the experiment, the TSPR group assigned a false life to Phillip. Phillip's history led him back to the time of the 1600's and told how Phillip was a supporter of the king and a devout Catholic. Phillip was married to a beautiful, but a cold-hearted and hateful wife, named Dorothea, who was the daughter of a neighboring nobleman. The fictitious story states that one day, when out riding on the edges of his property, Phillip came across a gypsy encampment off in the distance. There he saw a beautiful dark-eyed, black-haired gypsy girl named Margo. He instantly fell in love with her.

Not wanting to be apart from her, he secretly brought her back to live in a gatehouse near the stables of Diddington Manor, which was his family home. For quite some time he was able to keep his love affair with Margo secret, but eventually his wife Dorothea realized that he was hiding someone there and, upon looking, found Margo. Dorothea in a rage of jealousy accused her of witchcraft and of stealing her husband and had Margo arrested and put on trial. Scared of losing his reputation and possessions, Phillip did not stand up for Margo at her trial. Due to the charges, she was convicted of witchcraft and then burned at the stake. Afterwards Philip was riddled with guilt and stricken with remorse because he had not tried to defend Margo. It was said that he used to pace the walls of his Diddington home in despair. Finally one morning his body was found at the foot of the walls where he had "cast himself in a fit of agony and remorse."

Dr. A.R.G Owen, a member of the Department for Preventative Medicine and Biostatistics at the University of Toronto in the 1970's, was also a psychic researcher specializing in poltergeist cases. He also worked on the Phillip experiment and was the group's scientific advisor. In the introduction for the experiment, "Conjuring Up Phillip" he stated, "It was essential to their purpose that Philip be a totally fictitious character. Not merely a figment of the imagination but clearly and obviously so, with a biography full of historical errors." He wanted to make sure that there could be no historical records that would verify Phillip's existence.

After the experiment started, it went on for months without any success. Nonetheless the research group continued their experiment by sitting around a table, much like the common spiritualists did back in the 19th century. Then one day without warning, they slightly heard and felt a single knock on the table. Then the single knock was followed by a series of knocks, all heard and felt by all members sitting at the table. At first they didn't know what to think and they remained skeptical about the knocks. They all quickly changed their minds when the table began moving on its own around the room. One of the researchers spoke up to ask, "I wonder if Phillip is doing this?" A loud knock was heard as if in response to the question. Thus the ghost Phillip was created there in Canada.

The group devised a plan to indicate one knock as meaning "yes" and two knocks indicating "no" in order to communicate with the entity. Through this type of communication, the personality of Phillip came alive and he would end up telling them his story, which matched the fictitious life that the group had made up for him. As the experiment progressed, the so-called Phillip would cause the lights to turn off and on by themselves and members reported being touched by him. The group also noted other strange anomalies that also occurred.

It was also noted that the strange sounds and movements of the table seemed closely related to the thoughts of the group. If the group strongly agreed on an answer the knocks would be loud and quick. If there were doubts in the group for an answer, there would be a hesitation in strange sounds.

At the end of the experiment the members were not disappointed as they felt they had succeeded far beyond their expectations, however did they really prove that Phillip was created? Were their collective subconscious mind's really able to create a ghost or was it an actual entity they ended up conjuring up which played along with their Phillip story to gain their trust? This experiment was also documented on video and whatever the actual truth may be, it has proven an important historical account for the Para-research efforts in Canada,

Something interesting to ponder is: If a ghost is truly the soul of a person and a soul is pure energy then it cannot be destroyed only changed from one form or another. Einstein's theory is that energy cannot be created or destroyed just transformed. This is not fully true because a soul is a life force and a true form of energy. Where does the soul actually come from and what sets it apart from any other form of energy? Can someone just think about a certain type of ghost or soul long enough that they are actually able to create it into existence? The answer to these questions may vary with different belief systems, especially when it comes to the origination of the soul. Some believe the soul comes from God, which is also my belief system. Others believe it comes from a universal creator and then some just believe we are just born with a soul. If we however are automatically born with a soul then why do some healthy babies die either during the birthing process or shortly afterwards? Could this be due to the absence of a soul? Some people do not believe the soul continues on after the physical body dies but if a soul is energy and it cannot be destroyed, just transformed then the soul has to still exist after it leaves the physical body. Where it goes after physical death is a whole other story.

There are however a few things that set the soul apart from just any other form of energy. The soul has a conscious, which makes it unique because it has free will and free choice. It has the ability to make decisions thus making it accountable for the choices made. This soul's conscious also allows it to have its own unique personality and this personality along with its life force makes up the essence of the soul and in turn makes us who we are.

Whether the soul accompanies a physical body or is on its own, it is in my opinion, that a spirit cannot just be created by our mind. The soul is too powerful and what makes it so vital is that it has free will and that is something that no one can control other than the soul itself. Can a spirit take on the personality of another person while in death? Sure, because of its free will and choice. Why they may choose to do this is totally up to them and each one has their own personal reasons for why they choose to do what they do. Our minds may be able to create various ghost stories but it is my opinion that ghosts can and do take on personalities of other spirits. A soul is energy and it can transform itself, but only God can create or destroy it.

CHAPTER 9

"Children and the Paranormal"

Throughout the years, concerned parents who believe their children are being affected by paranormal activity or by what they believe to be a possible ghost have contacted OKPRI asking for our help. Some of these parents have stated they think their child may have an imaginary friend, while others claim their child is seeing a ghost that is mean or frightening. The worst cases are the ones that claim the ghost is causing physical harm such as bruises, scratches and other physical markings on their children.

Parents have occasionally reported seeing these entities themselves, especially when the entity is thought to be a passed friend or loved one. There have been many cases where these children have been able to identify the entity as a past friend, loved one or have identified them as such from photographs observed after their experiences once their parents have shown them these photographs. This provides them with a validation to their claims, especially if these people have passed before their children were born.

There are also children who experience paranormal activity because they are gifted and can see, hear and communicate with spirits. Sometimes parents are not always aware that their child is gifted and therefore think their child either has an overactive imagination or that the child is acting out for attention. Children like this are often times misdiagnosed with psychological disorders and are treated with medications. This is the first line of treatment by doctors and other providers for these children because modern science does not recognize the paranormal. Modern doctors, while clearly helpful in their practices, are all too quick to prescribe medications to cover symptoms without always getting to the absolute root of the problem. The metaphysical is not proven science and is based on theory alone. Medical science can only treat proven facts, based on evidence from controlled studies. Treating a theory would be considered experimental and could be considered unethical.

Some parents with gifted children are hesitant to take their children to a psychologist because they don't know if they can help them. Some fear that if their child's experiences are openly shared they will have their child taken away from them especially if their child has physical markings. What doctor in their right clinically scientific mind would believe a parent's story that a ghost had abused their child?

Whatever strange phenomenon cases there may be taking place with children, the fact remains that they have been affected by the paranormal for many generations. Since the 1960's there has also been what appears to be a growing number of cases that involve children who have been noted as being different or having different types of mental disorders. Studies have been done on children and there appears to be more and more signs of strange behavior with each generation of children that are born. Medical science blames the odd physical and behavioral changes on different things like processed food, contaminants in our drinking water, etc. There is another explanation however as some people believe that these children are part of a new type of spiritualistic movement. These children are a generation of children who are more aware and awakened to the spiritual world than their parents and grandparents before them.

The Phenomenon of Indigo Children

While there are many different people who have their own theory as to the unique behaviors of children, there has also been a label given to them as Indigo Children. There are many different characteristics that set an Indigo child apart from a non-Indigo child. These differences are in their unique abilities in creativity, empathy and then their ability to read minds. Indigo children are said to be highly sensitive with a strong sense of self worth and a strong feeling they their purpose in life is to make a difference in the world. They are known to be very strong willed and independent thinkers who prefer to do things their own way rather than comply with authority figures. Those Indigos with strong empathic gifts can easily detect or become in tune with the thoughts of others around them. They are also naturally drawn to matters concerning spiritualism, mysteries, the paranormal and the occult. Indigos usually think outside of the box since they are very creative and possess a certain wisdom and level of spiritual awareness beyond their years. They are often times referred to by spiritualists as an "old soul" and are said to possess gifts such as clairvoyance, clairaudience, clairsentience, clairalience, claircognizance and clairgustance. These six gifts are considered to be one's sixth sense or scientifically speaking as extra-sensory perception.

The Different Sixth Senses

These different sixth sense words are derived from the 17th Century French language with the word "*clair*" meaning "clear." Usually when these terms are referenced, they take on a spiritual or paranormal definition because they are senses that are extraordinary and not accepted by everyone. These extra senses also allow an individual to see, hear, feel, smell, taste and know things that the average individual normally cannot do with their ordinary senses. Below is a brief definition of each extra sense.

Clairvoyance is the ability to see things clearly.

Clairaudience allows someone to hear things clearly.

Clairsentience is the ability to feel objects, pain and emotion clearly or an ability to perceive extra tactile information. A person with this gift is considered empathic.

Clairalience is the ability to smell things clearly.

Claircognizance is the ability to know something without knowing how or why one knows the information.

Clairgustance is the ability to taste something without any physical object being placed in one's mouth.

While some people may consider these types of abilities a gift, some look at it as a curse, especially those Indigo children who choose not to embrace the abilities they have been given. This is especially true when they don't understand what they are dealing with. Indigo children typically have some of these gifts, but not all of them.

There is also a downside to being an Indigo child, as some of them are said to have social issues and often times do not feel like they fit in with other children. This can cause them to develop deep levels of depression and social anxiety. This however is not typically the case whenever they are around other Indigo children, as they seem to fit in better with those that are more like them. Indigo children have also been known to suffer from sleep disorders, such as insomnia and persistent nightmares. They have a tendency to be more visual, kinesthetic learners and they can remember best what they can picture in their minds and create with their hands. Most Indigo children are able to grow into adulthood without all their troubled childhood symptoms and most even retain their unique gifts.

Some psychiatrics believe that there is no proof or evidence for the existence of any type of Indigo children. They believe that children who have been classified as Indigo are merely troubled or disruptive children who suffer from psychiatric disorders such as ADHD (Attention Deficient Hypertension Disorder), ADD (Attention Deficient Disorder), OCD (Obsessive Compulsive Disorder) and even Autism.

Some feel that these children, that have been labeled Indigo by the New Age believers, see them as being something they are not. They believe the true source of the problem lies outside of psychiatric issues and stems from simple selfishness, arrogance and lack of discipline by the parents. It is also believed that the Indigo phenomena could also be the result of children influenced by television shows with the emphasis on magic, supernatural phenomena and fantasy.

So do Indigo children really exist or are they simply a group of troubled children who lack discipline and medical treatment for their conditions? I found myself seeking out the answers to this very same question when it came to my own daughter.

I began to notice unique behaviors with my daughter when she was about three and a half years old. Throughout the years since, I have learned that living with a sensitive or indigo child is not easy and can be a very difficult and trying time for any parent, especially if you do not understand what is truly happening. Children who are gifted usually start to show signs around the age of two to four years of age. No one knows for sure exactly how these gifts come about, whether they are passed down through the different generations or not. However, it does seem to be prevalent more so in certain families who have elder family members who also have gifts and abilities.

I learned through my dad that my gifts came from his Native American side of the family, as my great grandmother was once well known by many for her own unique abilities. She used to have people come to her for spiritual help and often times she would give them a reading by using tea leaves as a tool for spiritual insight.

Some people believe that ethnicity plays a major roll in those who are gifted, however there are accounts of psychic talents in all ethnic backgrounds. Some also believe children who are born with a veil or "caul," which is when a baby is born with their amniotic sac intact, or children who are born with reddish-pink markings on their foreheads, have been given special gifts to them upon birth. The veil and colored markings are said to symbolize a child with a "third eye."

My daughter, Sarah-Ann and my son Graysen were both born with a reddish-pink marking on their foreheads at birth, which lasted for about three weeks. At that time, I never thought about the marking symbolizing any type of psychic gift. When I asked my doctor about it, he was unsure of the source of the marking and thought perhaps it was a light birthmark of sorts that would eventually fade away. I spoke with my mother about it and she told me when I was born, I also had the same type of pinkish-red marking on my forehead, but it faded after about one month's time. She stated she had also questioned her doctor about the marking on my forehead and her doctor was unsure of the cause as well.

I began investigating the paranormal field when Sarah-Ann was around four years old. This was close to the time that I began to notice unique and strange behavior with her. She had always expressed her fears of the dark and of being alone in her room at night, because she said she would see ghosts. I figured her imagination was just working overtime and she was using that as an excuse to sleep in my bed. One night, however, I seriously began to think about the possibility of her being truthful about what she was experiencing.

Sarah-Ann was four years old and had a bad habit of getting out of her bed at night and sneaking into my room where she would get into bed with me. At that time, I was newly married to my second husband and this made for many very uncomfortable crowded nights. Sarah-Ann had always slept in a variety of awkward positions, so she was very hard to sleep with. I had tried for months to get her out of this bad habit. It took many nights of fighting with her for hours and placing her back into her own bed, but all of our efforts seemed worthless. She insisted on getting into our bed at any cost. Some nights, she would sneak into our room and fall asleep on the floor by my side of the bed where I would find her the next morning. I had even tried several attempts at locking my bedroom door where she couldn't come into my room, however this did not work either since she would sit outside my bedroom door crying and knocking until I either opened the door to acknowledge her needs and let her into my room.

Many parents feel their child is the best and above all others and, of course, I was always a proud mama who felt that way too. Sarah-Ann was a beautiful blonde haired, blue-eyed child, but she had such a stubborn streak in her. She had always been the type who refused to give up on something until her demands were met. She is still that way to this day as an adult! While she was growing up, I had always tried to be a patient and loving mother, but one particular night my husband and I had run out of our patience with her.

After fighting with Sarah-Ann for hours into the night to stay in her own bed, we decided to put her back in her bed and lock her bedroom door from the outside so she would not come out again for the evening. However, after doing so she cried and screamed and kept insisting that "the bad dark man" was back in her room and he was going to get her. At first I thought this was just her way of trying to come out of her room again, so after a few minutes I opened her door and she came running out grabbing on to me shaking uncontrollably and telling me she was angry at me for making her see "the bad dark man" again. She had mentioned this mysterious man to me previously, but I had just assumed it was her imagination and another attempt to sleep in my bed. I offered to go back in her room with her and lay down next to her, but she still refused. She truly felt like this bad man was going to get her whether I was there or not.

I began to question her about "the dark bad man" and she told me that the first time she had ever saw him was a long time ago when she had been laying in bed and saw him float from the laundry room past her bedroom. She said his hands were crossed over and placed together on his chest and he looked like he was wearing a long black cape. She said she had been seeing him for a while, but he had never came into her room until recently. The night he came into her room, she looked up and he was standing over her. I asked her if he had said anything to her and she said, "no." From the way her little mind was describing the whole situation, this "dark bad man" sounded like the typical shadow person type and normally shadow people are seen but not heard audibly. I couldn't fathom my daughter's imagination coming up with something like this on her own, especially since she didn't watch any scary movies or shows. Even the cartoon, *Scooby Doo,* was too scary for her at the time.

From that point forward, I began listening more to my daughter when she would tell me she was seeing or hearing a ghost. Through the years, I studied more and more about children and the paranormal and closely monitored my daughter's experiences. She not only saw spirits in various places, but she would hear them too. When she got to be around ten years old, they started making appearances in her dreams as well. It did not bother her that much to see or hear them. It was when they tried to make contact with her that she became really frightened. One thing that bothered her for years was spirit visitations when she was trying to sleep at night.

I found out Sarah-Ann had inherited some of my intuitive traits. Even if two different people have a lot of the same spiritual traits, they can each develop their own unique method of handling their fears. Sarah-Ann found comfort in wearing an eye patch over her eyes at night when she laid down to sleep. When I asked her about this, she told me it was to prevent her from seeing any spirits out who might try to come and visit her when she turned off her lights to go to bed.

Helping a child cope with their spiritual fears can be very difficult and I know this first hand from having to help Sarah-Ann along her spiritual growth. I have always stressed to her that not all spirits had bad intentions and most of them just needed some sort of help. Sometimes they even acted out in confusion, because they weren't fully aware of their situation. I told Sarah-Ann that if we were together at home or even out in public and she encountered a spirit who bothered her, she needed to tell them to leave her alone, see me for extra help and pray for God's help to not feel afraid.

One frustrating aspect for Sarah-Ann was always the fear of ridicule, non-belief or rejection by her friends or family members about the things she was experiencing. I have spoken to many parents who are dealing with raising children like Sarah-Ann and I always stress to them to be open and listen to what their children are telling them. Many children are afraid to speak out about what they are experiencing, due to potential ridicule and the fear they will not be believed by the adults they trust the most. I have come across many cases where many children are gifted and some of these children had disorders such as autism.

My two children are fifteen years apart in age. Sarah-Ann is now grown, but is still scarred from her childhood experiences with seeing and hearing ghosts. She is still very afraid to be alone at night by herself and does not like to sleep in total darkness. Her brother, Graysen is currently four years old and has already told me about a couple of experiences he has encountered.

One particular night, at about two o'clock in the morning, Graysen came into our bedroom and told his dad and I that he had just seen a man with a hat in his room. He said this man came through his bedroom wall and he had a dog on a leash. His bedroom wall faces a side street in the back of our house on a corner lot in our neighborhood. He told me this man came through the wall and started playing with his toys. Graysen said he told the man to stop but he wouldn't stop. I got up and went into his room, but I didn't see any man there. I asked Graysen where the man went and he said he didn't know. Thinking perhaps this might have been

Graysen's imagination, I put it in the back of my mind and went back to sleep.

It was around two-thirty in the morning about a week later when Graysen came back into our bedroom and climbed in bed with us once again. He told us he just saw the same man again and this time he was pulling on his dresser drawers. He went on to tell us he told the man to stop making so much noise, but the man kept slamming his dresser drawers.

During this same time, Sarah-Ann had a job where she worked until one o'clock in the morning. A couple of weeks after Graysen's encounter with the man and his dresser drawers, she had a similar encounter with the same ghost. It was 1:27 am when I heard Sarah-Ann yelling for me from outside her bedroom. Startled by her yells and worried about what was going on, I rushed into her bedroom to find out what was going on. She told me she was gathering her pajamas and a few other things before getting in the shower when she heard Graysen's dresser drawers opening and closing. She was surprised that her brother was awake at that hour, so she stepped around the corner to his bedroom to scold him for being out of bed.

Sarah-Ann described seeing a man who was around six-feet tall and wearing a hat. She said this man was a shadow figure and she saw him slumped over Graysen's dresser as he opened a drawer and then slammed it shut. Startled, she ran back into her bedroom and started yelling for me to come into her room. I looked in his room again, but saw no one except Graysen, fast asleep in his bed. Sarah-Ann was so shaken that she had me stay in the bathroom with her the entire time she took her shower.

A few days had passed. It was late, around 2 am, when Sarah came out of her bedroom to go into the bathroom to take a shower. She happened to glance into Graysen's bedroom as she passed by and briefly saw the shadow man once again. She ran straight into the bathroom and slammed the door. She told me about it the next morning. I asked her if her brother was asleep when she saw the man and she said, "yes." I teased her and told her it was nice of her to leave her brother alone in his room with a ghost!

Due to the trouble I had with Sarah-Ann growing up, I decided not to let Graysen know anything about my ghost hunting. When Sarah was little, she knew what I did. I couldn't help but think maybe her knowing caused more fear in her mind, because she understood that ghosts were real. I didn't want that to happen to Graysen, so when he came to us to say that he had seen this man, I had to wonder if his spiritual eyes were starting to open.

Graysen never called this man a ghost either. He had no idea what a ghost was since I had shielded him from knowing. To him, he was a regular man, but I knew what the man really was. I wasn't going to tell Graysen what he saw was a ghost either. I have also been really careful not to let him watch scary cartoons or movies. The last thing I wanted was to put fear in his mind and make him vulnerable to other worldly things. I couldn't help but wonder if these sightings were a start for him of the same my gifts and abilities that my daughter and I have.

Months passed after my son and daughter's sighting of this man. We had no further encounters with him. My guess was that he was a transient spirit who had wandered into our house and into my son's room just for a short period of time before moving on and finally leaving us alone. As more time went by, I tried to watch for further signs that Graysen had also inherited gifts and abilities like his sister. I will continue to pay attention to him and watch for these signs too as he grows and gets older.

Can children communicate while in the womb?

Two weeks before I found out I was pregnant with Graysen, I was lying in bed and saw a little boy beside my bed. He said, "Hi mama," and then passed right through me. I felt like this was when his soul entered my body. It was two weeks later when my pregnancy was confirmed. I already knew at that time that my baby would be a boy.

I was unsure if having another child was the right thing for me to do at that stage in my life. I was trying to finish my college degree, working full-time and in my mid-thirties. Two months prior to this, I had a small pea-sized tumor removed from my left breast and was also diagnosed as a type 2 diabetic. For the first two months that followed, I had mixed emotions about having another child. There were just too many other things going on in my life. I am one who doesn't believe in abortion, so I knew eventually I would have to accept my pregnancy and be happy about it.

During my pregnancy, Graysen actually communicated with me. He showed me an image of himself happily playing in the womb. When I was about seven months pregnant, Graysen came to me in a dream and told me he was coming early and there was going to be some complications with delivering him, but not to worry because he was going to be okay. When I was 35 weeks pregnant, I had gone in for my weekly stress test and they had a hard time locating Graysen's heart beat. They said it was weak. They tried some tests and said Graysen's biophysical profile should have been a score of eight out of eight, but instead he was at six. They wanted to keep me overnight to take more tests in the morning.

The morning came and after breakfast they did another test and said Graysen's score was now at two. They told me he wasn't getting the amniotic fluid that he should have been getting and they were going to take him by emergency cesarean section within the hour. I scrambled to get a hold of my family to tell them to hurry and get to the hospital.

At 2:23 pm, Graysen was finally born. The doctor said he was a lucky baby because the umbilical cord had been wrapped around his neck four times and if they wouldn't have taken him when they did, he wouldn't have made it. I felt relieved and blessed all at the same time.

I knew from the moment I had him he was special. Even then, I couldn't help but wonder if he was going to have my gifts and abilities too, especially since he had communicated with me during my pregnancy.

Strangely enough, while I was pregnant with Graysen, I encountered a woman in black. I was in my first trimester of pregnancy and was lying in bed when I saw a black tumbleweed-looking thing appear in my room beside my bed. I believe it was a ball of energy as it transformed into the head and torso of a woman. She had long black hair, pale skin and was wearing a black dress with long sleeves and a high collar. She was very angry with me and I didn't know why. She told me that the baby was her son and I couldn't have him because she was his mother. I told her to get out of my room and I started to pray. The woman disappeared.

I encountered this woman again while I was in the hospital the night before I gave birth to Graysen. I was sick with bronchitis the when they admitted me. I had been to my doctor six days prior and was given an antibiotic that wasn't working. I had called my doctor and asked for something different, but my doctor wouldn't prescribe me anything else until I had finished the antibiotic I was currently taking. Therefore, when I went into the hospital that Friday night, I was very sick and had difficulty breathing.

The hospital doctor immediately started me on a different antibiotic. At some point after falling asleep that night, I had stopped breathing. I awoke to hear this same woman tell me, "Christina, wake up! You have to wake up and breathe!" When I opened my eyes, I saw the same dark-haired woman dressed in a long black dress with the same long full-length sleeves and high-collar. The dress appeared to be a garment worn at some point in the 1800's. She had a concerned look on her face, but she smiled at me before quickly disappearing.

The next thing I knew, a bunch of nurses came rushing into my hospital room like a swat team. They honestly scared me as they rushed towards me in a panic and had me sit up. I asked what was wrong as they started to put an oxygen mask on me. They explained that their monitors showed I had stopped breathing for a short while and it sounded their alarms. From that point forward, they kept a close watch on my breathing and oxygen levels.

The third time I saw this woman was two weeks after I gave birth to my son. I was staying the duration of my postpartum recovery time at my friend's house. She was helping me since I had a C-section birth and was under strict recovery rules. At the time, I lived in a two-story apartment, so I couldn't climb the stairs. Staying at my friend's house was my best option.

I slept on my friend's couch with Graysen in his bassinet beside me. Behind the couch, there was a full standing cabinet/bar area with the kitchen sink built into it. The couch backed right up to the cabinet area and, while sitting or lying on the couch, you could only see the top half of the cabinet.

One night while settling down to sleep, I happened to look up and I saw the woman standing behind the couch in the cabinet area. I could only see her from the waist up. She was three-dimensional and transparent. I could see the cabinet right through her. As I looked at her, I saw her smile at me as if to say she had accepted me as Graysen's mother and she knew everything was going to be okay.

To this day, I do not know who this woman was. The only information I know is what she told me in the beginning about being Graysen's mother. I have always been skeptical about past lives, so I am not sure if she was truly Graysen's mother in a former life, or not. Since this last sighting, I haven't seen or heard anything else from this woman. Her appearance and Graysen communicating with me in the womb like he did has always made me question my son's connection to the spirit world and if he will prove to have the same gifts when he grows older.

It appears more and more children are growing up to be gifted and connected to the spiritual world. I have always wondered if this relates to the end of days when a great awakening will occur prior to the end of existence. This could also be because so many more people believe in ghosts these days compared to fifty years ago. People are no longer hiding their beliefs or personal experiences. Maybe because more adults are open to the idea of the spiritual world, it is causing their children to be more aware too. I never asked to be born with spiritual awareness, but I was. I only want to use my gifts for good and to always bring God into the brighter scheme of things. For a long time, I was afraid that having gifts and abilities meant that I was doomed to live in a fiery hell, but later, I realized that God can give us spiritual awareness and it's what we do with it that makes the difference. I was once asked a question that really stuck with me. When I use my gifts, am I using them for good or for bad? For God or for Satan? What I do with my gifts is what really matters and makes a difference. I always want to use my gifts for the good and to help enlighten others about spiritual matters and to let them know we have a wonderful God in Heaven who loves us.

I remember a case involving a child that my paranormal investigation team had researched in Oklahoma, in February 2009. It's listed on our website as "The House of the 6th Sense." This location was not the typical single-family residential location, but rather an apartment building. From what our group had learned, it was an apartment complex that had been around since the 1970's. In this particular apartment, we didn't find any history of deaths, tragedies, or other reasons for the land or building to be haunted. The current family living there contacted us because of the strange activity they were experiencing.

The family members were all experiencing minimal activity, except for the youngest daughter who was only eight years old at the time. Some of the paranormal claims the family was experiencing included seeing doorknobs turn on their own, a bathroom facet would come on by itself, and general feelings of being watched. There were various times when they felt as if they could not breathe. They described the air as feeling "thick and heavy." They reported that the hallway and bedrooms were the most uncomfortable places in the apartment.

I knew nothing about the case ahead of our arrival, except there was a young girl who had suffered a traumatic brain injury and had since been seeing and hearing things that most people typically don't hear and see. I wasn't sure if this little girl and her family were dealing with the same ghosts at each experience, or if they were dealing with different transient spirits that had been traveling in and out of this dimension for various purposes.

For privacy, I will call this little girl Jenny. When Jenny was four years old, she suffered a traumatic brain injury. Since her injury, she had been seeing different ghosts who visited her in her bedroom or when she was out in public. She had even stated that she saw spirits who would wave at her from the side of the road while she was riding in a vehicle. Much like the boy in M. Night Shyamalan's movie "The Sixth Sense," Jenny didn't quite understand what was happening to her or the extent of the gifts she now possessed. Out of all the ghosts she had encountered, there were three that seemed to hang around a lot. They were around so often that their presence would not allow her to have a peaceful home life. One of these spirits was Jenny's grandfather. He was there to try and help the family, especially since there had been a lot of disturbances taking place around Jenny.

One of the other ghosts around Jenny was a little girl whom she had become friends with, but this young ghost girl was connected to a woman who was not so friendly. Jenny had also seen a man wearing a dark coat with red eyes who would fight with the woman. Jenny said she would often see these ghosts come into her room from the hallway. Sometimes they came from her closet or the walls. They would sometimes linger around for a few moments and then disappear.

Jenny would try hard to ignore the woman that came to her in her dreams. Her appearance alone was scary. The woman was always covered in blood and wielding a knife. Jenny told us the little ghost girl she had befriended would sometimes follow her to school and to her grandmother's house. Concerned about the amount of anxiety and fear Jenny was experiencing, her mother asked our group to come out and investigate their home to see if we could find any answers about their haunting.

Our group arrived at the location unsure of what we would find. The family lived in an apartment complex where noise contamination from neighbors could negatively affect the results of the investigation. We were also unsure of what we would find with regard to the paranormal. The claims mainly revolved around Jenny, meaning she was the family member who most-often had experiences in the home. When we arrived, the entire family greeted us. Our group began to unload equipment as our case manager conducted an in-home interview with the clients. Next, I conducted a psychic walk-through of the location and took a few moments to sit down with the youngest daughter. I spoke with her about what she was experiencing. During this time, an EVP was captured that said, "Don't say." After my talk with Jenny, the children left with their father so the team could continue with the investigation without scaring the children or keeping them awake through the late hours. The mother and grandmother stayed.

A stationary video camera was placed facing directly down the hallway towards the bedrooms where most of the alleged activity was said to have been taking place. As our team investigated, the home seemed pretty quiet with the same comfortable feel of any normal home environment. Later on, once I had reviewed my recorded audio, I discovered I had recorded an EVP that said, "My girl". When the homeowner and homeowner's mother listened to the EVP, they said it sounded similar to the voice of their deceased father and husband. While conducting a photographic sweep, I saw a light anomaly shoot back and forth from the living room into the dining room area. I started taking pictures and was able to photograph that strange light anomaly.

The girl's bedroom seemed to be a very interesting focal point as well; since it was during this time that one of my team investigator's felt something had touched his leg. I started taking pictures of his leg, hoping to capture some evidence of the phenomenon as it was occurring when a strange mist-type anomaly showed up on the left bottom corner of one of the photos. We attempted to recreate this mist in a photo over and over again to determine a logical explanation, but the team was unable to determine a cause. During this time, an unknown vice was also recorded that was not heard by the team members at the time.

I felt the woman and child spirit were connected as mother and daughter and they had both died together. I had connected with the woman spirit during the sit-down phase of the investigation. She seemed quite agitated and showed me how she and her little girl had left their home in the middle of the night. They were trying to get away from her husband who had been abusive. Within a few minutes of their escape, the husband awoke to discover his wife and the young girl had gone. He quickly set out after them and gave chase. During the chase, the woman lost control of her car and wrecked, killing herself and her daughter instantly. At the time of the accident, the woman had a knife with her in the car for protection, just in case her husband had found her. She still carries it in death believing that she may still encounter her husband.

This woman spirit and her daughter had found the little girl, who lives in the apartment, and came to her for a reason they would not share with me. Perhaps it was because they were attracted to her energy or "light," so to speak. Maybe they felt she could help them. However, since finding the little girl, the woman spirit seemed to be unhappy and in a state of agitation.

There was also a man that had appeared in the client's home a few times. He fights with the woman spirit, but I wasn't able to connect with him to get any information. He wanted nothing to do with me and disappeared when I tried to talk to him.

I did feel there was one ghost in particular there who had good intentions. He was a family relative who felt to me like a father or grandfather figure. I had also smelled the scent of Old Spice cologne and asked the homeowner if her father had passed and if he used to wear Old Spice. She indeed verified the description I had given matched that of her father. The message he had for them was a bit personal, so I will not divulge it here. I can share that it was a very specific and special healing message solely for the homeowner.

After our investigation of the location, I had come to the conclusion that these spirits were attracted to the little girl for reasons of their own. It seems they had followed her from the place she had previously lived. One of my main concerns for this family was to help them understand what was taking place, but there was also the importance of stressing to them that their daughter had gifts. It was important for them to know she would eventually have to accept her gifts and to learn how to deal with them. I also let them know it was very important for them to be patient with her and listen to what she had to say. I added that children like their daughter often had trouble coping with her abilities, but the key to helping her to understand her gifts was not to be afraid of them, especially the spirits she would most likely encounter for the rest of her life.

Back in the summer of 2008, A&E debuted a paranormal television series called, "Psychic Kids: Children of the Paranormal." Chip Coffey, an American psychic investigator along with Chris Fleming and Kim Russo, hosted this series. It renewed twice with its second season premiering in December 2009 and the third and final season in October 2010. This series dealt with children who were experiencing paranormal phenomenon due to their spiritual gifts and abilities. The purpose of the show was intended to help these children harness their gifts and learn not to be afraid of what they were experiencing.

When I first heard about this show, I knew I had to watch an episode of it to see what it truly was all about. I was intrigued with knowing someone had finally come up with such a great idea for helping children who were having a difficulty dealing with seeing and hearing ghosts. I watched intensely as these kids and their parents shared their stories, some crying while others felt scared and ashamed of their issues. My heart went out to these children, because I knew first-hand what they were going through.

What blew my mind was what happened at the end of each episode. The children were given a camcorder and other pieces of recording equipment and were told to go hunt for the ghosts in order to face their fear. I have never been in favor of children investigating the paranormal. There are so many dangers involved in ghost hunting and I think by teaching children to "hunt for ghosts," it encourages them to encounter more dangerous situations than what they originally had to deal with. We have had people contact our group asking us if we would allow children to attend one of our public ghost hunting events or if we would host a private ghost hunt as a birthday party for their child. Our answer has always been, "no." Children already have many fears they have to face while growing up and there is no sense in adding additional fears or putting them in any unnecessary dangers. The show, "Psychic Kids: Children of the Paranormal," was accused of exploiting children and I can understand why these accusations were made. Perhaps this was the reason why the show only aired for three seasons before going off the air.

I do feel there is a need for children to be educated to a certain degree on the paranormal if they have gifts and abilities they don't understand or know how to deal with. Also, because these children need to learn to overcome their fears and not let any spirits scare them. In the same regard, I don't think a child's mind is always able to fully comprehend all aspects of the spirit world or what is completely involved with such spirits.

They say our children are our future, but how can our children be our future if they are not open to all aspects of the truth? After all, the paranormal is the norm, since it is something many people encounter, but it's just not something that is completely understood. It doesn't just affect adults, but children of every walk of life as well. The fact remains that more and more children are experiencing paranormal phenomenon and have specific gifts and abilities to hear and see spirits of those who have passed. However, with any newly discovered ability comes a special responsibility. It's how we, as parents of these children, develop our child's gifts and instill a responsibility within our children that makes a big difference on the positive outcomes of our children. The key to helping them face their fears is to be open and accepting while maintaining knowledge and positivity about the truth and what is really out there.

CHAPTER 10

Spiritual Warfare
"The Attack"

Throughout the years I've been asked by many new paranormal investigators if our team would mentor them and show them how to get started in the field. Before I agreed for my team and I to help them, I'd ask if they were prepared for what they might encounter. After asking this question, I would share with them a couple of my past experiences and advise them of the potential dangers involved. Since there are different types of spirit personalities lurking within the spiritual realm, one can never be certain what they are up against while investigating. I always emphasized the fact that some spirit types they might encounter could be good, some bad and some so evil, they could be dangerous. This would usually make them stop and think twice about their interest to investigate the paranormal. Some with more skeptical attitudes usually made comments regarding their disbelief in the possibility that ghosts could physically hurt someone. I always sat back and listened to their opinions, knowing their disbelief was from their lack of spiritual knowledge and experience in the field. As a mentor, I could only offer my advice and experience as a seasoned paranormal investigator.

Of course, there is nothing wrong with a healthy dose of skepticism, as long as the skeptic is empowered with facts. I completely understand their skeptic position, since I too was once inexperienced. I would find out later in my investigating years what true evil was. Once you are face to face with evil, you suddenly find that it tests your entire belief system and everything you thought you knew is tossed out the window.

I have never been one to be excited about battling against demons or unknown evil spirits, but when you are placed in a situation where you have no choice but to believe, you quickly appreciate having a higher power on your side. My higher power, of course, is God. I have to admit, in my earlier years of investigating I was always afraid if I started rebuking an evil spirit in the name of Jesus Christ or God, that I would anger the evil spirit and cause more havoc to occur. I was scared and did not know if I would be able to make the evil spirit leave. In the back of my mind, I had a smidge of doubt that made me wonder if perhaps God might not come to my rescue, because He might not approve of the paranormal work I was doing. I later found out that God is always on my side and always will be regardless of how other's opinions might have influenced my thoughts. My work in the paranormal field also taught me to trust Him more and call on him when I need Him.

There is a scripture in the Bible where God talks about how we wrestle with the principalities and powers of darkness. If you are reading this and you don't believe in God or the Bible, then that is your own personal choice, of course. For me, God is my all and has been my help, not just in times of trouble, but in my every day life as well. I have often wondered why I was born into a religious family. As I got older, I realized it was because I needed the spiritual experience that would help lead me along the path to where I am today. I especially find it helpful to have God on my side when investigating the paranormal field.

There are so many new paranormal investigators who jump right into the field without first being spiritually awake or having the spiritual strength to face the unknown. I have learned that it doesn't really matter how brave or grounded one thinks they might be when they choose to investigate the paranormal. In reality, no one really knows what awaits him or her at any given investigation. Typical ghosts are only the first part of the paranormal field. New paranormal investigators often do not stop to think about the darker entities and spirits that also exist. As mentioned previously, I have always firmly believed where you have good spirits, you will have bad spirits. There has to be a balance of energy. It's the universal balance and it won't be balanced unless both sides are present. It is dangerous to assume that nothing bad could ever happen to you. There is always a chance something could go wrong and to deny that possibility would only be lying to oneself.

For Christians who follow the Bible, there is scripture that speaks about different principalities, powers of darkness and the different types of spirits that are in our world. This scripture says in:

> *Ephesians 6:12, "For we wrestle not against flesh and blood, but against principalities, against powers, against the rulers of the darkness of this world, against spiritual wickedness in high places."*

Evil was born into the world when Satan thought he was greater than God. It is because of his arrogance that he and his angel followers were cast out of heaven. It was then that Satan and his fallen angels (demons) were unleashed upon the Earth to wreak havoc and chaos. It started with the great battle in Heaven.

Satan's name was originally Lucifer and he was a beautiful angel. His vanity and haughty arrogance made him believe he was better than God. It was then that he and his band of angel followers tried to take over Heaven. This, of course, did not please God and as the Bible says, God banished Lucifer and his followers from Heaven. Satan and his followers were then fallen angels. This story is found in the Bible in:

> *Revelations 12:7-9. "And there was a war in heaven: Michael and his angels fought against the dragon; and the dragon fought and his angels. And prevailed not; neither was their place found any more in heaven. And the great dragon was cast out, that old serpent, called the Devil, and Satan, which deceiveth the whole world: he was cast out into the earth, and his angels were cast out with him."*

God then gave Satan dominion over the realm of the Earth through the power of the air. Since Satan has control over the air or the outer realm of darkness, his influence is great over mankind. God has given mankind free will but Satan tries to influence that free will, just like he did with Adam and Eve in the Garden of Eden so very long ago. Not only does Satan influence mankind, he also commands and controls the other fallen angels that are in the earthly realm. These fallen angels are also the demonic spirits and evil unknown spirits that reek havoc on mankind and the earth.

Since I have mentioned how the devil can influence mankind, I want to stress that it that his influence is always in a negative way. There is a scripture in the Bible that mentions how Satan roams like a lion seeking who he can devour. This scripture is found in:

> 1 Peter 5:8, *"Be sober, be vigilant; because your adversary the devil, as a roaring lion, walketh about, seeking whom he may devour."*

The Bible also mentions Satan as being the "God of this world" and it talks about how that Satan blinds the minds of those who do not believe in God. This scripture is found in

> II Corinthians 4:4, *"In whom the God of this world hath blinded the minds of them, which believe not, lest the*

light of the glorious gospel of Christ, who is the image of God, should shine unto them."

The Bible even mentions God having a conversation with Satan about his good and faithful servant Job. When God asks Satan where he had been, Satan told him he had been going to and fro in the earth and walking up and down it. The scripture found in:

> Job 1:6-7 reads, *"Now there was a day when the sons of God came to present themselves before the Lord, and Satan came also among them. And the Lord said unto Satan, Whence comest thou? Then Satan answered the Lord, and said, from going to and fro in the earth, and from walking up and down in it."*

I haven't said all of this to preach a sermon but rather to enlighten you to the fact that evil is real and it exists in our world and Satan is the mastermind behind all evil. I also mention scripture so I can inform you about how my paranormal encounters led me to come face to face with true evil. Next, I will share a few stories of my encounters with spiritual warfare.

The Cemetery of the Damned:

It was in July of 2006 when I received a call from a woman that I will reference to as Susan for confidential reasons. Susan was the founder of a new group and was very upset when she called me and asked for our help with an investigation at a cemetery in Southern Oklahoma. She began to tell me about what had happened to her nineteen-year-old son, who I'll call Billy, again, for confidential reasons. It had only been a couple of weeks since they had been there, however the things they had encountered at a cemetery had scared her and her team members deeply, especially Billy. He was so shook-up that he promised he would never go ghost hunting again. As I listened to Susan, she described how they had found out about this small country cemetery and how they had decided to venture out one night to investigate. This cemetery appeared to be like most others, quiet and peaceful, but after starting their investigation, the team quickly changed their minds about its peaceful disposition.

Susan went on to say that her son wasn't in the best of moods that night. Earlier in the day he had a fight with his girlfriend and Susan thought perhaps her son's downtrodden mood is what had left him vulnerable. Susan and her team had split up into a couple of small groups to investigate. While collecting their data, Susan said she noticed her son had headed off to one particular corner and was crouched down in a sitting position. She watched him for a couple of moments and began calling his name. She felt like something might be wrong. Each time she called out to him, he wouldn't respond back to her.

A bit of panic and fear began to overwhelm her as she walked over to him. She gently placed her hand on his shoulder as she called his name out loud again. Susan said Billy suddenly stood up and looked directly at her. His eyes began glowing red and he starting growling at her. She found herself unsure of what do. Without any warning, Billy suddenly lunged at her and began to physically attack her. Others from the group immediately came over to intercede and were able to quickly pull Billy off of her.

Struggling, they took him outside of the cemetery gates and watched as he began to calm down and regain his usual personal characteristics. When Billy finally came to, he appeared to be confused and did not know what had just happened to him. The team told him about what had happened and he couldn't believe what they were telling him. He stated the last thing he remembered was walking over to the side of the cemetery before everything went black.

Needless to say, Susan was shaken pretty badly, but was lucky to have come out of the attack with no real physical harm. She and her group wrapped-up their investigation and headed back home. She explained to me that she was baffled by what had happened and she couldn't understand what could have gone so wrong from a simple cemetery investigation. Both she and her crew were shocked by the incident, especially Billy, who then told his mom he would never go ghost hunting again. This bothered Susan, because Billy had been investigating the paranormal field with her for a while and nothing like this had ever happened before. Susan decided she needed to seek some outside help with this cemetery since it was something she didn't know exactly how to handle. She had asked around about local groups in the Oklahoma City area who had extensive experience and was referred to my team. She decided at that point to make the call and request our help.

When I first spoke with Susan about her situation, I really did not know if I fully believed her story. It seemed a bit far-fetched from anything I had ever heard of thus far, especially something that intense occurring in a cemetery. Most new ghost hunters utilize cemeteries as a place to start investigating in until they can start getting their foot in the door into other places. Most cemeteries are considered harmless and some can even produce good quality evidence.

I continued listening to Susan's story as she claimed her son's incident was quite possibly a brief possession by something evil lurking inside the cemetery gates. While I believed that possessions were real, I also had never heard of one happening in a cemetery like this. In my years of investigating the paranormal and dealing with various people and personalities, the word "possession" was used and abused more times than I could count. I thought perhaps instead of a possession, her son had just overreacted to his own intense fear while he was in the cemetery. Regardless of my opinion, Susan seemed to be sincere on the phone and I could tell from the tone of her voice that she was still a bit shaken.

Susan finished her story and then asked us to come out to the old country cemetery to see what we could figure out. She was curious to know if our group could confirm some of the same strange experiences they had encountered. She recommended that I only take group members who were strong in their faith and also experienced in the field of paranormal investigations. She was worried about any new members or "newbies" as we call them, having trouble if they happened to encounter something bad like her team did.

During our phone conversation, I started seeing images of the cemetery and felt like there were four guardian-type spirits placed at each of the four corners. I also felt as if there was one grave in particular that was almost like the "heartbeat" for the cemetery. I described these images to Susan and also a few other images I was seeing. She confirmed the place I was describing was the same cemetery she had investigated. I was excited and thought perhaps there was something to this old cemetery after all. Upon concluding our conversation, we had planned a meeting time and I actually found myself excited about doing this investigation.

There were four of us from my team and four from Susan's team that went that night. We met at a local gas station off a near-by highway. After introductions, we all headed off to the cemetery. After a scenic drive, we arrived and planned how we would conduct our investigation. We all thought it would be best to split-up into two different groups with members from both teams working together in the same group. Before we got started, Susan showed us a picture they had taken from this cemetery the last time they had investigated there. The picture showed a man dressed in dark blue clothing sitting by a tree. He looked to be an older man with a gray mustache and beard. His ethnicity appeared to be African-American, which correlated with the history Susan had researched on this location. It was once an all black cemetery until sometime after the 1960's.

After we arrived at the cemetery, we walked up a long road that led to the gates. Even before entering, I was drawn to a large tree with a few massive branches that were low to the ground. I felt a tightening around my neck and I asked Susan if there had ever been any lynching done there at the tree. She confirmed what I was sensing and said the tree that I was feeling drawn to was the very same one that was used in lynchings. She also told me there used to be an old wooden church that had been built right by this tree but the church had since burned down a long time ago by arsonists.

I was already impressed with its history and was amazed at how this historic little cemetery could be so lost and forgotten. We entered the cemetery gates and each team took a side. As I walked alongside the graves, it actually felt peaceful to me. I couldn't help but notice a particular part of the cemetery had an open area with no headstones. I felt like there were several children buried there in unmarked graves and when I listened to bit closer, I heard a small child crying. There were many parts of this cemetery that felt so sad and then other parts that felt completely peaceful.

After a bit of time had passed, my group and I suddenly heard my name urgently being called. It was loud and clear, "Christy" and was heard off in the distance. This voice captured the attention of all of us, especially me since it was my name. At first, I thought I was being called by one of my team members who had possibly gotten hurt and needed my help. We all rushed over to the other side of the cemetery, but were surprised when we were met halfway by the other group who had also thought one of their names had been called. We discussed it and both teams stated they had heard my name and another member's name being called, yet no one on either team had called out to anyone. Upon review of my audio, I later found that my recorder had indeed picked up an unfamiliar voice calling out my name. During the time that I heard my name called, I snapped off a few photos and one of the photos showed a large mist all in the photo. Could this have been the image of a spirit we heard call my name?

Unsure at the time of what to make of the incident, we deemed it as an unknown occurrence and continued on with our investigation. I had felt drawn to the center of the cemetery, especially towards this one particular tree. I was carrying my electromagnetic field (EMF) meter, which had registered at zero the whole evening. There had been no base line reading within the cemetery from any nearby power lines or other man-made sources of energy.

As I entered the center part of the cemetery, I noticed some dark slender shadows flying from one tree to the next. I didn't quite know who or what they were, but I couldn't help but wonder if they were the cemetery's guardians that I had previously picked up on when talking to Susan on the phone. As I got closer to the tree, I happened to look down at the ground, which began to change right before my eyes. Where there had once been dirt, now appeared to be what looked like a large swirling black hole. I felt my head get a bit dizzy as I reached for the tree to make sure I could keep my balance. It was at that moment when I began to get spikes in the readings on my EMF meter.

I called out to an O.K.P.R.I. investigator on my team and asked them to start taking some pictures around me. I kept seeing the flying black shadows encircling us and I felt a very strange emotion come over me. I felt as if there was a demand for respect and acknowledgement that had to be given to a single unseen force. I didn't know who this was yet, but this spirit felt as if it was a leader among those spirits that remained Earthbound in this cemetery. I suddenly felt a change of energy throughout the cemetery as if someone had automatically flipped a switch. The peaceful feeling I had once felt earlier had now left and was replaced by chaos.

My team member who had been taking pictures around me during this time made a few comments about the images that his camera was capturing. I had asked him to keep taking photographs towards me until nothing else appeared in his photos. He finished taking photos after a few minutes so I walked over to him to see what the photographs would reveal. I was a bit shocked when I looked at the photos, because right there in the images were the long black and skinny shadows I had seen moving from tree to tree. It looked as if the figures were a two-toned black and brown color, possibly due to the camera's flash. They were positioned horizontally in the photographs, but were in different areas of each photo. I knew this had to be the shadows I had been seeing, however how could I prove that to anyone? I asked my investigator who took the photos to try to recreate the shots however when he did, the photos yielded nothing but the cemetery in its normal state. I didn't know what type of "creatures" these things were but I felt like we had possibly captured their strange images.

I didn't know why, but I also picked up on some sort of voodoo connection with this cemetery. The only thing that made sense at that time was perhaps there was someone or something buried in the cemetery that was strongly connected with the voodoo religion. I also felt like there were many souls in the cemetery that could not leave because they were being kept there by a stronger force. It made me angry, but also sad to think spirits were being held there and had not been given the chance to transcend. This meant all these souls were not earthbound which could also make things chaotic in this cemetery.

I saw an image of the soil under the grass and it looked tainted as if it were poisoned, in a sense. I didn't know if this vision of the soil was meant as a symbolic message or if it was to be taken literally. Overall, I just knew this cemetery was not a good or peaceful place anymore and the dead were not at rest here.

My team decided to meet up with the other group to find out how their investigation was going and to also compare notes on the night's activity so far. We showed them the pictures we had captured and I explained to them about the things I had experienced over by the tree. The other team had mentioned hearing audible voices and seeing human-like shadows, some black and some white, running in between the trees and bushes. I asked Susan if she had noticed anything in particular about the trees and she smiled and said, "You mean the shadows?" I nodded and told her I didn't know if she had seen them too or if only I had. She just smiled and said she had seen them. She said she was just glad we had actually experienced and validated some of the things she and her group had previously experienced. I told her that I was convinced this cemetery had some strange, unexplainable things taking place. I had no doubt it was haunted, but by what, I didn't quite know.

We decided to take a break for a bit and then split the teams back up again afterwards, but this time the groups would have different people. I was now working with Susan and two other members, one from her team and one from mine. Just as we were walking back into the cemetery, Susan called our team over to the side and asked us to follow her over to one area beside the fence line because there was something she wanted to show us. We agreed and followed her.

As she walked, she pointed to some headstones just a few feet in front of us. She began to tell us about what had happened to her son there and showed us the exact spot where it had happened. Susan then started to feel a bit dizzy. I happened to be standing beside her when, just as I started to turn my head to look in the other direction to see where we would go to next, I saw Susan falling straight forward on her face in my peripheral vision.

Luckily, her head missed hitting a headstone, but the ground had caught her forehead quite hard. I called her name while reaching down to help her up as other group members immediately came over to help as well. For about twenty seconds Susan was unresponsive before finally coming to. She kept saying, "Get it off of me! Get it off of me!" We sat her up and she complained about feeling dizzy again and said that something had physically attacked her. She felt like it was still with her.

I had placed my hands on her right arm to send her some positive energy. After about five seconds, Susan told me not to touch her. I took my hands off of her and asked, "why?" I was a bit shocked when she told me she had just felt a surge of electricity pass out of her arm and go into my hands. I told her I didn't feel anything different, so I thought I was okay. She said she hoped it hadn't, but still felt like it had. And now, she was worried that it was possibly with me now.

I really didn't know what to think about the incident that had just happened. I didn't know Susan that well and my logical mind had to question the circumstances of her fall, but it didn't make sense that she would fall forward without bracing herself. It is a natural instinct for people to guard themselves with arms extended in front while they are falling.

After that we took another short break to let Susan regain her full composure and we all discussed what had just happened. Since we didn't know Susan and her team very well, one of my members asked about her fall. They were wondering if perhaps she had just gotten a bit overwhelmed and excited and perhaps had just tripped over something and had fallen by her own account. I openly stated how I truly believed her fall was legitimate, because Susan had not followed normal body instincts of bracing herself or breaking her fall by putting her arms out in front of her before she went down. Susan's husband was also there and showed us a bruise that had started to form on her forehead. He was concerned she might have gotten a small concussion from her fall.

I asked Susan what exactly had happened to her. She said she was simply standing and listening to me talk when she began to feel dizzy. She explained how she felt as if someone had hit her really hard on the back of her neck when suddenly everything went black. The next thing she knew, we were helping her up off of the ground. I then explained to her the events as I witnessed them, including the fact that there was no one behind her that could have hit her, and it clearly wasn't one of us. She then wondered if the thing that had possessed her son, had also just attacked and possessed her.

Susan showed us a small medicine bag that she wore around her neck for protection, one that had one hundred-year-old Indian medicine in it. She told me that when she regained consciousness, she felt her medicine bag burning her chest. She explained it would do that whenever bad spirits were around. Susan revealed the medicine bag was part of her Native American culture and it was given to her by a medicine man. She said she never ever goes on investigations without it and felt as if the bag protected her from the negative spirit that night.

I listened in amazement as she told us a bit about her Native American tribal culture and their views on spirits. The depth of her knowledge fascinated me. I felt a bit disappointed in myself, because I didn't know more of my own Native American culture. My dad was between a half and three quarters Cherokee and Choctaw Indian, however no one in our family really passed on much about our Native American culture over the generations. I previously took a college course in Native American history, which taught me a decent amount about Native American culture, but I was certain reading about different cultures was much different than actually living the culture.

We decided to continue our investigation and, again, we broke up into two different groups before heading back out into the cemetery. As I was investigating, I noticed I was also having dizzy spells when suddenly; strange thoughts would come into my mind. On a couple of occasions, I heard a raspy voice that did not belong to me or to any of the investigators I was with. As more time passed, I started to get angry with the team for no apparent reason. Susan must have noticed the changes in my behavior, because she asked me if I was all right. I remember looking at her and feeling very angry with her too, but since I did not know her that well, I didn't want to confront her. I just ignored my emotions and told her I was okay. Instead, I explained to her there were moments where I didn't quite feel like myself.

Not long afterwards, I decided to be completely honest with her and explained how I was feeling emotionally. I confessed to her that I felt angry with her for some reason and how I just wanted to reach over and slap her in the face. I told her I had some thoughts of reaching out and physically attacking her too. This was absolutely out of character for me, as that was not my usual personality. I knew a dark spirit must have been trying to influence my thoughts and I had to shake it off and fight against it. I recalled my previous experience of knowing how negative spirits could influence one's emotions and, if the person wasn't strong enough, they could act-out on their feelings. I told Susan we would both be okay and I wouldn't let this spirit get to me.

I couldn't help but wonder if this same dark spirit was the same one that had attacked Susan that night in the cemetery. Was it possible that it was also the one that had temporarily possessed Billy and caused him to attack his mother? If so, why hadn't it tried to physically attack me like it did her the time it knocked her down? I asked Susan what she thought about it all and she told me that she felt it was the same bad spirit causing the trouble and she was worried that something bad might happen to me if I stayed in the cemetery much longer.

With the help of another trusted O.K.P.R.I. member, I was led outside the cemetery gates, per Susan's request. She wanted to give me some of her medicine from her bag and then she wanted to pray for me in her native tongue. I agreed and we sat down with Susan directly in front of me. She took some of the medicine out of her bag and told me to open up my hand. I did as she asked and then, there in my hand, she placed a broken, leafy herb-type substance. I didn't know what it was exactly, but I trusted she knew what she was doing. Sitting about two feet in front of me, she began praying in Cherokee. I found the language and prayer to be very beautiful.

Within a minute or so, I felt the medicine start to burn in my hand. I didn't know what was going on, but I assumed either my skin was having an allergic reaction to the herbs she gave me or her medicine and prayers were somehow working. As she prayed, she would emphasize certain words stronger than others and she made hand gestures towards me as if she were tossing something at me. I felt strange during those gestures, because I actually experienced what felt like a heavy pressure hitting me in the chest each time her hands motioned toward me.

After the prayer was finished, Susan told me to blow the medicine out of my hand and I did as she instructed. I felt a bit calmer and I thought perhaps whatever negative spirit had tried to attack me was now gone. It was already very late into the night, so we all decided to wrap-up our investigation and head home.

One of my team members showed me an unusual photograph he had captured while he was investigating. In one of the trees, there was a strange looking face. This face did not have full human characteristics, but instead looked more like a horrendous creature. Was this the dark spirit from the cemetery or just another one of the evil feeling spirits that was present and lurking in the cemetery? We weren't certain, especially since all we had was its face to look at. I couldn't wait to get home and thoroughly analyze every recording or photograph.

I told Susan this cemetery investigation was definitely going to be published on our Website and I already knew a fitting name for it. Due the events that had already taken place that night and the souls that were trapped there, I figured the appropriate name for it would be "The Cemetery of the Damned."

After we packed up all of our equipment and were getting ready to leave, we all discussed and agreed upon the idea of returning to investigate the cemetery again sometime in the future. We agreed to think about this decision first to weigh our options and agreed that this cemetery was not for any new or inexperienced investigators. It also should not be a place to recommend to others, due to the potentially harmful events many of us had experienced there. Finally, we all felt we wanted to figure out a way to release the souls who were trapped there. It had been such a crazy night and although our investigation was completed, I still had a few questions I wanted to ask Susan.

Everyone decided to meet at a local gas station up the road before heading home. Before I got in my car, I stood by Susan and we both were looking back up the road that led to the cemetery. We discussed seeing the same shadows dancing about, going between the trees and headstones. It was as if the spirits there were daring us to come back inside the cemetery gates again. I told Susan I was glad the investigation was over and she agreed. Finally, I told her goodbye and that I would be in touch with her.

I got in my vehicle. Little did I know, that night was just the beginning for me and I was face another nightmare over the next three months.

Things seemed to go downhill for me after our visit to the cemetery. I didn't know it at the time, but I later learned the negative entity that had attacked Susan had attached itself to me after all. It hadn't really left me that night in the cemetery like I thought it had. I found with each passing day, I became more and more irritable and found myself filled with emotional anger that seemed to come out of nowhere. At night, I would see and hear my bedroom door open and close and I would hear strange noises. My daughter and I both saw shadows passing throughout various parts of our house. I found myself uncomfortable when I was alone in my house. As more time went by, our whole family seemed to be on edge and fighting with each other.

Things in our house would either be displaced or completely disappear. We occasionally heard the voice of a woman. Except when she spoke, her voice sounded old and raspy. I also had horrible nightmares with events and images that were nearly unimaginable. Before going to bed at night, I would sit on the side of my bed and brush my hair. Occasionally, I found when I looked into the mirror of my headboard; I could see an old woman with long gray hair, squinty dark eyes, a long nose, and a very wrinkly face in the dim light behind me. I could even hear her laugh at me. Sometimes she would make a hateful comment. I knew right then that she was making a point to torment me.

At the time, I did not know where this nasty spirit had come from and didn't think it was from the Cemetery of the Damned. I was under the assumption I was free of spirit attachments that evening before I left the cemetery. As time passed, I spoke to Susan more often. Sometimes she would drop by my house for a visit. One particular day, she stopped by and I began to tell her the strange things I had been experiencing. She took a walk through my entire house to see what she could feel. Susan claimed she was psychically inclined and could see, hear and talk to spirits. As she walked down my hallway, she encountered an old woman who brushed passed her and felt the same bad energy that we had felt that night in the cemetery. My mind began to replay the events that had been taking place at my house and it became clear to both of us the terrible old woman who had been tormenting me and my family was the same negative spirit we had encountered that night in the cemetery and she had indeed followed me home. While we were discussing this connection, we both heard an eerie laugh as if it were mocking us. Susan promised we would take care of her once and for all and she would come back to my house another time to help perform a cleansing to rid my home of this evil entity. This would happen sooner than we both expected.

The Indian Boarding School

Before Susan was able to come over to conduct the cleansing, we had another collaborative team investigation scheduled at an old abandoned Indian Boarding School. My team and I had previously investigated this location a few times on our own about four years prior to joining Susan and her team for this particular investigation. Since the old school was on tribal land and belonged to the same tribe Susan and her husband belonged to, we were given permission to access this location and conduct an investigation. We were happy to have access to it again, as there had been many groups that had tried to conduct their own investigations, but failed at their attempts because they were not tribal members. Many of their tribal members were frightened by the old school due to the numerous sightings and strange occurrences that had taken place. The local tribal police even warned us about the ghostly dangers at the old school before we began our investigation.

On this particular night there were four of us who started the investigation, Susan, her husband, myself and another one of my team members. A few other members joined us a bit later on in the evening. Their work schedules had them working late so they would arrive a couple of hours after the investigation had already started. Strangely enough, even one of the tribal teenage boys who lived close to the school decided to drop in on us uninvited.

One of the standing rules I had established for my team was that no children would be allowed on any investigation and no member or accompanying guest would be allowed on an investigation unless they were at least twenty-one years of age. I had implemented this rule to avoid immaturity and liability issues, which could possibly arise at some point. Susan knew my strict rules, but explained it was tribal rule that no member of the tribe could be forced to leave any part of the reservation complex and he had a right to stay. This caused a bit of a dilemma, because when this teenage visitor arrived and made it known that he was interested in what we were doing, he insisted on coming along with us. According to Susan, we couldn't refuse his access, but we did tell him he had to follow our investigation rules. He informed us he knew of the areas in the school where "ghosts" would stay and he had visited the school on many different occasions, so he could show us where to go.

I didn't put much faith into what this teen was telling us, plus there was just something about him that did not sit right with me. I felt he had "darkness" with him and I questioned Susan about his mental capabilities. After speaking with her, I learned of her reservations about him as well and that this young boy had a history of dabbling in the dark arts quite often. Susan explained he was very troubled and had been into Satanism among other unthinkable things. She also confirmed he had "dark spirits" with him. Since we could not ask him to leave, our only option was to keep a close watch over him in case something unexpected took place. She suggested keeping a video camera recording him at all times, because she felt like stranger things were going to happen that night involving him. Heeding her advice, we allowed him to tag along, but kept our guard up the entire time. I learned more about the darker side of the spirit realm through this 16-year-old boy that night.

After investigating various areas of the old school, we entered the area of the old gym. It had always proven to be spiritually active and had a lot of haunted claims attached to it. The spiritual energy in the gym was said to be very high because some of the tribal members often held pow-wows there. Many people had reported hearing basketballs bouncing when no one was in the gym. Others reported hearing audible voices and seeing shadows moving about. We decided to monitor the gym area for a while and then conduct a "sit-down" for a bit where the team would sit with the energy in the room and attempt to make contact through various experimental methods. We noticed when we entered the gym that the teenage boy began to act strangely.

After walking about fifty-feet inside on the gym floor, a few of us watched as he looked upwards and then reached his right hand up quickly, grabbing a handful of an unseen object and pulled it closely into his chest. He squatted with his face pointing towards the gym floor. Both Susan and I looked at each other knowing that something was not right with the situation. Susan told me she was going to go over and have him sit by her husband during the sit-down, so he could keep an eye on him for all of us. She had a bad feeling that something was about to happen.

I continued to sit on one of the gym benches as Susan got the young teen situated. I couldn't shake the feeling that something wasn't right, so I followed my instinct to go across to the other side of the gym where Susan had gone. For some unknown reason, I felt like she was going to need my help should something happen.

With some equipment in hand, I went over to make sure everything was okay. As I approached closer, I saw Susan motioning for me to come and help her. There, sitting on the bench, was the young boy. He sat with his hands on his knees and his head was still dropped low pointing downwards at the gym floor. Susan was sending quiet signals my way letting me know something was terribly wrong, so I moved in closer and sat on the same bench behind the kid. Susan stood in front of him and began calling his name. He suddenly began growling as his hands dropped down to his feet and he began ripping up his shoes. I looked at Susan and suddenly realized what we were up against. Was this a true possession?

When I was twelve years old, I had attended a church camp where I observed a young teenage girl possessed by an evil demonic spirit. I was close enough at the time to witness the horrible events that took place when the preachers tried to cast the demonic spirits out of this girl, but I wasn't face to face with that demonic spirit like I was now here sitting on the bench by this young possessed boy. This was totally new territory for me and something I wasn't sure I knew how to handle.

If this was a true possession, I wondered what or who was the possessor? I suddenly did a check of my soul and of my faith and prayed a silent prayer to God for help. I had never come up against anything like this before, but I knew I had no time to question or doubt my faith or my abilities. I got a glimpse of this young teen's eyes and they were solid white as if they had rolled toward the back of his head. I felt a horrible fear come over me as I sat there and I was trying to prepare myself for the worst to happen. I honestly didn't know what I would do if this young boy lunged at me or tried to physically attack me. I knew I had to get those thoughts out of my mind, as this was spiritual warfare, a spiritual battle raging and this young teen was the one who was really under attack here. I couldn't help but think back to the one Bible verse found in

> *Ephesians 6:12, "For we wrestle not against flesh and blood, but against principalities, against powers, against the rulers of the darkness of this world, against spiritual wickedness in high places."*

I found myself praying again, asking God for his full protection and help for what we were about to encounter. I wasn't sure how we would handle the situation, but I held onto my faith and gathered strength for what we were about to encounter. Luckily, we had our video recorders going during this time. The following is a detailed transcript of the words and events that took place during this encounter. The name of this young teen will be changed to protect his identity. References to him will be under the name David.

Susan's husband and David are sitting on the bench as Susan approaches. David is sitting on the far end with his head down in his lap. Susan walks up to David.

(Susan) "David? David? Who are you?"

Susan bends down and leans in towards David.

(Susan) "Who are you? Talk to me. Talk to me. David? David? Are you David?"

A long growl emerges from David. Susan waves her hands around his face.

(Susan) "I don't fear you. I have no fear of you what so ever."

Another growl emerges from David as he reaches down and begins to rip his shoes.

(Susan) "That's not scaring me, as I have no fear of you."

David slowly raises his head to look at Susan.

(Susan) "Look at me. Go ahead. Look into my eyes, because I don't fear you. I'm not afraid of you. Who are you? Tell me your name."

David lowers his head back down and shakes his head, no.

(Susan) "Look at me. One who does not look in someone's eyes is a coward. Look at me!"

David growls again as he looks back up at Susan.

(Susan) "You're her and let me tell you right now, I don't fear you."

Susan waves her hands around David's head and shoulders.

(Susan) "I have no fear of you. Look at me in my eyes. I don't fear you, see, I'm not afraid of you. You need to leave him. You need to leave him!"

Susan had suspected the old dark white-haired female spirit that had been bothering me had followed me to the Indian Boarding School and had entered David and began using him as a host.

David's legs begin to shake as he lowers his head back down. He is growling and ripping at his shoes again. Susan continues to wave her hands around David's head and shoulders.

(Susan) "You need to leave him! You need to leave him now!

David growls loudly again as Susan motions for me to come over and sit behind David as he continues to growl. Susan begins lightly shaking David's shoulders.

(Susan) "You need to leave him! You need to leave him now! ...NOW! You need to leave him!"

Susan begins speaking in Cherokee.

(David, in a raspy voice) "It won't work!"

Susan continues to lightly shake David.

(Susan) "David, who's in you? Tell me! Talk to me! David, look up here at me!"

Susan motions for me to come closer and sit directly behind David on the bench. I had a gauss meter and I began measuring EMF readings emitting from David. The meter began alarming madly with readings spiking off the scale.

(Susan) "Why are you with him tonight? Are you afraid? Can you not talk?"

Ten-second pause.

(Susan) "Can you not talk to me?"

David whispers, but he cannot be clearly heard.

(Susan) "I cannot hear you, can you speak louder?"

Susan motioned for me to scoot closer to David. Susan's husband, Jim, turned on the flashlight he had mounted to his hat and he then began walking up towards Susan's side. The light briefly shone on David who then began to hiss and growl even louder than before. David began ripping his shoes again, but this time more violently. His hisses and growls kept getting louder and louder. He did not like the light and it seemed to threaten him.

(Susan) "Jim, turn the light off, turn the light off!"

David's growls and hisses continued, but decreased when Jim turned off his light.

(Susan) "Now tell me who you are. We're in the dark now. Tell me who you are!"

David growls, hisses and then produces a raspy whisper that cannot be understood.

(Susan) "Speak up. Speak your words loud. Who are you? Why are you here? Why are you attached to him?"

(David, in a raspy voice) "Because."

(Susan) "Because why? Did you come from Christy?"

(David, in a raspy voice) "No."

(Susan) "Did you come from Jake?"

(David, in a raspy voice and much louder) "No!"

(Susan, louder) "They why are you here?"

David's hands drop down to his shoes and he begins ripping his shoes again while hissing.

(Susan) "You can make all the noises and growls you can, because I'm not afraid of you. Go ahead! Growl all you want to!"

An investigator takes a couple of photos and David hisses.

(David, in a raspy voice) "No pictures!"

(Susan) "What do you want? What do you want?"

(David, in a raspy voice) "I just want... I just want to..."

(Susan) "You just want what?"

Ten seconds of silence

(Susan) "Why are you afraid of me? I'm just a simple person, so why are you afraid of me? Why do I scare you?"

David shakes his head with jerky movements.

(David, in a raspy voice) "You have…"

Five seconds of silence

(Susan) "I have what?"

David whispers, but it cannot be heard.

(Susan) "I can see it?"

David rips his shoes again as Susan stands up to give her legs a rest. She bends down and gets closer to David's face.

(Susan) "Well, I rebuke you out of him!"

(David, in raspy voice) "I won't go!"

(Susan) "You have to go!"

(David, in raspy voice) "You can't make me!"

(Susan) "I can make you, because I'm not afraid of you. I'm not afraid of you!"

David speaks again in his raspy voice, with his words louder and drawn out as if taunting Susan.

(David) "You can't make me!"

(Susan) "Oh, but I can and you know why I can? Because I walk in the light and you walk in the dark!"

(David) "Not true!"

(Susan) "It is true! This is not your place. It's not your dwelling. I'm with the light and you are with the dark. You need to pass over. You need to leave him!"

Susan laughs as she lightly shakes David.

(Susan) "Well I rebuke you. See, I can touch you. You don't do me any harm. I can touch you and I have no fear of you. You like to torment people don't you?"

(David, in a raspy voice) "Yes!"

(Christy) "Why have you tormented me?"

(David, in a raspy voice) "Because."

(Christy) "Because why?"

(David, in a raspy voice) "You have no business out here."

(Christy, not understanding) "What?"

(Susan, clarifying) "You have no business out here."

(Christy) "Ah! So are you saying that you are from here? We have friends here!"

David suddenly seems to be trying to awaken from his possession. He begins to violently cough and spit as if to get the spirits out of him, as is done in his Native American culture. Then, without warning, another voice is heard that is low and guttural in tone.

(David, in low guttural tone) "Shit!"

Susan and I bend down again to get closer to David. David continues to cough and spit and then tries to come back to himself again.

(Susan) "David? David? David? Remember what I told you about calling upon your grandmother? David! I know you can hear me."

David looks up at Susan for a brief moment before lowering his head back down. The palms of his hands are flat against the floor. David gasps for air and then suddenly laughs as he looks up towards Susan and Christy. His arms begin to shake and he seems to have slipped back into another personality.

(Susan) "Who are you? Who are you now?"

David's head lowers back down in his lap again.

(Susan) "David? David! You have to fight her out of you! David! Sit up! Rise up! She's got you bent over, rise up! David, rise up and look at me! Look at me. You're okay! Look at me!"

No response.

(Susan) "David, look up at me. Don't let her take over your body. Fight her! Do you hear me?"

An investigator takes a picture as David slowly rises up and sits up straight with his hands now on his knees.

(David, in a raspy voice) "No pictures!"

(Susan) "No pictures?"

(David, in a raspy voice) "Erase all of them!"

Susan knew that the light from the camera's flash bothered the spirit and for a minute, it seemed David had come back to himself.

(Susan) "Did you hear what I said? Why did you let her go into you?"

No response.

(Susan) "Can you talk to me?"

(David, as himself) "She's still in me!"

Susan rubs David's shoulder.

(Susan) "Well, you know what? I'll get her out of you, because I'm not afraid of her. Do you hear me?"

(David, as himself) "She's so loud!"

(Susan) "She's got bad magic and she has nothing on you. I'm not afraid of her. She walks in the dark. You need to fight her, David!"

David starts gasping loudly for air and then, with jerky head movements, he slowly looks toward the video camera, which captures his solid-white eyes. Susan and I knew what was happening. The dark spirit was taking over again, so Susan began shaking David on the shoulder.

(Susan) "David, look at me! David, you need to fight her! David? …David?

Silence for about ten seconds

David was, once again, no longer himself as everyone in the room could see the change in his demeanor.

David's head is still facing downwards toward the gym floor.

(Susan) "Now who are you? Who are you? Tell me your name! I'm eye level with you now, so tell me who you are!"

Long pause

(Susan) "What? You have no name? Tell me who you are!"

David's head rises up and begins to jerk as it moves from side to side. He begins to hiss again.

(Susan) "Who are you?" Are you the wicked one?"

David whispers but cannot be heard.

(Susan) "I can't hear you. Only cowards talk under their breath! If you're so powerful, then talk!"

(David, in loud raspy voice) "No!"

(Susan) "Then who are you? Who are you?"

(David, in raspy voice) "Just go!"

(Susan) "If you want to go home, just walk into the light. Are you trapped here? Why are you so mean?"

David's head rises up again and slowly turns. He begins to look around the room. Susan and I stand up again and bend over slightly. Susan waves her hand in front of David's face to get his attention, because she feared a sudden attack from him or on one of the group members.

(Susan) "Look at me, don't look at them! They are nobody. Look at me! Why are you here?"

David looks back up at Susan again.

(Susan) "Why have you been tormenting Christy?"

Silence.

(Susan) "You're a coward, because you won't talk. I called you a coward, talk to me. Why are you here? [Louder] Why are you here? You have no place here. This is not your home. It's not your dwelling and you need to leave!"

(David, in raspy voice) "Yes it is!"

(Susan) "No it's not! You need to leave!"

(David, in raspy voice) "I can't!"

(Susan) "Why can't you?"

(David, in raspy voice) "Lost"

(Susan) "You're lost? I want the truth now. Are you the person who has been tormenting Christy?"

(David, in raspy voice) "Yes!"

(Susan, much louder) "Why? Why? Why have you tormented her so much?"

Silence fills the room. David turns his body in the other direction away from Susan and I, as if to ignore us.

(Susan) "Don't turn away from me! Why have you tormented her so much?"

Susan and I went to the other side and stood back in front of David. Susan lowered her face back in front of David's. David violently jerks his head from side to side as if trying to get away from Susan.

Another group member was video taping the incident, so I motioned for him to come around to the other side to get a better view of David, since he was now facing the opposite direction.

(Susan) "You can jerk your head and keep your eyes rolled back, because I'm not afraid of you. I don't fear you remember? I'm not scared of you and you can't scare me!"

(David, in a raspy voice) "You have magic."

(Susan) "I have magic?"

I bent down and got in David's face.

(Christy) "I demand to know why you have tormented me, because I'm not afraid of you either and I rebuke you as well!"

David begins laughing in a whispery type of tone.

(Christy) "Laugh all you want, go ahead. Your time of playing games with me and tormenting me are through as of now!"

(Susan) "You know why?"

Susan motioned for me to help her. She wanted us to put our arms around David and form a circle around him while he was still sitting on the bench.

(Susan) "You know why? Because we put a circle around you! We put a circle around you and you know something? I rebuke you!"

(Christy) "I rebuke you as well!"

(Susan) "And I want you to go!"

David begins laughing in an eerie tone.

(Susan) "You cannot break our hold. Go ahead and try!"

(Christy) "It will not work!"

David continues to laugh.

(Susan) "You need to leave! You need to leave this body now! David! David! DAVID! You need to wake up and look at me! Rise up! Your grandma's here with you!"

Susan looks over at me.

(Susan) "Christy, don't let go of my hands."

(Christy) "I won't, but I have stuff in my hand. One of you guys come over and get this stuff please!"

(David, in a raspy voice) "I won't let him go! I won't let go!"

(Susan) "Don't break this hold Christy!"

(Christy) "I won't!"

A group member comes over and takes the equipment out of my left hand.

(David, in raspy voice) "I won't let him go!"

(Susan) "You can't, you can't break this hold! David! David! The wicked one goes away! The wicked one goes a way! Do you hear me? David?"

223

(David, in a raspy voice) "I won't let go!"

(Susan) "If you're so powerful, what's going on with you now? You won't show your face, you won't talk because you are sealed with the light! We sealed you in the light and you cannot do any harm to him, to me or to her! You are a coward and you need to go! I rebuke you and you need to go! David, you're there, come around! David! Raise your head up! David, come on, come on, she is gone!"

(Christy) "Come on David, wake up!"

(Susan) "Come on David, come on, she's gone!"

(Christy) "Come on David, wake up!"

(Susan) "Come on David! I'm not going to break this circle. David, come on. She's gone. You've got to fight her David! She's going to stay with you if you don't!"

(Christy) "Wake up David, come on, sit up."

(Susan) "Christy, you can use your hand but don't break the circle."

Both Susan and I tried to raise David's head up with our arms. We lightly shook David with our arms in hopes of bringing him back around to his normal self and to keep the dark evil witch-like spirit from maintaining control. Susan began to speak to David in Cherokee again.

(Susan) "David! Osiyo [hello] Come on David."

Susan looked at Christy.

(Susan) "Christy, I want us to lower our arms towards his butt and we're going to raise our arms up."

(Christy) "Okay."

(Susan, to the evil spirit) "Whenever we raise our arms up over his head, you are to be gone! You are to be gone out of him and we rebuke you. You cannot bother anyone in this room!"

David tries lunging forward to break the circle.

(Susan) "You are not strong enough to break our hold. You are not strong enough to break our hold! I rebuke you. We don't fear you. We think you are a coward. You pick on people and you like to torment them."

David started to look at Susan but then stopped and lowered his head back down again.

(Susan) "Go ahead and look at me. You can look at me in the eyes because I'm not afraid of you. Whenever we lift our hands up, you are to be gone out of this child and you are never to come back and work on people or work on their souls!"

David begins laughing again in an eerie tone.

(Susan) "Go ahead and laugh. Go ahead, because you think you are powerful, don't you? Don't you?"

Susan and I began to gently shake David again. Then Susan said she saw the spirit of David's grandmother, who was there trying to help.

(Susan) "David, your grandmother is calling you. Look at me, look at me, over here to your left! Your grandmother's calling you. Do you hear her? She's saying, 'David, David! Fight it, fight it!' Do you hear me? David? Let go of him, let go of him you witch! David, do you hear me? You ought to hear your grandmother; she's calling for you. Do you hear her? David, you need to open up your eyes and see your grandmother! David!"

(Christy) "Come on David, you can do it! She's here!"

(Susan) "She's here, come on David. She's here saying, 'David, I'm here to help you. David, David!' Leave him, you witch!"

David begins laughing hysterically in a raspy tone.

(Susan) "David! David!"

Susan begins to talk to David in Cherokee again, but David only hissed and laughed louder. Susan continued to talk to him in Cherokee. There was silence for about thirty seconds and everything seemed calm.

(Susan) "You can break, Christy."

(Christy) "Raise up now?"

Susan nodded, so we both raised our arms up over David's head, while keeping a circle formed. As we did, David began to violently cough and spit again. As soon as our arms were no longer touching David, he became weak and began to fall forward towards the floor, but we caught him. David began to cough and spit again.

(Susan) "David? David? Are you okay? Do you need to go outside? David, look at me. David, look at me!"

Susan gently touched his face with her fingers and brushed his hair away from his eyes.

(Susan) "I want you to go home, okay? Look at me. She's not with you now. Look at me. I want you to go home now. Do you hear me? She's not with you anymore so don't be afraid. Can you hear me? I'm going to have Jim walk you out the door. Go home, okay? Tell me that you're going to go home, okay? David?"

(David, as himself) "Yes."

(Susan) "Okay then, I want you to go home now."

(David, as himself) "She won't touch me or anything anymore?"

Susan gave him a hug.

(Susan) "No and that's why I want you to go home, because you don't need to stay here. You let her get in you. Yeah, you opened up and let her get in you and you can't do that."

Susan turned to look at Jim.

(Susan) "Jim, I want you to take him out of here and home."

Susan turned back to look at David.

(Susan) "David, I want you to go back home now, okay?"

David shook his head yes and then stood up and began walking toward towards the door. Jim and the other members took David outside of the gym.

The event only lasted a little over fifteen minutes, however it seemed to last much longer as it was happening. There were so many times we heard David growl or speak in another voice and this experience had honestly scared me. I was so glad I had never associated myself with any dark arts. I felt so relieved to be on God's side and fighting the good fight rather than walking and fighting on the side of darkness. I remember how close in proximity I was to David and how frightened I was whenever he looked directly at me with his solid white eyes. I thought, for sure, he was about to lunge and attack me. Quite honestly, I don't know what I would have done if he had. How does one prepare for something like that? Knowledge and experience are great tools when facing something this negative. Luckily, we had it all on video as proof of this event.

After the incident with David, all but Susan and I stood there in the gym discussing the events that had just taken place. We were both still a bit in awe and in shock. I asked Susan if she thought we had really gotten the evil entity out of him. She felt like the witch had left him, but there were more negative spirits that were bound to him and wouldn't leave. Susan said these other spirits were ones he had already had with him from his times of dabbling in dark magic. I asked her how she knew about David's dabbling and she told me she had known him and his family for quite a few years. They had spoken about David's unusual habits. Some of the tribal members even referred to his dark art practices as dealing in "bad medicine." Susan stated she knew for a fact that David had done certain "rituals," which had enabled him to bring forth bad spirits and the bad medicine.

We both discussed how the incident unfolded and agreed when David entered the gym, he had opened himself up to this dark spirit. We could only guess he had done it out of curiosity and to find out whom she was and what power she possessed. It was obvious David had been willing to let her take control of him, which is something she could not do with me in the past, since I kept my guard up, prayed and would not let her in.

As we continued talking, we felt the gym's energy begin to thicken. We began to look around the gym and noticed there were many spirits coming into the gym and heading over towards us. We didn't know where this dark spirit had gone, but we knew something had to be happening, because we saw elder tribal spirits and other Native American spirits filling the gym and surrounding us.

We stood a little closer together and watched as an elder spirit approached us. He was an older Native American spirit who appeared very gentle in nature. He asked me why I had brought the witch out here with us, since she was a bad spirit and they did not wish for her to be there. Other spirits around him agreed, but only the elder spoke. I apologized to him and told him I did not mean for her to follow me to the school or any place for that matter. I told him I knew she was bad, but she had followed me home one night from a bad cemetery and had since refused to leave me alone. The elder said he understood and accepted my apology and offered to help me. He asked us to leave the gym.

I wasn't sure just how this elder tribal member and these other spirits would be able to help me, but I felt I had to trust him and the others. I did not want to disrespect them in any way either, so I thanked the elder and the other spirits for offering their help. Susan motioned for me to follow her out of the gym. We left and headed out to our vehicles, which were parked about 500 feet from the gym and admin area. We needed to see if Susan's husband, Jim, and the others were back from taking David home and to see how the rest of the investigators were going.

As Susan and I arrived at our vehicles, we suddenly heard a raspy but familiar shrill voice yell out my name, "Christy!" After hearing this, Susan and I looked at each other and said, "Did you hear that?" We both nodded our heads and immediately knew it was the old evil witch. Susan encouraged me to ignore her, because she wasn't able to get to me now since the other Native American spirits were helping us to get rid of her.

We joined the rest of the group, who had returned from taking David home, and we all started talking about the strange events that had taken place with David that night. Most of us were still in shock and couldn't believe what had happened. During our conversation, all of us heard the dark evil spirit calling my name over and over again. Hearing her call my name sent chills up and down my spine. I knew I had to ignore her, but I also was curious about what it was that she wanted?

Part of me was tempted to take some equipment and head back into the gym to see what was going on and to see what I could get recorded, however the other part of me knew better and I would probably be putting myself in danger. Everyone in our group acknowledged hearing her voice and our theory was that she was, most likely, still in the gym and trapped there by the spirits who had offered to help me. I didn't know why she was frantically calling my name and I could only assume it was so I would come back in there so she could reattach herself to me, but I wasn't giving in to her.

The more she called my name, the more I felt she deserved what was happening to her, so I yelled out to her to shut up and to leave me alone. I also told her she deserved everything she was getting for the torment she gave me for so long. As moments passed by, her screams for me became more urgent as if she were running out of time. Then within about a five-minute period, we all heard her final scream and then nothing but silence. The air was calm and it was as if she had disappeared.

I couldn't help but wonder what the Native American spirits had done to her. Had the spirits in the gym really done away with her for good? If so, how did they do it? I knew there were just some things that we in the physical realm weren't meant to know but I was very curious. Now, I could only wait to see if the help the Native American spirits gave me had truly worked and if I would finally be rid of the evil witch.

I thought back to the time when I had the other nasty spirit, named Pamela, following me. This time the witch hadn't bothered me as badly as Pamela once had, but I believed that was only because I was better protected and better versed this time around on how to handle bad spirits when I encountered them. Prior to our investigations at the Cemetery of the Damned and the Indian boarding school, I thought I was pretty well protected, but I learned there are always new levels of protection to be discovered and utilized.

What most people don't understand is that it is nearly impossible to predict what you would do in a circumstance like this, until you are actually faced with it. After this incident, we only let a few trusted people we knew watch the video of this incident. They were all very shocked by what they saw. Each made similar comments about being aware of negative forces in the paranormal field, but stated they had never come across anything like that, ever. They also mentioned they really didn't know if they would be prepared for an encounter like that, if they were ever faced with one.

A few weeks had passed since that night's investigation and the incident with David and it remained a very vivid event. It also came to a point where it didn't matter how much time would pass; it would always be a night I would never forget. I was very thankful the Native American spirits had agreed to help me. Even though I didn't know how they did it, their help worked. I haven't seen or heard from the evil witch since that night in the Native American Boarding School.

I found it curious that our roles that night as paranormal investigators and Native American Spirits were reversed. We were the ones typically helping spirit and not the other way around. This incident helped me understand that those of us in the physical realm could work together with those in the spirit realm. Of course, I knew there was no way any of us in physical form could ever understand all the aspects of the spirit realm, but I was amazed by the things I had seen and heard from spirits and couldn't wait to see what else they had to share with me in the future.

I obtained a new level of respect for spirit that night. As a result, I made another permanent rule for my group. It stated that no member of my team would ever be allowed to provoke or test the spirits at an investigation. I knew negative spirits had the potential to be nasty and I didn't want any of my team members' behavior to be the cause for a physical attack. Most paranormal investigators I have spoken to had never experienced anything like this before, so I hoped I would never have to face something like this again. Little did I know, I would encounter a different, yet somewhat similar unexpected attack a couple of years later.

The Eldorado Haunting

In September of 2008, I received an email from the concerned sister of a family in Eldorado, Oklahoma, who was experiencing frightening events in their home. The couple was in their fifties and had purchased an old home they planned to fix-up and live in for their retirement. After reading the urgent email, I forwarded it to my case manager who immediately called this couple to see what they had been experiencing. After their phone conversation, my case manager called me to fill me in on some of the information and to let me know if our group would be taking this case or not.

The couple in this home was very scared and reported seeing apparitions, shadows, hearing audible voices, growls and strange sounds such as a huge wet dog shaking its fur. They had constantly heard footsteps walking around through various rooms and felt they were being watched, making them feel very uncomfortable in their own home. They even reported smelling foul and rotten odors. One morning, they had awaken to find their bedding covered in a urine-smelling liquid along with a strange symbol drawn on the female homeowner's forehead and right cheek. A white goo-like substance was found in the male homeowner's hair, which caused it to fall out in that specific area. These last two events are what prompted them to seek help with what they were experiencing in their home. They first consulted his sister and told her what had been happening. She began a search on the Internet for a reputable group that could help her family and they chose our group.

Our group began researching the history of this location and learned it was originally built in 1907. It was, at one time, a church and a parsonage. When the church closed down, the two buildings were combined and turned into a home. It was easy to tell from its design that it had once been two different buildings combined into one. The longest any family had owned the home was twenty-seven years. The shortest was two months. The home also had renters throughout the years too. We had also spoken with a couple of prior owners of the home who verified that the house had strange activity taking place within it, some mentioned similar activity as the current homeowners had been experiencing.

One day, the homeowners told us they were remodeling in one of the kitchen areas. The weather was cold outside, so they had all of their windows shut and kept their doors closed. While they were peeling some of the old paint off of the cabinets, a swarm of flies suddenly appeared in the kitchen and had surrounded them. They reached for some bug spray and began spraying the files in the air, but instead of dropping dead to the ground, they vanished into thin air. This was just one of many paranormal phenomena that had the family baffled and scared.

The female homeowner believed this entity was demonic in nature and was planning to have clergy come and bless their home, but first they wanted some answers. They wanted to know what was really haunting their home, so they could know the truth about what they were dealing with. They asked our team to investigate and planned to have a cleansing of their home done after we were finished.

When I had heard mention of the word, "demon," I couldn't help but wonder if they were just simply scared out of their mind and quickly jumped to that conclusion, or if it was, in fact, true. I had previously encountered many homeowners that didn't completely understand the paranormal and how rare a demonic haunting is. Many of them would automatically assume their troubles were created by a demonic presence. Of course, in all my years of investigating, I've never taken their assumptions lightly as I know from experience in this field that anything is possible and one can never be too careful.

Our group usually stayed booked with cases three to four months in advance, but when this investigation request came in, we knew we had to put it at the top of our priority list. Ironically, just a couple of days before we were scheduled for a different residential investigation, the client had cancelled, which left an opening for that Saturday. We called the Eldorado couple and told them about our recent opening and they were thrilled. They asked us to come out to their home that weekend and help them. We agreed and set-up the details of our trip over the phone.

Normally, I am not given any details of our cases before and even during the majority of an investigation. My case manager handles all the details and client relations. However, in this instance, he felt I needed to know a few of the facts on this particular investigation for safety reasons, since what the homeowners described seemed beyond a typical haunting. After learning about a few of the ins and outs, I scheduled a group meeting for that Friday night. I felt it was necessary and only fair of me to let the group know about the potential dangers of this case and caution them about what we might be encountering during this investigation. I always give my team members the option of opting-out of any case if they ever feel uncomfortable. I wrestled with the decision to let particular members go, but I also did not want to deny them the opportunity to learn about potential demonic cases like this one. They had to gain their experience somehow, so I agreed to open the case to all members, as long as each one followed the rules of respect and no provoking of any spirit in case it turned out to be a nasty one.

At our meeting, my case manager and I advised the entire team about the strange phenomenon reported at this house. I warned everyone about the potential dangers and informed them that the homeowners believed a demonic entity might be present. I gave them all the option to sit-out this investigation and if they felt like they were not mentally or spiritually prepared for what our team might encounter. I also wanted to let them know this could be just like any other investigation and the homeowners could simply be exaggerating the dangers. We wouldn't really know until we were there on location and conduct the investigation. One of my newer members, who was still in training, decided she would stay at home while we went. She didn't feel comfortable enough with her knowledge in the group to attend the investigation. I was very proud of her for her honesty and we all promised her we would keep her posted on the night's events.

I was still skeptical about this investigation, being a demonic case, but I also couldn't shake the reservations I had about this it either. So far, after nine years investigating the paranormal, I knew anything could happen, especially after all of the crazy experiences I had in the past. I didn't want to go in with a disbelieving attitude and take the risk of us putting ourselves in danger if we weren't careful. I knew I had encountered bad situations in my past with negative entities, but I felt I was also spiritually strong and prepared in case we should encounter something horrible.

I made sure I prayed and asked for God's help before we left that Saturday to make the three-hour drive to Eldorado, Oklahoma. I wasn't going to make the same mistake I had with the Indian Boarding School a couple of years prior by not putting God first in the investigation's prayers. I have learned to put God first and pray and ask Him for His help more and more with each year that passed, especially before I conduct an investigation.

All my investigators seemed lighthearted, as usual, and we enjoyed our long road trip. We stopped for dinner and to got a few snacks for the long night ahead. When we were about thirty minutes away from the residence, my case manager received a call from the homeowners. They frantically told him about some strange activity they had just witnessed. They were walking down one of their hallways to go to another room when they were stopped dead in their tracks, because they saw their clothes hangers start to shake in an open closet. They said they had also heard strange sounds like pops, footsteps and growls earlier that evening. They were very nervous about being there alone without the team. They told my case manager they would now be waiting outside for us, because they feared for their safety if they were in the house any longer.

When we finally arrived, we saw the homeowners standing under their carport patiently waiting for us. They saw us pull up into their driveway and immediately came over to our vehicle. They began to tell us more about the things that they had just experienced. After speaking with them, we could tell they were badly shaken. We wanted to do an interview with them and asked if they would be willing to show us some of the places they had experienced the strange activity. They agreed, but only if we were in the house with them.

We followed the homeowners into the two-story home. We could tell it was quite old and knew why the homeowners were remodeling it. Age had taken its toll on the turn-of-the-century home and it was definitely in need of some repair. We began an in-home interview with them and recorded their experiences on video in each of the rooms they had experienced activity. After our in-home interview, the clients turned the house over to us and told us to lock up when we were through. They had made plans to stay over night with some relatives who lived in a neighboring town.

While a few of us were inside with the homeowners, some of the other investigators began taking some photos outside. They had experienced a few strange things in the back yard. Two investigators were taking photographs of the side and back yard area of the home and both witnessed seeing a tall shadow pass in front of them. A few seconds later, as they separated several feet from each other to cover different angles, one of the investigators audibly heard a low but guttural voice yell to her to, "Get out!" She told the other investigator about it and asked him if he had heard the voice too, but he denied hearing it. He walked a bit closer to her to discuss what she had heard and to snap a few photos in the direction of the voice, when suddenly they both heard the same low guttural voice yell again, "Get out!" Unfortunately, neither investigator had their audio recorder turned on at the time and it was not captured as evidence. Upon review of the photographs taken, one in particular appeared to show the face of a strange image. Recreations of this black and red image were attempted but the photograph was unable to be duplicated.

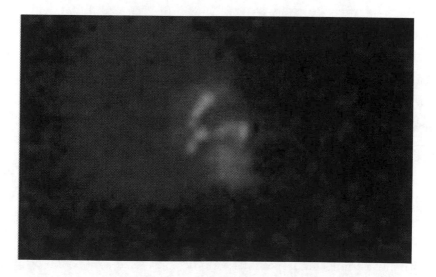

While a few of the investigators were continuing to do outside sweeps, I did my normal routine of conducing a psychic walk-through of the home. This walk-thru consists of myself and a couple of other investigators going from room to room listening and paying attention to anything I may pick up on psychically while the other investigators take note of my findings. Normally, one of the investigator's who follows me is my researcher. This is so the researcher can take notes and find documentation later on that might validate any information I receive.

During my walk-through, there were a few significant things that stood out to me. In the dining room area, I saw the room change and five men were sitting at a dark wooden table. There was a young white male sitting in the middle to one side. He appeared to be a leader of sorts and had a short military haircut, piercing blue eyes and wore a red robe. Then I saw an old book that had a brown leather binding sitting open in front of him. Candles were burning in several areas on the table and I heard chanting with words I could not understand. I felt like these men had summoned some sort of demonic entity. I believed this to be true when suddenly; I saw a hideous-looking creature standing before the leader. I heard him command the creature to perform an act of vengeance and murder and after the task was done, it was to return to him. Then in a flash, I saw a man being attacked by this demonic entity, causing his death.

I relayed this to my team, who was documenting the information. Something my team has learned, throughout the years of working with me, is if something I saw concerning spirit message doesn't make sense at the time, it might become clear later on when the historical research is completed.

We were investigating the upstairs area of the home and went into the master bedroom since it was an area the homeowners had claimed to be very active. I began taking photos in the room when my camera captured a strange light anomaly off of the stand up furnace that was in the room. Normally a strange light like this could be considered a reflection off of a metal surface but after analyzing this one, I didn't feel that was the case with this photo. During this time we were also getting emf spikes and we were able to record a few class c evps.

We continued our walk-through in the spare bedroom. It was the next major area where I received interesting information. It was here that I saw a little girl around the age of six sitting on the floor playing. She was in a light pale-looking yellow dress, nice socks and black dress shoes. She looked up at me and smiled; then her face suddenly changed into this same hideous-looking creature I had seen earlier. It lunged forward at me as if it was going to attack, but before it could, it quickly disappeared.

I described how it was ashen-gray in color and that it had large orange-brownish-red eyes and a large mouth with jagged teeth. It really didn't have much of a nose but it did have several growths beneath its chin with large horn-type appendages protruding all around its neck. When it lunged at me, I heard it snarl and growl and found myself quickly taking steps backwards. I knew then that we weren't dealing with any normal ghost. I felt as if we were dealing with something much more powerful. I knew we had to be careful with the way we handled the remainder of our investigation and our presence around this entity.

Almost immediately after the creature had lunged at me, I became physically ill. My head began to hurt and spin. My stomach was nauseated and I began to break out in a light sweat. I called the team together in the living room and split everyone up in two teams, so they could conduct their sweeps to collect all sorts of data. I spoke with them about what I saw and cautioned them on the situation at hand. I had decided to go with team two, because I felt I needed to get out of the house for a while and see if my symptoms would subside.

Team two went outside and we set up our foldout chairs to prepare for our wait. This home was in a rural country setting, so the whole area seemed a bit dark without any city lights to provide extra illumination. It was quiet and each of us could hear the sounds of the night, including a few cows off in the distant pasture. As we sat, we had casual conversation and one of my investigators kept feeling like she was being poked in the back of her head. We didn't quite know what to make of it, so we continued our conversation. It was cut short a couple of times when we heard rustling off in the bushes beside the house about twelve feet from where we were sitting. We also heard what sounded like an audible growl and our first thoughts were that it was an animal off in the distance. We got up to investigate the rustling and growling sound, but we found no animal present or other source for the noise.

We continued to talk and I began to feel even more ill. My head was hurting badly and I became even sicker to my stomach. I started to break out again in a light sweat and felt like I needed some air. I told my team how I was feeling and the longer I sat there, the worse I felt. I got up thinking that maybe if I got up and walked around for a bit, I would feel better. I excused myself and walked in front of our parked vehicle.

Suddenly, I became weak, dizzy and felt like I was going to fall down. I leaned over the hood of the van to keep my balance. After a minute, one of my team members came over to check on me. For confidentiality reasons, I will call this female investigator, Lindsey. I told Lindsey how I was feeling and she suggested I lay down on the bench seat in the van. I agreed and did as she suggested, hoping the sick spell would pass.

As I lay there, I kept seeing the face of the same hideous creature I had seen upstairs in the house. I also kept hearing a low guttural growl and a high-pitch hiss. I felt myself becoming very angry, irritable and wanting to reach out and choke one of my team members. I knew these thoughts and emotions were not my own. Red flags went up and I immediately knew I was under heavy spiritual attack from this entity. I began rebuking it and commanding it to leave me alone. I prayed to God, asking Him to deliver me from this evil presence. I pictured protective shields all around me. The stronger I tried to make them, the sicker I felt. I also heard a voice over and over again telling me to stop fighting and let it have control. I kept saying, "No" and continued visualizing my protective shields and I continued to pray. At one point, I saw my shields flickering like light struggling to stay on, but was about to burn out. I kept praying, asking God to help me fight this creature.

When my investigator and friend, Lindsey, came back over, she offered to get me some water. I thanked her and decided to sit up for a minute to see if I would feel any better. I told her I was very angry and felt like choking someone and that I knew I was under attack by this demonic entity. She looked at me with a shocked look on her face and said I had a "wild look" in my eyes. She could tell I wasn't completely myself. I reassured her I was fighting it and wasn't going to let it take control of me.

Lindsey said she would be right back with my water and before she could walk off, I felt the sickness suddenly release. When Lindsey was returning to the van with my water, I suddenly heard her call out my name in an urgent panic. I immediately jumped out of the van to render my help. Once she reached the van, she gripped the side door and very quickly called my name three times. Within seconds, Lindsey fell backwards and hit the ground. I was almost to her side before she fell, but wasn't quite fast enough to catch her before she hit the ground. We all heard the loud thud of her fall, which caught the other two investigators off guard. The other two investigators came running towards us. Looking back on this incident, I noted when Lindsey fell backwards; she hit the ground hard but didn't, in any way shape or form, try to brace her fall. If she had, the validity of her attack and fall might have been questioned.

The other two investigators and I, at Lindsey's side, were all in complete shock and wondered what had just happened to her. I checked her immediately for a pulse and to see if she was breathing. We all noticed Lindsey's body was very stiff and her limbs were positioned out straight outwards, like a board. She didn't appear to be having a seizure either. I knew Lindsey quite well and knew she didn't have any medical problems that would make her collapse like this.

As Lindsey lay there, she was unconscious and unresponsive. My mind raced trying to think of a logical explanation for her present state, but couldn't think of anything. About a minute had passed since she had fallen and I was starting to panic while trying to get her to regain consciousness. I didn't want to imagine the worst, however deep inside of me; I knew this entity must have been the one to cause her fall.

Then suddenly, without warning, we heard a growl emerge from out of her throat as if to threaten us to leave her alone. I immediately knew what was wrong with her. My belief was confirmed and I knew it was now trying to take control of her. I began silently praying and kept telling the entity to leave her alone. I desperately needed God's help to deliver Lindsey from this evil and demonic presence. I had some of the other investigators light me some sage too and I let it burn in my hand and put it next to Lindsey. I was trying all avenues to help her.

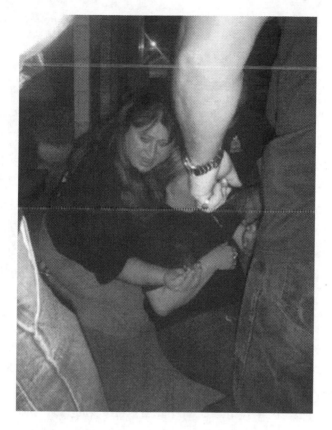

The more I prayed the more the entity used Lindsey's vocal cords to laugh and growl at us. I asked one of my investigators to get one of the other guys from the inside team to come help me get her up and off the ground. She was too stiff and nearly impossible to move without the extra hands. Help was there almost immediately and one of my investigators, who also had some experience in spiritual matters, came over to assist me in trying to bring Lindsey to full consciousness.

Without any warning, Lindsey's body suddenly became limber and we heard a long raspy breath come out of her mouth. Her eyes began to flutter and she awoke to full consciousness. I knew the demonic entity had finally released her and a wave of relief came over me.

The whole incident only lasted for a little over four minutes, but at the time, it felt like such an eternity. When Lindsey finally came to, she was complaining about pain in various parts of her body. I knew she would be sore, especially the next morning because of the hard fall she had taken. She questioned us about what happened to her. When we told her, she was quite shocked about what had just transpired. She informed us the only thing she remembered was standing beside the van when she suddenly felt very dizzy, as if she were drunk, so she started calling out my name. She remembered grabbing on to the side of the van to keep her balance and then suddenly everything went black. Next, she saw this ugly looking creature grab her face and it began telling her to acknowledge it. As she described the "creature," it sounded just like the one that I had encountered in the upstairs bedroom. Lindsey said there were a couple of times when she heard my voice talking to her, but she said she couldn't respond because it felt like she was in a dream state and couldn't wake up.

After we made sure that Lindsey was okay, we asked her if she wanted us to get her to a hospital. She said, "No" and that she would be okay, but she did want to sit out for the rest of the investigation. Our group talked about wrapping up and going home given the circumstances that had already occurred that evening. We had driven a long way and I knew the homeowners were counting on us to conduct a complete investigation, but I also knew they would understand if we left early, given what had happened. I knew everyone on the team was a bit rattled too, so I had everyone take a group vote about leaving or staying to complete the investigation. Everyone voted to stay and finish, but some didn't want to go back into the house, so they volunteered to stay outside.

Once the investigation resumed, the team heard audible voices, another growl and an odd laugh. I went back in the house with part of the team. I had to continue being the fearless leader even though I knew the dark entity was still in the house with us lurking in the shadows. I had to be strong and not show any fear. Whatever it was, it was definitely nothing nice. It was demonic, in my opinion, and something I really wanted no part of. I was no demonologist and I honestly did not have enough faith in myself to go up against this demon on my own. It was very hard for all of us to finish our investigation.

Normally, I don't burn sage at a location, but I felt the urge to do so once we finished our investigation. I silently prayed for the homeowners and asked God to bless the home. I was not only physically drained, but emotionally as well. I was ready to leave and head back home. The whole evening had really taken a toll on me and I was just glad to be done.

On the way home, we talked about the evening and two of my investigators didn't know if they wanted to continue investigating anymore. Lindsey was one of them. I personally couldn't blame her, given the circumstances and everything she had been through.

I went to bed that night and had horrible nightmares of the "demonic creature" chasing me. No matter where I ran or where I hid, it continued to follow me. Not only did I have horrible nightmares that night, but every night for the next week. I spoke with Lindsey during this time and she reported the same type of nightmares. Were our dreams just a product of our emotions brought to the surface by our subconscious fears? I personally didn't think so, since I had dealt with spirit for so many years.

This case bothered me and I knew I had to find some answers, so I contacted a couple of clergymen for guidance. After explaining the case to them, they told me they agreed we were dealing with a demonic presence of some sort. I had my group researcher look into the meaning of a symbol that had been drawn on female homeowner's cheek. She found that the symbol closely resembled another that was used to represent one of a hierarchy of seventy-two demons captured by King Solomon. This demon also resembled the one Lindsey and I had described seeing.

According to legend, King Solomon of Israel captured seventy-two demons and sealed them in a brass container and threw it into a lake to hide from the Babylonians. Eventually, they found the vessel thinking there was treasure inside and broke it open, releasing the demons. It was said that King Solomon studied demons and some believed he had the knowledge and power to utilize them to do his bidding. While the thought of a "holy" king messing with around demons seems a bit odd, documentation states he used his knowledge and powers for Godly reasons.

Still not satisfied with just the answers I had received from the clergymen, I went ahead and contacted a well-known Demonologist, John Zaffis, to see if he could provide some sort of logical explanation for the events that had transpired that evening in Eldorado. After explaining it all to him, including the symbol that we were researching, and the incident that happened to Lindsey and I, he told me it sounded like we were dealing with some sort of lower demonic minion.

He explained in the demonic realm, there are different levels of demons and each demon type had legions of demons under them. Lower ranking minions could take on the characteristics of higher-level demons. He thought that might explain why the negative entity we encountered closely resembled the well-known prince demon, Belial.

When I asked him why there were only two of us that were spiritually and physically attacked, he asked in return if I had any gifts or psychic abilities. I told him yes and also mentioned that my investigator, Lindsey, was a strong sensitive. He told me that was the reason we were attacked. He said people like us were natural targets for negative entities, such as this one. He referred to the old saying; "Take down the strong holds first," which meant it needed to affect those with spiritual gifts first before it went for the weaker spiritually minded ones. He further explained how it wasn't a good idea for people like me with strong spiritual gifts to be around negative energies or to even investigate places that had bad energies, because they would always target me.

I knew his words were true, because of all my past experiences. However, I also felt it was a risk I would have to take in order to help those in need. I thanked John for his time and advice and ended our conversation. Still baffled by everything, I finally came to the conclusion this negative spirit was definitely some sort-of demonic entity, but I didn't know to what extent. I made up my mind that a few of us needed to go back to finish this investigation completely and in depth. I also wanted to conduct more extensive research, not just on this location, but on the demonic entity that was there too. I wanted answers for this case!

During this same time, we had been working with a reporter from one of the local news stations. The reporter had been working on an assignment where he had been writing paranormal related stories published on a webpage called, "The Ghost Writer." This web page covered strange cases of paranormal phenomenon taking place in Oklahoma. To maintain confidentiality, I will call this reporter, Shawn.

Shawn had already written several stories about O.K.P.R.I. and some of the places we investigated. He was supposed to be with us at our initial investigation in Eldorado, but ended up not being able to make it that night. A couple of days after our investigation, Shawn got in contact with me to ask how the investigation went. He also wanted to know if he could do an interview with a few of us and use some of our video footage for his story. I agreed and met with him to give him the full story.

I described the events from that night. During my interview, I explained that we weren't completely sure what we had encountered that night, but clergy and John Zaffis had suggested it was perhaps a demonic minion of sorts. I further explained that we were still conducting research and hadn't come to a full conclusion for the case. For the sake of our team's reputation, I wasn't comfortable with putting everything out there for the public about how our encounters that night were with a full-fledged demonic entity, especially through the local news media. I was confident it was demonic in nature, but wasn't certain how to present that information to the public, nor did I know if I wanted to allow a reporter to determine how to represent it in certain terms. I especially felt this way since the word "demon" was already used far too often in the paranormal field. A group can also become a laughing stalk among other investigative groups if they were ever to announce a demonic entity encounter before concluding all investigations and research on a location. Even then, the research and evidence had to really hold strong against all logical explanations in order to support the claim.

Intrigued by our story and by the video evidence we revealed to him, Shawn couldn't wait to get the story out there. I did ask Shawn to approach this story with regard to our professionalism and be careful with how he put it together, as I did not want our group to be under any scrutiny. Come to find out, his story would have repercussions on our team later on.

The title of his story became, *"The Demon of Eldorado"* and as I feared would happen, other paranormal teams began calling us fakes and liars, especially one team leader in Oklahoma who was notorious for publically slandering other teams any way she could. Many groups had learned to avoid this woman and any dealings with her out of mistrust, so luckily most did not listen to her criticism of our team. We were glad when her presence within the paranormal community faded away by the year 2012 along with all the trouble she brought to others.

Regardless of some of the negative comments received, our team never officially classified our investigation in Eldorado it as a demonic haunting. The media had through Shawn. However, we all had our strong suspicions about what we experienced that night, but we also knew if some of those same ridiculing teams had experienced what we had, then they too would be at a loss for a complete and thorough explanation.

Later, Shawn decided to go out to the house in Eldorado to conduct his own video investigation. He took his wife along with him and spent some time inside the home recording video. They kept cameras recording inside while they went outside to record for a while. He stated that the house seemed very quiet. He was really disappointed and didn't think he would have anything on his video footage when he went to review it.

About a week later, he called me and was shocked to let me know that his camera had recorded some strange sounds in the house along with a low gruff sounding voice in several sections of his video. He, too, became a full believer that something strange was taking place in the Eldorado home.

We spoke with the homeowners about their case and they asked us to come back after about two months of time. Only a few of us had agreed to go. I was hoping that nothing negative would happen again. I decided to go, but only if I was fully rested and had strong spiritual shields in place, just in case. Only two of the original team members present that first night had returned with me. I knew I needed to put some closure to this case and figure out exactly what was there if possible.

Just as before, the homeowners greeted us. After showing them all the evidence and research from the prior investigation, we gave them their own personal copy and they left us on our own to investigate again. Unexpectedly, the house was very quiet, but I caught a few glimpses of the so-called little girl. I never saw her change into the creature and I didn't take the time to confront her. Strangely enough, there were also a few other souls that had been deceitfully enticed to come there by this demonic minion who once was portrayed as this "little girl." All spirits present were lost and wandering souls looking for answers and hope, including that of a young woman who had committed suicide many years ago. The evening overall, however was very quiet and nothing out of the ordinary happened.

Upon review, our evidence did reveal a few voices, some asking for help, some as random conversations and then, of course, the voice of the unknown negative one telling us to get out, along with a few other vocal threats. I was glad it hadn't tried to attack us that night, but my question was why? Why had it attacked on the initial investigation, but not on the secondary? The answer was soon revealed to me when I was approached by a couple of team members who were still upset over the attack that had taken place that night with Lindsey and I.

I was told that one new member we had recently taken into the group had been provoking the entity that night. It happened early in the investigation when myself and a couple of the other investigators were inside interviewing the homeowners. This particular member had stood out in front of the house and started cursing at the dark spirit, telling it to come out and show itself, all while calling it bad names and challenging it. Then I was told this member had written the words, "come play" on the side of the house with a crystal that had left markings that could still be read.

On top of all of this, the same team member performed some ritual of casting stones on the front porch of the home. The group members who came forward about this had the whole incident on an audio recording. They played it back for me and also clipped the portions of audio for these events and sent them to my email. I was livid and immediately confronted the group member about this.

He denied all accusations and retained his "not guilty" status even after I played the audio proof for him. He knew he had put Lindsey and I in danger that night by provoking the dark entity. He also knew our group rules consisted of no provoking or antagonizing any spirits that might be present. I immediately dismissed this member from the group. If he could not be trusted, then he did not need to be a part of our team. The attack made sense and I understood why we were attacked on our initial visit, but not during any other visits that followed.

Two years had gone by and during that time we continued helping the family with investigations at their Eldorado home. Each time we investigated, we gathered more and more evidence. I was also able to help a few souls who were trapped to crossover.

A&E's national cable network show heard about our Eldorado case and called me to discuss filming a special episode of our investigation there. They flew myself and another team member out to Southern California to do some filming for this episode for a show called, "The Haunted." They also had a film crew come out to Eldorado, Oklahoma, to film the location. They liked working with our team and decided to do other case specials with us.

Afterwards, we were contacted by the BIO channel's producers for a show called, "My Ghost Story, Caught on Camera" and our team filmed a couple of episodes about other significant cases we encountered. It would seem that my group's popularity was growing and our hard work and dedication to our clients was paying off. No matter what our group did throughout the years, we never wanted to loose site of what mattered most to us. Our goal has always been, and always will be, to help our clients, any spirits present at a location and to gain further knowledge about the paranormal.

I find comfort in times of trouble or when up against any dark entities that are controlled by Satan when I think about a couple of scriptures.

> *James 4:7, "Submit yourselves therefore to God. Resist the devil, and he will flee from you."*

> *Romans 8:31, "What shall we then say to these things? If God be for us, who can be against us?"*

There has always been a spiritual war raging since the beginning of time. The question we have to ask ourselves is, "Are we really prepared for a possible spiritual attack?"

CONCLUSION

My goal for writing this book was to be able to share my knowledge and experience with others who might be interested in the paranormal and spiritual realm. I also wanted to be able to help those who were in need of answers perhaps about a haunting or a paranormal experience that has left them baffled. Throughout the years I have had many people, clients and friends alike, who have asked me various questions about paranormal issues. I knew I needed to get my story and experiences out there and put in writing and published into a book so others could have some answers and insight into my experiences and further knowledge about the paranormal realm.

I hope that every person who has read my book has been able to find valuable information here that will help them either with a personal haunting or experience or with any other spiritual type issues they may be experiencing.

I also wanted to stress in my conclusion that there is always power in prayer and one's faith in God if they just believe in Him and call upon his name. Never be ashamed of who you are or what strengths or weaknesses you may possess. God is always willing and able to use someone to help another if we let Him. If God can use a little shepherd boy named David to kill and defeat a giant named Goliath, He can help us do anything in our lives if we just ask Him! He gave his son Jesus to die on the cross for our sins so that we might be able to one day live in Heaven with him. Never loose faith or sight of God's love for us and know that for all of us who believe in Jesus, Heaven awaits us on the other side one day when our time on earth here is done. God bless you and always keep the faith!

Personal Message from Christy Clark:

Thank you for taking the time to read my book. I hope you have enjoyed it and I hope it has been helpful to you. We are all on a spiritual journey and knowledge can be a powerful tool to use along our way. I do plan on writing a sequel to this book in the near future so be on the look out for another upcoming book! If you have any questions concerning a haunting you may have or if you have any questions about any area of my book, please feel free to contact me at my personal website at: http://www. christyaclark.com or through O.K.P.R.I. at http://www.okpri.com or at my personal email: christyokpri@hotmail.com. Feel free to also contact me regarding any personal comments you may have about my book or any other area of interest you would like to discuss. I am also available for interviews in all areas of media interest that may arise too.

As always, God bless you and remember God loves you regardless of who you are or what you may have been through. God is a God of love and mercy and is always available to hear our earnest prayers and requests. All we have to do is ask Him!!